STARLIGHT CAFE

STARLIGHT CAFE

❖

ROB ALEXANDER

Written and produced by Rob Alexander

Cover image by Renato Waru

Published by Stickleback Productions

A catalogue record for this work is available from the National Library of Australia

Starlight Cafe

ISBN: 978-0-6451337-0-7

For dear Sarah, Harriet, Aman and brave William whose humour will remain with us forever.

ACKNOWLEDGEMENTS

I have to thank my awesome wife, Ros. Your encouragement and patience in humouring me by reading drafts over the long journey has made this book possible. Also to Deb Bennett who's support has been invaluable in getting me to the finishing line. Thank you both so much.

CHAPTER 1
MULTIPURPOSE MOBILE INFORMATION CENTRE

Jack clung to the pole. He braced again, pushing his heels into the floor. The ropes lost their slack and his feet left the ground; he dangled in the air trying to keep his balance. He leaned into the pole but another yank pulled him sideways. Poles clattered around him as he fell to the floor.

'Stop messing around and hold the pole straight or we'll never get this bloody thing up!' Ben yelled.

'Piss off! You pulled too hard. Nearly ripped my arms off!' Jack shouted back.

They had struggled for over an hour with the mass of slippery white plastic sheets. It had sounded an easy way to make money when Jack first told Ben about the job. He'd put up tents as a kid but this was so much bigger. The plastic sheets heaved like ships' sails. As soon as one side was erected, a pole or rope came loose and another side fell apart. It took another twenty minutes until the marquee stood at an uncomfortable angle.

Jack rocked the marquee; it swayed but remained standing.

'I think it's more Leaning Tower of Pisa than Taj Mahal.'

'Why do they call this place a Multipurpose Mobile Information Centre?' Ben asked.

'Dunno, good marketing, easily impressed clients.'

The marquee was one of many stretching the length of the exhibition hall. 'The latest in real estate development', the exhibition promoters promised. 'An exciting new life for the whole family'.

Banners spruiking 'Lakeside Gardens', 'Executive Grove' and 'Paradise Springs' hung above each marquee. The best of them displayed plastic palm trees, deck chairs and coloured umbrellas.

Ben stepped into the aisle to admire their Bueno Vista contribution with a warm glow. Bueno Vista leaned into the aisle so that it dominated the regimented row of competing marquees. *A job well done*, he thought. *Worth the sweat and dust*. Combing his jet-black hair with his fingers, he stretched his six-foot frame to relieve the ache in his back. He wished he looked as good as Jack, gleaming like he had just stepped out of the shower. 'You're made of bloody Teflon; nothing ever sticks to you.'

Jack laughed. He was short and wiry with blond cropped hair and sharp blue eyes. He looked younger than his twenty-nine years and was still asked for ID at pubs. As a child, his lack of height was an obsession. He'd tried tying bricks to his ankles and hanging them over the edge of his bed for hours on end. It made no difference except for sore ankles. Mates called him 'short arse' and his mother didn't help by saying he had a 'compact frame'. Jack had a quick temper and learned attack was the best form of defence early on. His Uncle Pat was a street fighter and taught Jack how to fight back. When Pat visited, he'd get Jack to practice with him. 'Come on boy, move those feet. Jab left, duck right. Now jab again. That's the way Jack. Keep your guard up. Knee to the groin, good boy.'

Jack and Ben had both attended Parkhurst Comprehensive School. After teaming up during a school bullying incident, they discovered a shared passion for *Star Wars* and became close friends. Jack was Luke Skywalker as he felt the force was in him and he convinced Ben to be Chewbacca due to his height and strength. Jack occasionally forced other classmates into supporting roles during school lunch breaks. He made them re-enact classic scenes. Ben, shy by nature, was glad Chewbacca only had to growl.

The first time Jack visited Ben's house was a surprise. They always reached Ben's house in Theobald Street first on their way home from school. One day, Jack asked if he could see Ben's new *Star Wars* poster. Ben looked apprehensive but led him through the back door into the kitchen. Jack sat down at the narrow kitchen table watching Ben clear a single breakfast bowl and spoon covered in dried-out Weetabix. As Ben placed it in the sink Jack could see a jumble of dirty plates and cups. He looked around at the peeling wallpaper and stained carpet tiles, then caught the pungent whiff of cat's urine. 'Where are your parents Ben?'

'Dunno. Mum's got a new boyfriend and stays at his place sometimes. Dad doesn't live here anymore. It's OK, she leaves me money so I can look after myself.'

Jack didn't stay long. His mum was surprised when he gave her a hug as he walked in the back door. 'What have you been up to? Fighting again I suppose,' she said, ruffling his hair. Jack dropped his school bag and slumped in a chair, watching his mother peel potatoes. He couldn't get the image of Ben's sad surrounds out of his mind.

Their friendship ended when Jack was fourteen. Ben started missing school and became secretive about his movements. After he was absent for two consecutive weeks, Jack asked their teacher where he was. 'Ben's left school and won't be coming back; didn't he tell you?'

'Where's he gone then? He didn't say anything to me about moving.' His teacher was usually brusque and hard as nails but his question made her look uncomfortable. 'He's not coming back and that's all I can tell you. I'm busy, please shut the door behind you.'

As Jack walked up Theobald Street, he saw a large van with doors wide open parked outside Ben's house. A sofa was being carried into the house and a family of strangers stood in the garden. He stopped and stared from the other side of the road. Ben had been a close friend and he couldn't understand why he hadn't told him he was leaving. Jack walked away from the house, kicking an empty beer can. It landed in the gutter with a clatter. His sadness gave way to anger at Ben's betrayal.

Two years later, Jack left school. His father wanted him to take an apprenticeship with Langs Construction. He loved the construction business and had secured an apprenticeship for his son at Langs heavy construction equipment division. Jack had other plans after becoming obsessed with a television home renovation show "Under the Hammer". He dreamed of starting his own business as a self-employed handyman. His father was disappointed and told him he was throwing a good career away. But he supported Jack by buying him a basic set of tools. Jack called his business Hammer & Nails.

After struggling to stay afloat for the first few years, he gradually built up a steady business with maintenance contracts for local schools.

The news from the Department of Education came without warning: "Procurement of all maintenance work must be provided by licenced companies approved by the Department for Education".

Jack showed the email to his girlfriend Julie. 'This is a real kick in the guts. The operations guy at Campions Grammar said they'd been given no choice and Blackstone Engineering have been given the contract, starting next week. It's going to be the same with all the rest. Hammer & Nails has never needed a licence before and I don't have the qualifications to get one.'

Julie had met Jack three years earlier when he visited Brascoe Solicitors for advice on executing his grandfather's will. Julie was an only child, her circle of friends restricted by her mother's approval. She'd never met someone like Jack. He was open, frank and full of confidence. He had an infectious laugh and she looked forward to hearing his latest excuse for visiting her office.

Though she loved her parents, Julie felt suffocated by them and moved into a shared house when she started practicing law at Brascoe's. Her parents tried to talk her out of seeing Jack, wanting her to meet people with a similar professional background. Her mother was horrified when she found out that Jack was from the council estate and had gone to Parkhurst. When Julie announced that she and Jack were buying a house together, her mother burst into tears and her father refused to help them move in. Julie accused them of snobbery and said she wanted nothing more to do with them unless they changed their attitude. They had barely spoken since.

After the school maintenance work had finished, Jack tried to find work as a general handyman. He left his business cards with real estate agents and hardware shops but with the downturn in the economy, work was hard to find.

One day he answered an ad on the "Local Jobs for Local People" website:

> "WANTED - *Experienced Multipurpose Mobile Information Centre (Marquee) installer*
> *Phone Sid Slater Real Estate on 01462 327391*"

He was drinking in the Pig & Whistle when Sid Slater texted him:

You've got the job. Be at the exhibition hall no later than 7.30 am. Exhibition stand 36, Bueno Vista. The marquee is in a crate, assemble by 8.30 and I'll see you there. Sid.

Jack pocketed the change and picked up his pint. As he turned to find a seat, he glanced around and noticed a vaguely familiar figure hunched over a table in the corner. He wasn't sure but when the man looked up, he knew it was Ben. He walked over and sat opposite him. 'Ben! How are you? Where have you been all these years?'

Ben flushed. 'I've just been away, moved back a while ago.'

'I tried to find out where you'd gone when you stopped coming to school. I was pissed off that you didn't bother saying goodbye or anything. I thought we were best mates. Where did you move to?'

The question caught Ben off guard. He felt embarrassed, his face turned a deeper shade of pink. 'Sorry Jack.' He stared at his half-drunk pint and slowly ran his fingers up and down the glass. Then he glanced up. Jack remembered those sad brown eyes. He broke the awkward silence. 'Where are you living now mate?' Ben slowly sipped his beer and shifted in his chair. 'I managed to get a council flat in the Towers and I've started looking for work.'

'Look, if you've got nothing on and want to earn some cash, you could help me put up a marquee at the exhibition hall. I've got to go now but it would be great if you could give me a hand and we can catch up.'

'Sure, when do I start?'

CHAPTER 2
SID'S AUCTION

Sid Slater cruised to the entrance of the exhibition hall and parked his immaculate BMW in the disabled parking area. He checked his few strands of dyed black hair were in place and slipped on a yellow jacket. Emblazoned across the jacket's breast pocket in lime green, it read "Sid Slater Real Estate, An Honest Deal". Sid put his mobile to his right ear, revealing a fat gold bracelet that glinted in the sun. His crooked smile looked about to crack beneath his pencil-thin moustache.

Sid loved the real estate business. His life was deals, commissions, minimal effort, no scruples and zero compassion. Grabbing his briefcase, he adjusted his sunglasses. He was so engaged in his phone conversation that he tripped over the kerb.

'Shit!' He recovered and looked around to make sure no one saw his mishap. Then he strode into the exhibition centre. Scanning the hall, he sighted his Multipurpose Mobile Information Centre leaning into the aisle to greet him.

He found Jack and Ben inside the marquee, engrossed in a game of poker.

'Christ, this marquee is a shamble! Straighten the bloody thing up, it looks like it's trying to escape. And step on it. My clients are here in an hour. I need every banner erected and the Bueno Vista brochure stand set up.'

'The lean is a feature,' Jack said, 'it stands out in the crowd.'

'Looks like shit. Straighten it before it falls over,' Sid snarled. 'You'll find the rest of the stuff in the boot of the Beemer. Don't put finger-marks on my paintwork.'

'Hang on, the deal was we put up and take down the marquee, nothing about setting up stands.'

'Look, deadshit, if you want to get paid, do it and make it snappy.'

'Tell him to get lost,' Ben whispered.

Ignoring Ben, Jack snatched the keys dangling on Sid's pinkie finger and marched out to the car. He and Ben spent the next half hour setting up stands, laying out brochures and agreeing to never work for Sid again.

Sid came back to the marquee, red-faced.

'The bloody exhibition is about to open and where are my staff? I told them to be here at nine o'clock. Christ, I've got an auction to run in Melton and no one's here to look after my fucking tent.'

'Don't you mean Multipurpose Mobile Information Centre?' Jack replied with a smirk.

Sid ignored him and started to pace up and down the aisle, muttering to himself.

When his mobile rang, he scrambled to pull it out of his jacket.

'I said 9am on the dot!' he screamed. 'Get your arse down here in thirty minutes or don't bother turning up Monday.

'It's not my fault your kids in hospital, I've got a business to run. I'm not a bloody kindergarten!' Sid closed the phone and slammed his fist on one of the display tables. Brochures scattered to the floor.

'You two, pick these bloody brochures up.' Sid waved at the floor.

Jack winked at Ben and ambled towards Sid.

'Hey Sid, looks like you're in trouble mate. What if me and Ben take care of things for a while? Until your lazy staff arrive. We can give out your brochures and cards, charm the buyers. At least you'll have someone here. Cost you a bit extra—say another twenty an hour for both of us till your staff arrive?'

Sid stared at Jack with his cold, calculating chicken eyes. Then he looked at Ben. Ben's t-shirt said: 'Kill Democracy'. He shuddered. He was up for a fat commission at the auction in Melton but he had also lined up potential buyers at the exhibition.

'Alright Jarred, I'll accept your terms.'

'It's Jack.'

'Well, whatever your name is. Hand out the flyers and keep your mouth shut. Get their names and numbers, that's all. I'll contact them afterwards to discuss our new house and land packages. You can show them the plan on this display but any other questions, tell them I'll phone. Keep to what I've said and don't stuff it up.'

'We need our pay in full now,' Jack said, holding out his hand.

'When I get back!' Sid snapped.

'Now or we leave.'

Sid hadn't planned to pay them for a couple of months but he knew a checkmate when he saw it.

He removed a fat wad of folded notes from his back pocket. He licked his finger and carefully counted out the notes. He threw the money on the display table and checked his watch. 'Don't forget to smile, makes 'em trust you.' He left at a sprint.

'Nice one,' Ben sniggered. 'Take that stupid jacket off and let's get out of here.'

Jack shook his head. 'It won't be for long. And, besides, I've never sold a house before.'

Ben sighed.

The exhibition doors opened and people began drifting in. Jack took up his position beside the Bueno Vista banners. A couple in their late twenties headed straight towards him.

The man grabbed Jack's hand and gave it a vigorous shake.

'Don't tell me, you must be Sid. I can always put a voice to a face.'

The man gave Jack a knowing smile, exposing perfect bleached-white teeth.

'I'm Dean Crouch, spoke to you on the phone.'

The smell of garlic and cigarettes wafted over Jack as Dean spoke. He took a step back as he shook Dean's outstretched hand.

'Mate, the Bueno Vista development looks great,' Dean continued. 'Me and Naz have talked it over. If we can get the elevated half-acre block next to the Bueno Vista health club and karaoke bar, you've got a deal. Of course, you'll have to make the garage a triple. We need space for the two Porsches and Naz's new Range Rover.'

Ben stared at the woman standing next to Dean. She

looked like a goddess as she twisted strands of ash-blond hair in front of her deep-blue liquid eyes. Her skin glowed like a lightly basted chicken. Naz was perched on top of bright yellow Louboutins complimented by a skin-tight leopard-print catsuit that showed off her well-toned body.

Dean grasped Naz's hand. 'I nearly forgot. This is Narelle, Naz. She was a regular at my solarium. You may have heard of it? Dean's TanTastic Solarium? We fell in love over a tanning machine and now we're married and wanting a bigger house to start a family.'

Narelle smiled at Dean. 'Plus, we need more space for the home gym. The Peloton alone takes up a normal- sized room.'

Ben decided Narelle was better when she didn't speak; her voice would crack a walnut.

'And if you extend the garage,' she continued, 'we'll have space for a jacuzzi next to the tennis court.'

'Well, you've made a brilliant choice.' Jack said, warming to his theme. 'The good news is that you will own one of the few blocks with water glimpses. Our structural engineers assure us that the block supports a double-storey house. No problems.' He smiled.

'What do you mean?' Dean said, looking confused. 'You've already confirmed we have two storeys. That's why we selected the Embassy French Provincial with marble bathrooms, granite kitchen tops and all appliances. You sent the specs.'

'And it will work perfectly Dean,' Jack replied. 'The landfill they used to cover the old tip is very stable. With deeper footings, you won't have any movement.'

'But your brochure said, "built over pristine land"'

Ben turned away to rearrange the brochures in the stand, trying not to laugh.

'Dean old buddy, it's prime real estate. The stuff on top is pristine, taken from a conservation area. We had to pay off the greenies to remove the last bunch of humpbacked swamp frogs in existence before we could get it. Slippery little buggers. Not a soul will know this exclusive piece of land was ever a tip.'

'I'm excited about the water glimpses, you didn't mention on the phone that there was a lake on the estate.'

'Dean, the water glimpses will be superb from the second storey. And even when the wind blows in your direction, there's hardly any smell. We've cleaned the place up a treat. I've even seen ducks there.'

Narelle wrinkled her nose. 'What sort of smell?'

'When I say a lake, I suppose a series of ecological ponds would be a better description. Quite normal for a reticulated wastewater treatment plant.'

Narelle gasped and clutched her throat. Dean's eyes swivelled behind his Oakleys. One whiff from a sewage farm and Narelle would be off. Already she was tugging at his sleeve in alarm.

'Er, look Sid, we need to discuss a few things. Get back to you, mate.'

Jack and Ben watched as Dean and Narelle sped towards the Paradise Found stand. Paradise Found's banner boasted: House and Land Packages for Executives who Dare to Dream.

Ben felt a tap on his right shoulder. He turned around.

A crisply dressed woman in her late thirties held a Sid Slater Real Estate folder under her arm. 'Hi, I'm Mandy, work for Sid Slater Real Estate. Sid told me you were holding the fort. Thank you. The miserable bastard was panicking because he had an auction on. He's also expecting a couple to come and close a deal.'

'That wouldn't be Dean and Narelle with two Porsches and a Land Rover?' Jack asked.

'Oh god, you've met them. Crass, with new money? Sid reckons they're dead certs though.'

'Maybe not, they didn't seem keen on the Bueno Vista location after I spoke to them. I saw them wandering towards the Paradise Found stand.'

Mandy raised coiffed eyebrows. 'You cannot be serious? Sid will go nuts. You'd better get out of here before he gets back.'

'So, you don't think we'll make it in the real estate game?'

Mandy frowned. 'You should skedaddle before Sid gets back.'

CHAPTER 3
FRANK'S NEW CAR

Frank tapped the steering wheel as he peered over the boom gate toward the guardhouse, waiting for Barry to finish his coffee. Barry brushed cake crumbs from his trousers, straightened his cap and sauntered over.

Barry used to work in the main building of Mack 'n' Morti's Fast Food head office as a stationery clerk where he earned a ruthless reputation. He made sure every floor had the correct number of pens, paperclips and notepads in the cupboards. With thorough detective work, he compiled a list of suspects who used stationery for private purposes. He would pass the list on to Dennis, his manager. Each time he delivered it, Dennis sighed and changed the subject. One morning Dennis announced to Barry that his dedication had been recognised and the company was promoting him to guard the car park boom gate. They gave him his own kettle and microwave, so he wouldn't have to come back into the main building to make lunch. Barry wore his new uniform with pride, especially the peaked hat featuring a red embossed metal security badge.

Apart from the CEO, Barry diligently checked all passes. It didn't matter how many times he'd seen them before. If any of his old stationery suspects drove in or someone upset him, retribution was swift. He would examine their car pass in detail, shake his head and take the pass into the guardhouse. For an interminable time, he slumped in his chair, checking the offending pass against an imaginary list. The hapless victim would then arrive late for work.

Today, Frank was lucky. Barry waved him through.

Frank parked between blue lines in front of a sign that read "Reserved—F Wilson (Manager)". Like his silver turbo-powered, all-wheel-drive Audi, the sign was brand new. Not even Barry could upset Frank today. He breathed in the intoxicating new car smell combination of leather, wool carpet, wood grain and scented chemicals. He had intended to buy the basic model but Anton, the Audi sales executive, offered him a great deal on the Sports GT. Anton upsold him floor mats, a limited-edition Audi cap and headlight protectors. The options cost an extra two thousand pounds. Anton assured Frank he'd get his money back if he ever traded in the car.

The monthly car lease payment made a big dent in Frank's salary but he didn't care. He bared his teeth in the rear-view mirror checking for stray muesli grains, then adjusted his new look 'running bonfire' hair and straightened his tie. When he got out, the door closed with an expensive clunk. Frank stroked the silver paintwork on the warm bonnet and re-read his prized reserved parking sign.

He joined Mack 'n' Morti's Fast Food franchise chain nine months ago. At twenty-eight, he was one of the ambitious young guns of the corporation known as 'the turks'. Frank's cut-throat actions saw him survive the first cull of fresh-faced intakes. He was now on his way up the ladder. He loved the culture of Mack 'n' Morti's where there was no misguided sense of loyalty. If you didn't cut it, you were out.

Company policy required young executives to have a mentor. Frank was allocated Craig Robinson, Manager for Franchise Development.

'Stupid people, these franchise bunnies,' Craig told Frank on his first day. 'They actually think they run their own business even though we tell 'em what to think, what to say, what to sell, what to charge.

'Then they pay us over two hundred grand for the privilege. They don't own the real estate and, of course, we can flick 'em if they don't perform. You've got to give it to Mack 'n' Morti's, they know how to run a business.'

Frank knew from office gossip that Craig was on his way out. In his early forties, he'd become a 'has-been' but Frank wanted to stay in his good books until he got closer to the big boss.

The lift doors opened to the executive level on the fifth floor. This was the home of Mack 'n' Morti's fast-talking American CEO, Chuck Adams.

'Hey Sal,' Frank said to Chuck Adams's bored-looking PA. 'I'm here to see the big man. Is he in a good mood or what?'

'Go straight in Frank,' said Sal, concentrating on her nails. 'They're about to start.'

Frank opened the door to a large wood-panelled boardroom with windows on one side overlooking the car park. On the walls hung several large contemporary artworks. A long, light-coloured wooden table dominated the room. Twelve high-backed faux-leather chairs surrounded the table. The CEO of Mack 'n' Morti's sat at the head of the table riffling through the monthly report. Chuck was from the US parent company. The company had sent him over to establish the chain in England. He wore slim-fitting tailored suits that showed off his muscular physique, which he admired every morning in the shower. His shock of red hair was thinning but he'd booked in for hair plugs when he returned to the States. If things went to plan, a junior vice president's role was in the bag on his return. Competition from the local fast-food chains had been tougher than expected but Chuck was ruthless.

He worked out with weights at the company gym each lunchtime, except on Fridays. Chuck knew that over seventy percent of American adults and eighteen percent of children were overweight and he wasn't going to let it happen to him. He reserved Friday for what he called the 'Chuck Chaser'. His chaser required senior managers to don shorts and T-shirts and run laps around the office car park.

It was his PA Sal's favourite form of entertainment. She would stand at the fifth-floor window as Chuck jogged past underneath, followed by his puffing team of managers. The third lap always took its toll on Mike Binks the accountant and Chuck invariably turned around to spur him on. He jogged on the spot with his pasty-white, freckled knees pumping up and down like pistons and screamed, 'Hup-hup-hup-hup! Let's keep it together boys!'

Then he returned to the front of the team, increasing the pace. He encouraged them on by singing out the company battle cry: 'Whose burgers do we like best?' And the team would refrain, 'Mack 'n' Morti's cos they don't taste shit like all the rest.' Then they'd chorus: 'Mack and Morti, Mack and Morti' as they sprinted or staggered past Barry's gatehouse.

Mack 'n' Morti's was established when its hugely profitable parent company, Vine Tobacco Inc., needed to diversify. Vine Tobacco was a global player in the cigarette market but after some massive financial pay-outs to victims of lung cancer, the tobacco industry started to look risky. Litigation was ongoing so Vine Tobacco decided to move into other markets. Research showed fast food was a good strategic diversification. With its large customer base and poor government food regulations, the company believed it could subtly expand business into a younger demographic.

Their research showed over 250,000 fast food outlets in the US alone. Over eighty-five million fast food meals were eaten per day with twenty percent of those eaten in the car. Customers also drank around fifty gallons of soft drink each year. On any given day, thirty-four percent of children ate fast food.

Vine Tobacco's international president was Newt Grimble III. He told his executives that, 'if people are going to get fat from fast food, then they should do it eating our burgers. Health freaks are a serious threat to our way of life. Our company goal is to keep 'em fat and happy. People, this is what I call a real growth industry.'

Chuck stood up as Frank entered the boardroom. The other meeting participants were busy settling themselves around the table.

'C'mon in.' He grabbed Frank's hand in a vice-like grip.

Three quick pumps and he let him go. Frank joined the rest of the team at the table.

Chuck sat down again and looked at his team. They were young, handpicked and hungry. He'd entrusted them with the company's most confidential plans and strategies. With his firm hand and clear vision, they were on course to meet their aggressive targets.

'OK everyone, let's get this show on the road,' Chuck barked. 'First, guys, let's reconnect our collective energy force field.'

They joined hands around the table in preparation for singing the company song. Team-building exercises were part of the global culture at Vine Tobacco and Chuck had carried this through to Mack 'n' Morti's.

'We, loyal followers of founding father Abe
Fitzhugh
Promise that when times get tough,
And things get rough,
We're gonna kick ass till our enemies' spew spew.'
The team then unlocked hands and punched the
air, yelling,
'Hit 'em left, hit 'em right,
let's fight fight!'

Chuck looked around at the grinning, flushed faces of his team and said, 'Gentlemen, let's begin. I wanna show you the new ad campaign. It's kicking goals for us in the US, so I've decided to give it a shot here.'

Chuck nodded to Pete Crabshaw, one of the top talents in the room. Pete dimmed the boardroom lights and pointed the remote at the wall-sized screen.

The screen came alive with a close-up of tanned, curvy supermodel Mishka Stellofski sitting under a palm tree by a swimming pool in a skimpy red bikini.

Mishka pouted and, with half-open eyes, offered up a Mack 'n' Morti's burger to the camera lens. She looked hard into the camera. "Darlinks, your childrens are precious. Zay will love our Mack 'n' Morti's healty burgers. So good for zem." Then she winked and the picture zoomed back to a shot of Mack 'n' Morti's restaurant nestled in a stand of palm trees. The camera panned to children eating burgers as they laughed and played beneath an artificial waterfall. Then the screen faded to black and Pete turned up the lights.

'Whoo!' Frank said, pushing himself back in his chair. 'That's brilliant.'

Chuck sat forward, waving a finger around the table. 'We're going big with this one. Buses, halfway up buildings and on bloody big billboards everywhere. The works.'

Everyone slapped the table and cheered.

'OK, on with the show.' He looked around the table until he found Frank's mentor, Craig Robinson. 'You can kick it off Craig. Tell me about our new franchise opportunities.'

Craig looked nervous. Last month he'd failed his target and Chuck threatened him in front of the team. He'd been working seventy-hour weeks and hoped he'd done enough to get back into Chuck's good books. He ran his hands through his hair, then opened his report and read out the summary:

'We are continuing our policy of establishing franchises in new development suburbs. That is, all suburbs with a population of over ten thousand. I am pleased to report that with one exception we've achieved our target. Real estate is secured and we are negotiating with potential franchise operators.'

Craig sank back in his chair, wiping his sweaty palms on his trousers under the table.

'Tell me about the exception Craig,' Chuck demanded.

All eyes turned toward Craig.

'Um, a developer is in partnership with a real estate operator. He's entered into an exclusive deal with the Burger-a-Day chain. From our research it appears they have negotiated a deal that gets them a cut in the franchise operation.'

Craig took a swig of water and continued.

'The Burger-a-Day group must be feeling the pressure from us. They are trying to tie up exclusive deals with developers in exchange for profit share. This is the first one we've come up against but we don't want this to become a trend.'

'How did the developer stop us from buying the real estate in the first place?' Chuck asked.

'He worked with the agent who negotiated total control over prime commercial sites in the new suburb for five years. The same as they do with a shopping complex. All fast-food outlets in this area are now tied up, so it looks like we may not get a presence.'

'Bullshit!' exploded Chuck, thumping the table. 'What's this guy's name? You get back down there and negotiate. If he doesn't wanna play ball, then we'll have to get rough and kick ass. I won't stand for one exception in our franchise strategy.'

The room went quiet. Craig looked around the table for a friendly face but his colleagues were all staring at their laptops.

'Are you up to this Robinson?'

'Yeah um, of course Chuck, yep um of course. The agent partner working with the developer is Sid Slater, um, he's behind the Bueno Vista development. Yeah, of course I'll sort it out, Chuck, it's done.'

The tension eased. Chuck turned to Mike Binks, who was sitting beside Craig. Mike reported on current deals with the food suppliers.

'Thanks Mike. Now give me an update on stage one of the Hook 'Em Early campaign.' Chuck turned to Pete Crabshaw.

Opening a file marked Top Secret in large red letters, Pete adjusted his glasses and glanced around the room. 'Nashton Bakery is running at over seventy per cent capacity for small buns designed for the toddler program. We've introduced further security measures including increasing the number of guards. The security perimeter fence at the rear of the premises is underway. So, there's no way the opposition will get access to the secret recipe.'

'How are they selling against the standard burger bun?'

Pete Crabshaw flicked over a page and read, 'Production is up twenty per cent over last month. Sales outstrip standard kids' burgers two to one in our trial locations. The buns proved so popular in our trial that the kids eat the buns and leave the burger. We're putting it down to the top-secret ingredient.'

'I don't like anything that might attract attention to the buns in this project,' Chuck said, partly to himself. 'We're a test case for a worldwide release and we've gotta be vigilant to protect the secret recipe.

'We're no different to any large fast-food manufacturer or confectionery company. We gotta keep our recipe safe. I wanna run a think-tank session on this tomorrow. You all need to come up with at least one good idea to explain why they are leaving the burgers. Apart from that, these results are excellent. The Hook 'Em Early campaign looks like a success. I can tell you that the boys back at Vine are taking a keen interest in this project.'

'Fantastic!' Frank slapped the table.

'Way to go!' Craig chimed in.

'So, let's hear it for the kiddies!' Chuck laughed.

'Yeah, let's do it for the kiddies!' everyone chorused.

Chuck waved his hands to get the team to settle back down. 'OK, let's move on. Give us the financials Bill.'

Bill was Director of Finance and gave a breakdown of the financial reports. Frank Wilson followed, reporting on competitor intelligence and a list of competitor outlets opened.

'Burger-a-Day has opened two new outlets, one at Mill End and the other at Finchley Mews. The one at Mill End is the closest to us, half a mile away but it's not on a traffic route so won't have a significant impact.

'Burger-a-Day are going nowhere fast since we opened up next door in Smeaton. Since the health inspector's report, it's barely half full during the lunch period. Once we launch the Toddler Burger, it will be history. That's all the new competitor news for this month Chuck.'

Frank closed his report and turned to Chuck.

'I don't want to tread on anyone's toes here Chuck but I can't believe we've allowed some two-bit operator to compromise our major strategic plan. How about I prepare an in-depth analysis on Burger-a-Day? It will give us a clearer focus on the way they operate, look for their weak points, find some dirt. I'm sure we can sort this Sid Slater guy out.'

'That's what I wanna hear guys, solutions not problems.' Chuck smiled and squeezed Frank's arm. 'Craig, you get some help from Frank on this one.'

'Judas bastard,' Craig mumbled under his breath.

CHAPTER 4
BURGER BREAK

Through steady drizzle under a slate-grey sky, Jack and Ben made their way across the exhibition centre car park.

'Hey Ben, I'm starving, there's a Mack 'n' Morti's over the road.'

'I can't stand that fast food crap,' Ben moaned. He trailed reluctantly behind Jack as they headed for the outlet's glittering entrance.

'What do you want?' Jack asked him as he browsed the shiny menu. A young girl, dressed in Mack 'n' Morti's gleaming red uniform gave them a bored smile from behind the counter.

'Don't care, it all tastes the same and I know I'll feel like shit afterwards.'

Jack ordered two Morti Blasters, jumbo chips and a cola meal deal. They settled into a bright red vinyl-covered booth. Above them hung a huge poster of Mack and Morti beaming down on them and clenching huge burgers between their sparkling, perfect teeth. Their pink jowls reminded Ben of Sid Slater.

Ben unwrapped his Morti Blaster and sighed. 'Look at this waste. Why do they use so much paper and cardboard? What's wrong with a proper plate? I'll tell you what's wrong with a plate,' Ben continued, ignoring Jack's attempt to speak. 'Costs too much in labour to wash it. Instead, a fancy wrap one minute, rubbish the next. Mack 'n' Morti should pay for creating so much waste.'

Ben was on a roll.

'These fast-food places take no responsibility for the environment or people's health. It's profits and more bloody profits. You know Jack, they could stick a fried dog turd in this bun and suckers would eat it. I reckon this stuff should have health warnings like "this food is crap and will make you fat".

'Look at that!' Ben was speaking louder than he realised as he pointed to a tubby toddler in the booth opposite. 'They have to bribe kids with a free toy to get them to eat this cat food. Imagine if my old man offered to buy me a piece of Lego every time Mum dished up carrots. I would have enough to build my own Legoland, plus perfect night vision.'

The toddler's mother turned around. She had heard every word Ben uttered.

'What's your problem?' she growled. 'If my Leon wants burgers, he can have 'em. They don't do him no harm, so shut your face and mind yer own bloody business.'

Ben looked at the toddler stuffing burger and chips into his face, then at his mother jammed in the cubicle.

'Looks like you've had a few too many burgers yourself,' he muttered.

'What's that, deadshit?' The woman struggled to free herself from the booth.

Jack kicked Ben under the table. 'My friend said he must get another burger for himself.'

In the excitement, Leon started to choke on a mouthful of burger. His mother slapped him hard on his back and his head hit the table. Leon exploded with a wail, spitting a mixture of chewed chips and burgers.

Ben rubbed his shin and went back to picking at his chips.

'You told me at the pub you had a partner now Jack.'

'Yeh, Julie. We met at a solicitor's office where she works. I don't know if you remember my grandfather but he died a few years ago and I went in to talk about his will.

'I remember him. He used to work at the lost luggage department at Kings Cross Station. He told us all those stories about the weird stuff people handed in. So, tell me about Julie.'

'I couldn't take my eyes off her. She has this amazing smile and was so smart and easy to talk to. She was the most beautiful girl I'd ever met. When we met at the solicitor, I kept asking stupid questions trying not to leave. I made up excuses to get more appointments and eventually plucked up courage to ask her out. She was living in a flash shared house and was a qualified solicitor. I didn't think I stood a chance but had to try. We've been together for three years now. How about you Ben?'

'I went out a few times with someone from work but it didn't last long. She was a real party animal and I didn't want to get pissed every weekend, so we broke up. Anyway, I'm okay with my own company.'

'Maybe things will pick up once you get settled.'

'Well, I won't hold my breath. I guess we'd better get moving. Can you drop me off?'

They emptied the tray of wrappers and cups into an overflowing plastic bin and left.

The drizzle had turned to heavy rain as they hurried across the street to Jack's orange van. Displayed along the van's side were big dark-green letters that said: Hammer and Nails. Underneath in smaller print, No job too small: Phone 0342 123 231.

Jack got into the van and unlocked the passenger door. He dropped Ben off at The Towers flats. 'Thanks a lot Ben, you saved my bacon. Let's catch up for a beer soon.'

Ben gave a small wave and walked to the entrance of the flats. Jack continued home, only the swish of windscreen wipers breaking the silence.

CHAPTER 5
RETIREMENT

What's Uncle Stan's car doing here? thought Jack as he pulled up behind Stan's car. Fresh red paint ran along the battered front wing of his uncle's old white Austin 1800.

Looks like he's scored a new victim.

Wish he'd get his eyesight tested.

Jack walked into the kitchen and hugged Julie. Stan was sitting at the kitchen table warming his hands on a mug of tea.

'Look at the state of you,' Julie said. 'Did you put up the marquee by yourself?'

'No. Remember I told you about my old school friend Ben. He came and gave me a hand.'

'Do you want something to eat?'

'We got a burger at Mack 'n' Morti's.'

'Can't see what people see in that rubbish,' Stan grumbled. 'Why don't they eat healthy food anymore? That's why my business is slow, I reckon.'

Stan had run the Starlight Cafe for more than thirty years but trade had fallen away over the last two. His menu and decor hadn't changed from the day he and his wife Ruby opened. The same tables and chairs, even the original paintwork. He was happy with the way it looked and reckoned revamping the interior was a waste of money. Besides, he thought the regulars would be upset if he changed anything.

These days, Jack thought the Starlight Cafe looked seedy. After years of cigarette smoke, the bright-yellow walls had turned a streaky brown. The smell of rancid oil permeated everything. Stan would not admit it but even the regulars were starting to desert him. They'd found a bright new place round the corner that sold all sorts of fancy bread and pastries. The new place was shiny and clean, the staff well trained and polite.

'What have you been up to Stan?' Jack asked.

'Had another round with the neighbour's cat this morning. Missed it by a couple of inches at most. It managed to get another bird before I could find my catapult in the drawer. Bastard of a cat. I'll turn it into gloves when I catch it.'

'I can't believe you're still after that cat.'

'It stalks the birds and I like to feed them. And I don't like having the mangy feline in my garden. I'll get it one day.'

Everyone who knew Stan knew about his obsession with the neighbour's cat.

'Why aren't you at the cafe today Stan?'

'It's been a bit quiet.' Stan stared down at his hands. 'I was telling Julie. I'm thinking of hanging up the apron. I want to spend more time in the garden, do a bit of fishing and travel. I'm thinking of selling the business.'

Jack couldn't believe his ears. For as long as he remembered, Stan had run Starlight Cafe. He had fond memories of Stan making him giant milkshakes after school. His

Auntie Ruby, who died five years ago, used to let Jack choose a cake from the display case whenever he dropped in.

'Uncle Stan, I can't believe you're talking retirement. I thought we'd have to fish you out of the deep freeze when you finally carked it. Why don't you take a holiday before you decide? Give yourself a chance to think it through. I bet you'd miss it in a matter of weeks.'

'No Jack, been thinking about it for a while and it's time for me to give it up.'

A silence fell on the kitchen, broken only by the clink of cups.

Stan stirred more sugar into his tea. 'Julie was telling me things are a bit quiet for you. I wondered if you've ever thought of owning a cafe. You don't make a fortune but it'll bring in a good bit of weekly cash. We could work out a fair price and you can pay me in instalments once you've got the hang of it. I'd be happy to show you the ropes—how to order supplies, what to charge and so on.'

Jack thought his uncle was joking but Stan's face was serious.

Things had hurtled downhill fast for Stan last year. It was after the Edgware Senior Citizens' bingo outing incident. They'd stopped by the Starlight on their way to bingo and ordered takeaway sandwiches for their lunch. He wasn't prepared for such a big crowd but rather than give up much-needed business, he fished out the packet of salami he'd put in the bin that morning. *It'll be all right*, he thought. *It's only a couple of weeks past its use-by date and this stuff lasts forever.*

Disaster struck at the bingo hall. When the caller

announced, 'two fat ladies, eighty-eight' in the first game, Doris Whitmore slumped over her bingo card with a terrible groan. She clutched her stomach and handbag and staggered up the long corridor to the toilet where she was violently sick. She groped her way back to the main hall only to meet Gladys Brompton shuffling past her, looking wild-eyed. The women exchanged sympathetic groans and passed without speaking. None of the senior citizens managed a full house. A continuous stream of groaning men and women shuffled from the bingo hall to the toilets over the course of the afternoon.

Following this disaster, the health inspector paid a surprise visit and conducted a thorough inspection of the cafe. Stan received orders to clean the place up and fix a faulty fridge. He also had to attend a course on food preparation and hygiene.

The incident shook Stan's confidence and tarnished his reputation. He noticed several of his regulars walking straight past his door and felt a dark cloud descend on him. For the first time in thirty years, he thought about closing the Starlight Cafe.

Stan leaned back in his chair, waiting for Jack to digest his proposal.

'You've caught me off guard Stan, let me have a think about it and I'll give you a call.'

Stan nodded. 'I'll be off now,' he said, pushing his chair away from the table. 'Thanks for the cuppa Julie. Give me a call Jack.'

The old man searched through his large bunch of keys and, after several attempts, found the correct one for the driver's lock. He got in, turned the starter and the engine spluttered into life. Stan jammed the gears into reverse and the car rose on its suspension. The car snaked backwards down the wet driveway, scraping the gatepost before knocking the rubbish bin over.

As Stan drove home, he reflected on his offer. *Maybe I only need Jack to keep it ticking over instead of selling it straight away. I might just need a holiday, time to think. What would I do stuck at home all day? After all, it was just bad luck about the salami. I'm sure the regulars will come back eventually.*

There was a screech of tyres as Stan went through a red light.

His thoughts turned to another possibility. *What if Jack loved running the cafe and didn't want me anywhere near it? What would I do then? I don't want a showdown with my nephew.*

As Stan pulled up to his house, he caught a glimpse of his troubled face in the interior mirror. He shook his head and pushed the thoughts to the back of his mind.

When Jack came back inside from walking Stan to his battered car, Julie was making a pot of tea. Jack got the milk from the fridge and sat down at the table thinking how short and thin his Uncle Stan had become, old grey trousers hanging from his belt. 'Why do you think Stan wants to give up the cafe? That place is his life.'

'It's your mum. She's been at him for ages to give it up. She wants him to join the senior citizens' group—not the Edgware one, of course! Why don't you give your mum a call?'

'I will after dinner. By the way, I picked up tickets for

Battle Proms at Hatfield Park on Sunday. We'll be able to see the Spitfire and cavalry in action.'

'That's great. They've got a fabulous orchestra. I'm so looking forward to it.'

After Jack finished eating, he settled himself on the couch to ring his mother. He went through their usual small talk and during a lull in the conversation, changed the topic to Uncle Stan.

'He told me he was thinking of retiring. I thought he was in that cafe for life.'

'I know Jack,' his mother replied. 'But he's starting to forget things and I'm worried that he'll cause another incident. Someone could get seriously ill or die next time. Imagine that on his conscience? It's just not worth the risk. Plus, the place needs a good scrub, someone younger to take it on. He's in his eighties and should be taking it easy. Since Ruby died, he does nothing but work and never takes holidays. We're worried about him Jack, he needs a new interest. I'm going to get him to come on holiday with me and your dad. If you're interested in buying it, I'm sure he'd let you have it for a bargain. But of course, don't do it unless you want to.'

'OK Mum, I'll think about it. Hope you and dad have a great holiday and catch some decent fish.'

Jack ended the call and wandered back to the kitchen, where Julie was working on her laptop at the table.

'I don't know the first thing about running a cafe, Julie.'

Julie shut her computer and moved her chair closer to Jack's. She held his hand and kissed him gently on the lips.

'Do you like what you're doing now Jack? You've built the business up over the last few years and it's awful to see it crumble so quickly. Wouldn't you like something that's established, just needs a bit of modernising to build it up? Do you really want more handyman work over the next fifteen years?'

Jack sat back in his chair with a look of surprise, then tapped the table with his fingers.

'I'm not sure. Sometimes I feel like one of those hamsters on a treadwheel; you keep running but it all looks the same. I do get sick of unblocking kids' toilets; you can't imagine what they block them with. And I wouldn't miss the late-night call-outs because some turkey forgot to turn the lights off.'

'So why don't you want to take up Stan's offer?'

'Do you think he's serious?'

'Of course. Why do you think he came over today? You won't be going in cold; Stan will show you what to do.'

Jack stood up and paced the kitchen. He thought back to his childhood at the cafe. Stan and Ruby behind the counter, laughing and chatting with the customers. The cafe decorated with posters of faraway places. Each table had a small vase holding a fresh flower from their garden. Stan would sit Jack near the window. 'Here you are sir,' he would say as he delivered his nephew's favourite banana milkshake and vanilla slice.

Jack grinned at Julie. 'Let's do it. But on one condition.'

'What's that?'

'We have to do it together. I'll run the cafe but you do the accounts.'

He stuck out his hand to shake. Julie laughed and took it. 'It's a deal. You'd better talk to Stan in the morning and find out what sort of agreement he wants to put in place. Now let's go to bed.'

CHAPTER 6
SANDWICHES

Jack tossed and turned. He dreamed the Starlight Cafe had expanded to ten times its size. Waiters whizzed between the tables on roller skates distributing loaves of bread, tubs of butter and slices of ham. He tried to catch them but they were too fast. He ran into a large white kitchen ablaze with fluorescent lighting. Stan stood in a long white coat loading up trays. 'Stan, stop it! We haven't made the sandwiches yet!'

Stan laughed hysterically and kept loading up trays. 'I've found the answer, the way to make our fortune. We'll call these the SSDS, a world first.'

'What are you talking about, Stan?'

'Leave it to me laddie. Be a good boy and go back to your milkshake and vanilla slice. The "Sensational Starlight Deconstructed Sandwich" will soon be born.'

As Jack tried wrestling the trays away from Stan, the alarm clock went off and he shot bolt upright in bed.

'What's wrong, Jack?' Julie said, rubbing sleep from her eyes.

He let out a long, slow breath and told her about the dream.

'Oh, that's so funny Jack, maybe you should suggest the SSDS to Stan.'

Jack had a quick breakfast with Julie, then left for the cafe. He parked outside the cafe with a feeling of anticipation and excitement. 'Well,' he said to the steering wheel. 'This is the first day of a new life.'

The Starlight was in a small, nondescript block of shops on a busy road close to the city. On the left Mrs Edgecombe's florist shop burst onto the street with colourful displays of flowering tubs. On the right stood Henry Gardner's dark, masculine tobacco shop. Windows filled with pipes and exotic cigars in rough-sawn boxes.

As a kid Jack loved going into Henry's shop, looking at the pipes and the various special cleaning implements. He couldn't get enough of the smell of the tobacco and cigars. They smelled different to cigarettes, conveying a hint of the exotic. Their brands had strange-sounding names that conjured up images of pirates and sea adventures in the Caribbean.

Jack liked old Henry. When he turned twelve, Jack joined a fishing club and decided that he needed to smoke a pipe like the other fishermen. He told Henry it was a present for his father. Then he stole a couple of his dad's cigarettes and stuffed the tobacco into the pipe. Every time he drew, his throat burnt as if on fire. After several attempts he gave up and consulted Henry. When he explained that the cigarette tobacco was giving his dad a sore throat, Henry laughed.

He reached under the counter and gave Jack a small tin of sweets.

'You might like these Jack and if your Dad would like to pop in, I can recommend the right sort of tobacco.'

Jack still remembered what the tin label had written

on its lid: 'Pavilion Soothers. Helps relieve smokers' sore throats.'

He could still taste the sting of tobacco as the cold early morning air hit him in the face sending a shiver down his spine as he left the van. Starlight Cafe's bleak windows framed the door. They were grubby and smeared and the shopfront looked sad and neglected.

When he opened the door a waft of warm, stale air engulfed him. Stan's frail figure stood behind the counter.

'Come on, we've got work to do.'

'Ready when you are Stan, can't wait to get started.'

'Hurry up and grab an apron, we've got sandwiches to make.'

'I have reliable suppliers Jack. Suncrust Bakery sells the cheapest bread; it's a bit doughy but I've had no complaints. Make sure you use Jimmy from Donny's Small Goods, he'll look after you.

'Now Jack, let me see you make a ham sandwich.' Jack laid out two white pieces of bread and placed three wafer-thin slices of ham from the packet on both slices. He was reaching for the lettuce when Stan pushed his hand away. 'No, no, no, you've put enough ham on that for three sandwiches,' he moaned. 'Use the cheaper ingredients to fill it up. Just give 'em a taste of the expensive stuff or you'll never make any money. And you'll have to speed up in case there's a sudden rush of customers.

'Move over, let me show you how to do it properly,' Stan sighed.

With a flick of his knife, he scraped a miniscule amount of margarine from a large container. In one fluid action he smeared two slices of bread and placed a single slice of ham and a scrap of lettuce with pinpoint precision. He cut the sandwiches in half and wrapped them in a few seconds.

After the sandwich-making lesson, Stan moved Jack onto the espresso machine. He showed Jack how to turn on the machine and guided him through the steps in making a coffee.

'OK Jack, now let's see you make me a coffee.'

Jack used the doser to fill the portafilter.

'Are you trying to send us broke Jack, that's far too much coffee. Tip some back, my customers like their coffee nice and weak.'

When Stan's wife, Ruby was alive, she had made Stan introduce burgers and chips. They purchased the hamburgers and chips frozen, so they were quick to cook and it improved the profit.

'When do you change the oil, Stan?' Jack, poked at lumps in the murky brown oil sitting in the chip pan.

'Oh, every now and then,' mumbled Stan. 'It doesn't go off; in fact, it gets better with age like a good wine.'

They served burgers and chips to customers on plain white plastic plates. Jack had to be careful not to leave the burgers cooking for too long, otherwise the fat streamed out and the burgers shrank to thin discs of gristle. To Jack's surprise, the burgers brought in a steady flow of customers.

No accounting for taste, he thought.

'I'll see you tomorrow Jack. Make sure the door's locked before you go. I'd give you a hand to clean up but your mothers invited me for dinner and I don't want to be late.'

Jack closed the door behind Stan and began wiping

down the espresso machine. Doubts gnawed at his stomach as he looked around the grubby interior. He'd thought the cafe would attract more customers and started to wonder about Stan's claim of loyal regulars. He decided the only thing loyal was the oil sticking to the walls and the grime crusted on the table edges.

Stan arrived at his sister Mary's house and rang the doorbell.

'Hello Stan, come in. George won't be long; he's closing the greenhouse.'

Stan followed Mary into the sitting room.

Mary and George had recently retired after selling their successful printing company. They lived in a large, comfortable house on a private estate. Stan stood with his back to the fire warming his hands. 'You know, Jack's a bit wet behind the ears. He means well but running a cafe takes brains and hard work. Not sure if he's got what it takes.'

Mary sat upright in her chair.

'Stan, it's incredibly good of you to sell the Starlight to Jack. Julie says he will work hard, especially now you've shown him the ins and outs. It's not like the cafe is starting from scratch. You've given him a loyal customer base and a couple of weeks training to get the hang of running the cafe. You're always around if he has questions. Starlight Cafe could be the making of him and Julie's worried about Jack. He's been busting himself to find work but it's harder and harder to find. It's time to wind down, Stan. None of us are getting any younger.'

'OK, I'll tell him he's on his own in the morning. What if he forgets to order enough bread or milk one day, though?'

'Stan, you've got to let go. Jack will manage.

'Now Stan, before we sit down for dinner, I have a surprise. George and I have booked a six-week fishing and coach tour holiday.' Mary handed Stan a brochure.

Pilkington's Tours—Come with us for the ultimate fishing tour. Our friendly expert guides will make this the experience of a lifetime.

Stan flicked through the brochure. 'Looks wonderful Mary. When do you and George leave?'

Mary smiled and handed Stan an envelope. 'Open it Stan,' she urged. Stan took out a ticket and read: 'First-class ticket for the Pilkington Ultimate Fishing Tour—Mr Stanley Renshaw.'

Stan's eyes started to water. 'Mary, I don't know what to say.' He hugged his sister and whispered, 'Thank you so much.'

Stan broke the news to Jack at their morning tea break the following morning. He thought Jack would panic and beg him not to leave. After all, Stan was the old master and his nephew the apprentice. But Jack seemed genuinely excited.

'Now, don't forget if you look after your regulars, they'll look after you. That's always been my motto.'

At the end of the week, it was time to say goodbye. Jack had purchased a Rod 'n' Fly fishing tackle box and filled it with cans of beer as a thank-you gift. He presented it to Stan at closing time.

'Oh Jack, you should have kept the money for the cafe.'

Stan's eyes started to fill again. His whole working life was tied up in the four walls of the cafe.

'I'll miss this place you know. Now, if you need anything: advice, a hand, anything, let me know and I'll come back straight away.'

'Thanks, Stan, I expect you to drop in some fish!'

It was time for Stan to leave. He unclipped the bundle of keys from his belt and handed them to Jack.

'Take care of the old place, won't you?' he said, looking around the greasy walls.

'Of course Stan. I know it's been a rush but as soon as you get back, we can sign the contract of sale and I'll start paying you for the Starlight.'

The cafe door burst open and in came Mary and George.

'Hey, Stan! Thought we'd celebrate your big day! How about coming down the club? We can get an early dinner and hit the pokies.' George put his arm around Stan. 'Come on mate, we've got a bit of fishing to plan.'

Stan looked reluctant to leave.

'Have to clean the cafe first, then I'll meet you there.'

'Don't be daft, you're retired.'

'Go!' Jack pointed to the door. 'I'll clean up. Go start that new life of yours.'

Stan suddenly appeared much older, looked lost but George grabbed his arm and steered him out the door. Mary gave Jack a wink and was gone.

Hope he's all right. I feel like I've thrown him out of his own home. Jack finished cleaning up, turned off the lights and locked the cafe door. He stood back, staring at the

Starlight with a mixed feeling of apprehension and excitement. 'Well, this is it,' he muttered to himself.

Jack met Julie at the Rose and Crown to celebrate the new venture. He spotted her through the crowd, sitting in the snug. Jack made his way over, passing a rowdy group of young men in suits playing snooker. Supporters perched on stools, cheering the players when a ball was potted.

'You look exhausted Jack, let me get the drinks.'

'Thanks Julie, a pint of Tennents and bag of pork scratchings would be great.'

Jack ripped open the bag of pork scratchings.

Julie took a sip of lager.

'Did Stan give you another lecture?'

'No, he was fine. Mary and George picked him up and he seemed happy enough. I'm just surprised at how little we made. The money we took barely covered the cost of ingredients. Maybe it was a slow week. Still, the first thing I need to do is close for a couple of days, give the place a good scrub and update the menu.'

'You're right Jack but there's another thing that I think you should do,' Julie's cheeks turned pink.

'What?'

'You said yourself that a lot of Stan's regulars have stopped coming in. The cafe got a bad reputation after the senior citizens' incident. We need an Under New Management sign in the window.'

Jack stopped eating. 'Stan would be devastated.'

'From what you've told me, the place won't cover your wages unless we attract a lot more customers,' continued Julie. 'And anyway, you only need the sign for a couple of weeks, he'll never know. I love your Uncle Stan but he's let the place go and people won't eat there unless they see it cleaned up and with a new image.'

'I know you're right. I feel like I'm betraying Stan but we don't have a choice. We can barely afford to close even for cleaning. We'll be hard pushed to get it cleaned over the weekend.'

'I don't think we can do it alone Jack. We need help if you want to open by Monday.'

'I could give Ben a call. He did a good job helping me with the marquee at that exhibition.'

'OK, you better ring him tonight.'

CHAPTER 7
CAT PROBLEMS

Stan felt tired but couldn't get to sleep. He re-arranged his pillow and pulled up the sheets. He started counting sandwiches but nothing worked. Eventually, he turned on the bedside light. The clock read 3 a.m.

I'll have a cuppa and shuffled to the kitchen.

Stan sat in his striped flannelette pyjamas under the stark glare of the fluorescent lighting. He felt old and alone. He was going to miss Starlight Cafe and morning banter with his loyal customers. As he stared at the teapot, tears trickled down his cheeks. The taste of salt filled the corner of his mouth.

'What have I done?'

He let out a huge sob. This hadn't happened since Ruby's funeral and he had no way of stopping it. *Stupid old fool, senile worthless idiot.* The tears continued. From the corner of his eye, he caught the shape of something moving in his back garden. He wiped his eyes with a sleeve and flicked on the outside light. At once he spied the neighbour's cat stealthily crossing his lawn. Grabbing the teapot, he opened the door and ran screaming into the backyard. The cat streaked towards the fence in terror, then yowled as the teapot shattered against the fence, splattering tea over the palings.

'And don't come back, you lousy, moth-eaten heap of shit!' Stan screamed at the top of his lungs. 'I'll get you next time.'

His neighbour's upstairs window flew open.

'What do you think you're doing, you stupid old bastard. It's 3 a.m., for Christ's sake, have you finally gone raving mad? I'll call the police if you don't shut up. You need certifying.'

The neighbour disappeared, slamming the window shut.

'Piss off!' Stan yelled at the closed window and walked back into the house.

He felt better now and looked around for the teapot to make another cup of tea.

'Bugger.'

CHAPTER 8
FRESH PAINT

Ben caught the 292 outside his flat at 7.30am. He sat at the top, in the prized front seat. He'd been scrolling through the Morris Hunt recruitment agency website when Jack rang. He'd enjoyed seeing Jack again and had said yes to the job without hesitation. Ten stops later, the bus pulled up and Ben looked across the road at the cafe. He could just make out two people through the murky windows. He crossed the road and tapped on the door.

'Come in Ben, thanks for helping out.' Jack put down his broom. 'Come and meet my partner, Julie.'

Julie wore green overalls and a shower cap. 'Hi Ben, great to meet you. Jack has told me all about you.'

'Oh, hi Julie, thanks for the job.'

'We'd better get started. Ben, you take that bucket and start cleaning the walls and ceiling. Julie and I will start on the skirting boards and windows.'

Ben mounted a ladder and grabbed a sponge from a steaming soapy bucket. As he reached up to wash the cornice, hot water streamed down his arm.

'Oh shit,' he groaned, as the hot suds soaked his armpit. The wall reacted to Ben's scrubbing by sending rivulets of dark-brown water rushing to the floor.

Jack stood back looking at Ben's wall. 'That's one wet

armpit for Ben but a major step forward for Starlight cafe.' Julie rolled her eyes.

'Yuck.' Julie emptied another blackened bucket into the sink. 'Look at all that dirt.'

With each bucket of black water, the years of grime started to fade and bright-yellow walls appeared. Jack attacked the windows with a powerful degreaser. Shards of light started to show through and the cafe began to look brighter.

Ben finished cleaning the walls in the afternoon. His next job was to tackle the greasy chip pan and grill. He drained the oil into waste containers and scraped out thick layers of sludge containing lumps of fossilised objects at the bottom. It took Ben till early evening to clean the pans and hotplates back to bare metal.

Exhausted, they sat at a table admiring their handiwork. The streetlight opposite the cafe flickered into life and headlights from passing cars shone brightly in the window as they passed.

Jack looked up at the clock. 'It's after six o'clock, hadn't realised it was so late.'

They sat staring out of the window, each deep in their own thoughts. The 292 double decker pulled up at the bus stop with a wheeze and the doors opened. Several passengers left the bus carrying a mixture of shopping bags and backpacks. The bright-red paintwork of the bus glowed as the doors closed and it continued its journey.

'You know, this must have been what it looked like when Uncle Stan opened in the seventies,' Jack said, looking around at the bright yellow walls.

Ben found a can of cooking oil in the storeroom. 'Hey, do you want something to eat?'

'Yes please, I'm starving,' Julie said. 'What are you offering?'

'I've found this cooking oil and there are burgers and chips in the freezer.'

'Do you know how to use the equipment, Ben?'

'Sure, they taught us at, er, school,' replied Ben, blushing.

He poured fresh oil into the pans, gathered ingredients and began cooking.

Ben served the burgers, feeling nervous. 'That old oil must have been there for a hundred years, these chips should taste a bit different. The meat's still rubbish, not much I can do about that.'

Jack sampled the burger. 'Hmmm, meat tastes like crap but you're right about the chips. They're delicious.'

'Stan's chips never tasted like these,' Julie said. 'They're great!'

Ben sat back, feeling a sense of pride.

Jack finished his burger. 'Hey Ben, now we've spruced the place up I'm worried I'll be swamped with new customers. If they come and I can't serve them quickly enough, they won't come back. I've only cooked for friends. Do you want to come in around eleven and make the burgers and chips?'

'Sounds great, I'll bring my food hygiene certificate.'

CHAPTER 9
UNDER NEW MANAGEMENT

Stan squeezed his eyes shut, willing himself to stay asleep. He had been dreaming of Ruby. They were in the Starlight working side by side. Ruby had her red hair up in a neat bun and wore an apron covered in pink roses. She had been telling Stan how excited she was about their holiday in Torquay when the dream began to fade. Stan opened his eyes.

He peered at the clock; 6am Monday morning. Stan showered and dressed as if he was going for work. He was on autopilot, repeating the routine he had done five days a week for thirty years. He walked down the steep carpeted stairs into the narrow hallway and grabbed his hat and overcoat from the oak hall stand. In semi-darkness he scrambled for the cafe keys on the hook by the front door. Confused, he turned on the light to see the hook was empty. His autopilot switched off and he felt overwhelmed by a feeling of loss. *Silly bugger,* he told himself.

He remembered his sister Mary's words. 'Stan, unless Jack calls you it's important that you leave him alone so that he can stand on his own two feet. You can go and see him after you get back from holiday.'

Stan usually had breakfast at the cafe while he was getting ready to open. He wandered into his kitchen and turned on the kettle. *I'm sure there's something I forgot to tell Jack. That front door lock's a bit iffy. He might not know how to jiggle the key.*

Stan couldn't help himself. Starlight was like a magnet. Ignoring his sister's advice, he decided to drop in and give Jack a hand on his first Monday morning. The coach for his fishing trip holiday wasn't leaving until lunchtime so he had time to drive to the cafe and ensure the lad got off to a good start. He felt calmer now, as he fell back into his usual routine. It was still dark when he arrived at the cafe but something looked different.

Good boy Jack. He's washed the windows, had been meaning to do that for a while.

There was a new sign in the window but it was too dark to read it. Stan fished in his pocket for his spectacles and put his face closer to the glass. He felt a sharp pain in his chest and started to feel faint as he read and re-read the words:

Under New Management.

How could he do this to me? I've passed on years of experience, given him a golden opportunity and this is how he repays me!

He stared at the sign in case he'd been mistaken but the same cold message glared back.

Stan clenched and unclenched his bony fists. *The regulars won't stand for it; they'll leave in droves. It'll serve Jack right.*

Stan thought of staying to confront his nephew but he was too churned up to think straight.

He walked back to his car muttering and drove to his sister's house in a foul mood. He banged on the front door until he woke Mary, who opened the door in her dressing gown.

'What's going on Stan? Are you feeling ill? Come and sit down.'

Stan struggled for the right words. 'New, under, Jack, sign, bloody management, traitor.'

'Slow down Stan. I can't understand a word you're saying.'

Stan tried again. 'Bloody management, sign, under, new, bloody management.'

Mary looked puzzled. 'Do you mean there's an under new management sign at the cafe?'

'Yes, your son has stabbed me in the back. I can't go on holiday while he ruins the Starlight.'

'Don't be so dramatic Stan. I'm sure Jack didn't do anything out of malice. I expect he's excited about running the place and wanted to show customers that he's new and you're not cancelling your holiday. We've paid for it and you can't back out at the last minute.'

'The regulars won't like it; you mark my words Mary.' Stan waggled a furious finger at Mary. 'He's got no right putting that sign up, it's a total lack of respect for all the hard work I've put in.'

'It's his problem, not yours Stan. You're retiring and sold him the business, remember? Sit down and I'll make you a cup of tea. Have you had breakfast?'

Stan pulled out a chair, suddenly exhausted. 'I've built

that business up over thirty years and he'll wreck it in a few weeks.'

Mary reached across and took her brother's hand. 'You've got to give Jack a chance Stan. It's only his first day. Once you've had something to eat and drink, you need to go home and get your bags ready, or we'll miss the coach. You can sort it out with Jack when you get back from holiday.'

'Well, he hasn't heard the last of this, I'm telling you.'

Stan locked his door and carried his suitcase to Mary and George's waiting car. He placed the case in the boot and sat frowning in the back seat.

'And another thing, the Starlight isn't—'

Mary held up her hand in front of Stan's face. 'Stop it. We're on holiday now Stan. I don't want to hear another word from you about the Starlight.'

Stan fell silent, sinking back into the seat.

CHAPTER 10
A NEW START

'What do you think?' Jack posed, hands on hips, showing off his new look: black jeans and black shirt.

'Very hipster, nice change from the overalls and boots,' Julie said, laughing. 'Good luck! Give me a ring and let me know how it's going.'

Jack put his arm around her shoulder and kissed her lightly on the lips. He pulled on his fleece and hurried out to the van.

They'd bought a home in a narrow street full of solidly built pre-war terraced houses. The small front garden had been concreted over to provide off street parking. Jack backed the van carefully into the street between crowded parked cars. He drove holding the flat of his hand up to shield his eyes. The sun had begun rising on a cold windy day. Joining the main road towards the town centre, he could see traffic at a standstill ahead. In the distance he saw the flashing lights of a police car and a policeman directing drivers around an accident.

'Come on, hurry up!' Traffic was at a crawl as Jack waited impatiently in the queue ahead of him. Once past the accident the traffic cleared and Jack floored the accelerator. '*Can't believe I'm late on day one. Hope the delivery man doesn't bugger off.*'

Jack shivered as he opened the van door, leaving the warmth behind. He picked up two empty beer bottles that lay discarded in the cafe entrance.

Wouldn't hurt to find a bin, would it?

He unlocked the cafe door and turned the lights on. The fluorescent tubes crackled, then flickered and light flooded the room. *Bring it on. I'm ready for you customers!*

A delivery van pulled up. The driver opened the van and carried through trays of bread and rolls into the cafe.

'Blimey, the place looks a bit different. Think I prefer the old colour; this is a bit bright for my taste.'

Next to arrive was Santo, the vegetable supplier.

'Wow! Looks great Jack. Hope it goes well for you and give my best to Stan.'

Jack started preparing everything the way Stan had taught him. Sandwiches wrapped, cakes sliced, eggs boiled, containers filled with ingredients ready for the day's trade.

OK, 7.30. This is it. Hope it's not too busy before Ben gets here.

The clock ticked over to eight before the first customer entered. He was a pasty-looking man in his early forties, wrapped up in a large brown overcoat.

'Tea and a muffin,' he mumbled as he sat down to read the paper. Jack brought the order over to him, then pretended to clean the next table. He smiled whenever the man looked up but the man didn't speak, drank his tea, ate the muffin and left.

The morning rush didn't materialise and the cakes and

neatly stacked sandwiches remained untouched. Jack started pacing behind the counter.

'Where are they? It's as bad as last week,' he said when he phoned Julie.

'I'm sure they'll come Jack. Got to go, sorry. Talk later.'

Ben arrived at eleven and looked around.

'Is the rush over Jack?'

'Hasn't started yet Ben but it's bound to pick up at lunchtime. I'm going out to see how the place round the corner is doing. Can you look after the place for few minutes?'

'Sure.'

Jack returned, looking sad.

'The place is packed. They've got three people serving at once. It's so swish, all chrome and lights. I pinched a menu. Look at it. More expensive but people don't seem to care. Their average sandwich price is almost eight pounds! They've got fancy breads I haven't even heard of. Let alone the ingredients: smoked salmon, capers, imported Slovenian goats' cheese. Where do they buy all that stuff?'

'You've got curried egg Jack.'

By lunchtime, a few regulars had drifted in. 'Looks cleaner but it won't be the same without Stan you know,' said a woman on a walking frame.

'These chips taste a bit funny,' another customer said. 'Lost all their flavour, not as good as Stan's. He served real chips.'

'You mean that rancid flavour of dead rats?' Ben mumbled from behind the metal divider that separated the grill area from the rest of the cafe.

The divider was high enough to hide the griller from

customers. Behind it stood a long preparation table for burger and sandwich-making. Two double-door fridges and a freezer lined the back wall.

'Ben, it's four. How about I make us a coffee and we close up?'

'Sounds good to me.'

'I can't understand what went wrong today. The cafe looks so much better, why aren't they coming in?'

'It's the first day Jack. Word will get around.'

'I guess, Ben. I need to be patient and build up the regulars. Can you come in for the next two weeks, say eleven to four o'clock? I can pay you cash.'

'That would be great. I've got a job interview later in the week but that's all.'

By Thursday afternoon there was no improvement in customer numbers. Jack slumped at a table while Ben made them coffee. 'I don't get it Ben, what am I doing wrong? This is no better than when Stan ran the place.'

Ben chuckled quietly to himself and poured out coffee flamboyantly from a great height.

'Are you all right Ben?'

'Never better Jack, now drink your coffee.'

CHAPTER 11
GOURMET SPECIALS

Ben arrived early the following day.

'Thought you might like to take a break, get some fresh air. Go on, I'll look after the place, take your time.'

'OK Ben, thanks.'

Ben wanted to repay Jack's support and had come up with a sure-fire plan. He quickly unpacked a large bag of goods he bought from the local gourmet grocer the night before. He spruced up the sandwiches with new ingredients and laid them on the display shelves. If the sandwiches took off, he planned to change to fancier bread and rework the sandwich names with Jack. Ben was certain word would get around about the great sandwiches at Starlight Cafe. It would give Anton's Deli round the corner some real competition. He started to daydream about long queues stretching into the street when Jack reappeared.

'Anton's is packed, Ben. They've got such a big range of sandwiches plus toasted focaccias. I don't know how we can compete unless we completely change the menu.'

Grinning, Ben shadow-boxed past Jack, punching him in the arm.

'You worry too much mate, things will pick up, believe me.'

Jack wondered if Ben had been drinking.

'Hope so Ben, we're getting killed.'

An elderly man in a threadbare Harris tweed jacket scanned the cakes. 'Got any coffee scrolls mate?'

'No, only vanilla slices and custard tarts,' Jack replied.

'How about a delicious cheese and tomato sandwich?' piped up Ben.

The man shook his head and studied the vanilla slices. 'I'll have a pink vanilla slice.'

'Are you sure you wouldn't prefer a nice sandwich?'

'No, I want a vanilla slice.'

'Don't know what you're missing,' Ben continued.

'Are you deaf, I said I don't want a sandwich.'

Jack rushed to hand over the vanilla slice. The man wandered off to sit at a table, shaking his head at Jack.

The next customer was young, a snappily dressed businesswoman in a hurry. She inspected the neat row of sandwiches and selected ham and pickle.

'I'll take this and a takeaway flat white please.'

Jack made the coffee and, as he put the plastic lid on the cup, Ben sidled up beside her.

'Are you sure you wouldn't like that sandwich to eat-in?' he asked. He swept his arm toward the empty tables for effect.

'No, I'm in a hurry.' The woman gathered up her coffee and sandwich and made for the door.

Jack looked at Ben. 'You feeling alright?'

'Never felt better.'

The lunch trade began slowly. Ben paid great attention to anyone who bought a sandwich. He hovered around their table asking if they felt comfortable.

'What's in this bloody sandwich?' asked Norm Vendy, one of Stan's regulars.

'Ah, cheese and tomato with that extra bite,' Ben beamed.

'It's bloody awful, thought the cheese was off,' said Norm, screwing his nose.

'Yeah,' said the lady from the next table. 'I ordered chicken and avocado but it tastes all salty.'

'That's because it's our specialty called Hint of the Sea,' Ben explained. 'It contains chicken, avocado and anchovy.'

'Well, it tastes horrible. I want one the way Stan makes it or my money back.'

Norm took his sandwich apart.

'You've put bloody capers in mine, no wonder it tastes funny. You can give me a proper one or I want my money back as well.'

Complaints started from the other tables.

'Why did you put this black stuff in my egg and lettuce sandwich?' moaned another regular.

Things were starting to turn ugly. 'But that's olive pesto and hot chilli sauce. It's a delicacy in Greece,' Ben explained.

'You can stick your Greek flavour up yer arse. I ordered an egg and lettuce sandwich. How hard can that be?'

Ben retreated behind the counter, looking for support from Jack who glared at him, not speaking.

The crowd at the counter grew. Jack grabbed the unused bread, making replacement sandwiches and refunding money. Ben tried to help but Jack stopped him.

'Throw all the stuff you've made in the bin and keep out of my way,' he snarled.

Ben unpacked the rows of specialty sandwiches. Humiliation consumed him as he threw them in the bin. The two men didn't speak for the rest of the day despite Ben's attempts to apologise.

'Ben's an idiot, he'll send me broke,' Jack said to Julie when he got home. 'Now even the regulars aren't likely to come back. He's wrecked the business before I've even started.'

'I'm sure Ben was trying to improve things. If you're that unhappy, why don't you let him go?'

'No, I said I'd give him two weeks and besides, I owe him.'

'What do you mean Jack?'

'Nothing, just something that happened at school. It's a long story. I've no idea what he put into the ham and chutney,' Jack continued. 'They were the worst. The customers hated them. Next they'll be suing us.'

'Are you sure he put anchovies in the chicken and avocado?' Julie tried to hide a smile.

'Bloody piles of 'em. He called it his gourmet special: Hint of the Sea. One customer gagged, had to drink four glasses of water to get rid of the taste. They would have lynched us if we hadn't given them a replacement *and* their money back. I can only think he wrote down some ingredients from Anton's Deli but had no idea how to use them, the idiot.'

The following day the regulars kept double-checking that Ben hadn't made the sandwiches. Business remained slow.

Jack counted the day's meagre takings. 'I'll give it another week, then do some advertising.'

CHAPTER 12
SQUASHED CAKE

Harry Cleghorn had cased the cake shop in Stoke Street for a couple of days. Only a few people wandered by during the day. The new shopping centre in the high street had reduced customers in the small shopping strip to a trickle. The joint looked perfect; cash only and nearly deserted between 11 and noon. But fear stilled gripped Harry on this, his first robbery.

Uncle Ned had summoned him the previous week to discuss his future.

'Harry, I promised your father I'd look after you and it's time we had a serious talk. Against my better judgement I agreed to you going to college. Now you've got that nonsense out of the way I've decided you need a proper job. It's time to join the family business.'

Harry sank back in Uncle Ned's Chesterfield armchair in despair.

'Now Harry. I'll start you off with something small to get your hand in. A holdup in a small shop in Stoke Street is perfect. There are only four basic steps we need to go through:

1. Case the joint—make sure the shop is empty of customers and the street is quiet.

2. Have a plan—spot the till, check the route for a quick getaway.
3. Exits—check the exit doors are clear.
4. Surprise—the element of surprise, rush in and shout a lot.
5. Take off—once you've grabbed the cash, don't hang about.

It's easy, all you have to do is remember the word CHEST.'

He agreed that Harry didn't have to use violence if he didn't want to.

Harry checked the shop once more before venturing inside. All was quiet so he burst through the door like Uncle Ned had instructed but the counter was empty. Harry waited for a few minutes pretending to inspect the fairy cakes, then went to the till. He couldn't work out how to open it. The noise of a flushing toilet sounded. He was so nervous that beads of sweat began pouring down his face. The cake shop was stuffy and his heavy overcoat made things worse. He wore it because he thought it made him look more dangerous and it helped hide his cricket bat. He heard a door creak from the rear of the shop and a frail, elderly lady tottered out.

Harry shouted, 'This is a holdup!'

He didn't brandish the cricket bat as Uncle Ned suggested, in case the lady had a heart attack.

She looked at him and smiled. Then she reached under the counter and lifted out a boxed cake. On top of the box was an address written in large letters and she thrust it into his hands. She was hard of hearing and struggled to read Harry's lips.

'Yes dear, I know it's a pickup but you don't have to shout'.

Harry tried to explain he wasn't there for the cake but she kept smiling.

'You look extremely hot dear, are you coming down with a fever? Now, come with me and I'll make you a nice cup of tea.'

Before Harry could protest, she grabbed his hand and led him to a table. Other customers entered the shop and Harry's resolve collapsed. He sat in silence as the elderly lady fetched him his tea and a donut.

'You young people are always on the go. You should stop rushing about. I'm not letting you go until you've drunk all your tea and eaten that donut. You can take that cake and deliver it when you feel better.'

Harry finished eating, showing her the empty plate and gathered up the cake box. He thanked the lady for the tea and left the shop. He was going to dump the cake in the nearest bin but it was too big to fit in the slot. He looked at the address—Starlight Cafe—and realised it was close by. Well, he might as well get one thing right today and deliver the cake.

It was another cold grey afternoon and the Starlight was empty. Ben had gone to buy cooking oil from the wholesaler and pick up a cheesecake from Stoke Street. Jack was busy cleaning the counter. He glanced up as he noticed a man in a long overcoat walk past the window several times and peer in.

Harry had found the cafe from the address on the cake box. To his surprise it was completely empty except for a short, harmless-looking man behind the counter. Maybe he could make up for his failure at the cake shop. He felt nervous and again patted the cricket bat under his coat.

The coast was clear. He opened the door and slid round the frame to catch Jack by surprise. The bell above the door clanged as the belt of his coat caught in the door handle. He fought with the door and shut it behind him with a slam, then straightened his cap and dark glasses. He strode to the counter with the cake under one arm.

Harry thrust his other arm down the front of his long overcoat. After a few seconds' struggle, he managed to drag out the cricket bat.

He balanced the cake in one hand and raised the bat over his head.

'Hey you! Don't do anything stupid or I'll crack your skull open like a coconut. I'm not afraid to use this. Hand over all your money and you won't get hurt.'

Jack placed his cleaning cloth on the counter.

'Well,' he said calmly, 'there's a tenner in the till and I've got another five in my wallet. No, wait a minute, make that two in the wallet, I gave three quid to the Scouts annual raffle when they dropped by.'

'Don't believe you, you must have more than that. Don't mess me around, I'm dangerous.' Harry tried to look fierce.

Jack shook his head.

'Sorry mate, you might do better at a bank.'

'You must be joking; what sort of business are you running here? You must have more money than that.'

'Take a look for yourself. Jack opened the till and Harry peered inside.

'That's pathetic, what if I wanted a cup of tea and only had a ten-pound note? You can't be serious.'

'My mate Ben will be back in a minute; he might have a bit more money but not a lot. He had to buy more cooking oil. You might like to come back this afternoon when we've had more customers through.'

'So, what am I supposed to do?' Harry said, getting agitated. 'Sit in the corner and wait? Or give you a ring to see if you've managed to make some money?'

He was getting more worked up, waving the cricket bat in the air. It had taken all his nerve to get this far.

Jack made his move. Harry crashed to the floor as Jack caught him with a right cross to the side of his head. As Harry writhed on the floor still clutching the cricket bat, Jack leaped over the counter. He trapped the bat under his foot and was about to deliver another punch when he heard a loud crack. Under his foot the handle of the cricket bat lay broken on the floor. Harry rolled over, looking despairingly at Jack and began to sob. Confused, Jack didn't know what to do.

Ben appeared through the door.

'What the fuck's happened?' He looked at Harry, curled on the floor with a cakebox under one arm and the handle of the broken cricket bat in the other.

'Oh, it's OK,' this bloke here came in and wants to rob us. Think he's a few biscuits short of a packet.'

'What sort of a robber is he?' Ben whispered, staring down at Harry. 'He looks a bit emotional.'

Harry's shoulders heaved and he let out a series of low moans and sobs.

Ben bent over him. 'Sit up mate, don't try anything funny.'

Harry struggled to a sitting position and offered Ben the flattened cake box.

'This delivery is for you,' he spluttered.

'That's our cheesecake, I've been around to the cake shop and she said someone picked it up. How come you've got it?'

Harry's right eye was so swollen from Jack's punch that it had closed. 'You wouldn't believe me if I told you.'

'You gave him a real belting Jack.' He let out a slow whistle staring at the closed eye. 'And all he had was a kid's cricket bat.'

Harry started crying. 'My eye is burning; I can't see anything.'

Ben helped Harry into a chair.

'Why don't you make him a coffee Jack?'

'He hardly deserves a coffee.' But he went over to the espresso machine and started grinding the beans.

Ben drew up a chair opposite Harry. 'Tell me mate, how long have you been doing this robbery stuff? You don't strike me as the type.'

Harry no longer cared and blurted out his day's disasters. 'I'm new to this, you're my second job. Well, if you could even call the first one a job.'

'Why's that?'

Harry explained his first attempt at the cake shop and how he ended up with the cake delivery box.

'Look,' he said. 'Call the cops and get it over with. I can't face trying another holdup, I'd sooner go to jail.'

'What made you want to start robbing in the first place?'

Harry dabbed tears from his rapidly swelling eye.

'My whole family are career criminals and proud of it, they go back generations. My cousin Mick, he's doing a couple of years for GBH, says I'm an embarrassing Nancy boy. I went to college instead of joining the family business and did a diploma in Marketing. Passed my exams and got a job with Leyton Fabrics but they found out about my family. They thought I'd be trouble and sacked me. I've been trying to get another job but no one's interested once they find out I'm a Cleghorn. I don't have any money and now my family say they're going to throw me out unless I join them. So last week, my uncle gave me tips on holdups, nothing violent. Just scare a few people he said but I'm not up to it. I can't even find a decent weapon. Had to borrow this cricket bat from my nephew. He's gonna kill me for busting it.'

'You could go on the dole,' Jack suggested.

'I can't do that. My uncle would lose face if I did that instead of joining the business. He's been like a father to me since I escaped from the cult.'

'A cult, what cult?' demanded Jack in surprise.

'It's called the Children of Gliese 581c. They believe in a being called Vimwa who lives on Gliese, a habitable planet twenty light years from earth. The cult leader Adrian says Vimwa would send him a sign when we could start the inter galactic journey. Adrian attracted a lot of followers, including my parents.

'When he decreed that all women under twenty-five had to visit him in the attic to see if they were good breeding stock, I'd had enough. I reported them but don't know what's happened to my parents or the Gliesen sect since.

'I love my uncle but I want to have a legitimate career I can be proud of. There's no way out for me, I don't know what to do.'

Harry started to wail.

Ben got up to find him a box of tissues from behind the counter where Jack was finishing a fluffy cappuccino.

'Do you really want to call the cops?' Ben whispered to Jack.

Jack looked at Harry, who sat slumped across the table. He hadn't even tried to make a run for it. 'Yeah, he sure as hell looks sad. I don't think I've got the heart.'

Jack and Ben came back to the table and Jack handed Harry the coffee. He clasped it with both hands and sipped thirstily.

'Don't worry mate, I'm not going to ring the cops. I know what it's like being broke.'

Harry looked up in disbelief. 'Thank you so much. I can't believe it. It's very decent of you. Thank you, thank you,' he sobbed.

'What's your name?'

'Harry, Harry Cleghorn.'

'I'm Jack and this here is Ben. Um, sorry about the eye.'

Harry squinted out of his good one. 'I deserved it. You were bloody quick, so fast that I didn't see it coming.'

After the coffee, Harry perked up. 'So, how did you two get into the cafe game?'

Jack explained the story.

'Trouble is, I can't attract customers.'

Harry gazed around the cafe with his good eye.

'I don't think you've got a hope. I cased Anton's Deli round the corner a few days ago. It was packed to the rafters: inviting, cosmopolitan and trendy. No matter how much you clean this place up, it's still going to look dated. You can't compete unless you change the image. Believe me, this is something I know about from my marketing course. You've got to have a good image as well as great products to sell.'

'My food is good,' protested Jack. 'The sandwiches are fresh, the burgers no worse than anyone else's and Ben's chips are crisp and crunchy.'

'You've got to understand that it's not only the quality of the product but the way it's sold that determines success.'

'You mean fast food outlets like Burger-a-Day?' Jack said.

'Exactly.' Harry warmed to his theme. 'Those international fast-food chains know how to market. People don't buy Burger-a-Day for taste or because they're good for them. They buy them because of clever branding. They target the youth market: convenience and price. Burger-a-Day know that image is more important to people than quality food.'

'Yeah but where does that leave me? Do I wait for things to pick up or tell Stan I don't want to buy the Starlight?'

Harry sat up straighter.

'If you want this place to make money you need to make major changes. Think about what you're selling and who you want to target as customers. In other words, you need a re-branding plan.'

Harry's words echoed around the walls of the cafe. The robber-cum-marketer talked sense.

Jack broke the silence. 'Look Harry, I figure you owe me for stress and fear when you tried to rob me. Can you help me with this re-branding idea? I can't pay you much now but if your plan works, we can figure something out.'

'I don't know what to say.' After the events of the day, Harry expected to be sitting in a cell rather than giving marketing advice. But his choice was simple. Persevere with crime or come up with a plan to save the cafe. He couldn't face the anguish of another robbery attempt. And if he continued to fail as a criminal, he faced his family's scorn.

'Let me have a think about branding options. We can meet here on Saturday morning at around ten and I'll present some ideas.'

'Give me your driving licence,' Jack demanded. 'You know, a little bit of insurance for me. If you turn up as promised, on Saturday, I'll give it back and that's the last time we mention the robbery.'

Harry's bargaining power was low, so he handed over the licence. He picked up the pieces of the broken cricket bat and left the cafe.

'The guy's right you know Jack.' Ben placed the closed sign in the cafe door window. 'Whatever you do, it's got to be radical. Even if the Starlight picks up, it's never going to compete with Anton's.'

'Yeah, I know. Stan's way of running things is in the past. I want to make this business work and make the Starlight the best cafe in town. It's my future.'

CHAPTER 13
DISAPPOINTMENT

Ned Cleghorn was head of the Cleghorn crime family. He was a big, barrel-chested man with a broken nose from too many fights. His deep-brown eyes and slicked-back steel-grey hair gave him the air of a Mafia boss.

His dad had been a sergeant in the British Army. That was before the court martial for selling his armoured tank to a North African warlord during World War Two. Ned's father drilled the virtues of smart dress, shiny shoes and short hair into Ned from an early age. In public, Ned wore a dark, tailored double-breasted suit complemented by matching silk tie and black shiny shoes.

The Cleghorn family were well known in the borough of Hackney. With few jobs around, many Cleghorns resorted to petty crime, becoming regular faces at the Magistrates' Court. Ned was different; he had a talent for numbers and came to the attention of their bookmaker neighbour, Jim. Jim employed young Ned at the Kempton Park racecourse running errands and calculating odds. Ned's racing ambitions grew and he bought shares in greyhounds to race at the Hackney dog track. He narrowly escaped a conviction for bet fixing, then diversified and became a boxing promoter. His business interests expanded and he began employing members of his family for their dubious skills. If a Cleghorn ran into trouble, Ned 'sorted it' as he was fond of saying.

Ned moved from Hackney to a comfortable three-bedroom house in a leafy street in Stoke Newington with his family. Harry walked past the Jaguar XF parked in the driveway and rang the doorbell.

Ned's wife Caroline answered the door. 'Come in Harry.' He bent down and kissed her on the cheek. The familiar smell of her perm and Chanel No 5 wafted his senses. As the matriarch of the Cleghorns, Caroline provided support and love to her family in times of trouble.

'Good to see you, Harry. Sorry to hear things didn't go so well love. I told him it was a bad idea.

'He's in the study; I'll bring you some tea.'

Harry entered the study and Ned beckoned him to a chair. Ned sat behind his desk. He leaned back in the chair with his fingers in a steeple position as Harry clutched the sides of his chair.

'Didn't go well, I hear, Harry.'

'I burst into the cake shop like you said but there was no one behind the counter. It threw me off.'

'What did I say? Case the joint. It's not much bloody good bursting in if there's no one to fucking hold up, now is it?' Ned said in an exasperated tone.

'No.' Harry clenched his fingers and stared down at the carpet.

'And what happened after that? How'd you get that black eye?'

'Well, 'Harry stammered, turning crimson. 'It all went wrong at step four. I cased the place properly. I burst in, shouted a lot and demanded their cash but they didn't have any. When I wasn't looking this bloke jumps over the counter and, quick as a flash, belts me in the eye. I was lucky they didn't call the cops.'

Ned liked his nephew but couldn't understand why he didn't embrace being part of the family business.

Deep down, he'd known Harry would fail. He'd still hoped that somewhere in Harry, the Cleghorn genes might surface when he held a weapon in his hand.

'I'm extremely disappointed in you Harry,' Ned said, in a tone of resignation. 'Still, at least you had a go. It might be better if you have a go at the import–export side of the business now. You could do a bit of driving for the family.'

Harry came out in a cold sweat. Ned's import–export business was run from an old warehouse hidden away on an industrial estate. It was full of cheap imported goods the family re-labelled as luxury items. The cheap whiskey from Estonia sold as Glenfiddich Experimental Series had been highly profitable. Harry knew that driving meant taking the lorry to meet fishing trawlers coming in under the cover of darkness from Europe. Then he would have to ferry the suspect goods back to the warehouse.

Ned continued. 'I'll send Vincent round to sort it with the boys at the cafe. Give 'em a gentle slap for your black eye.'

'No, please don't do that Ned. They didn't call the cops. I have an idea that I'm sure will interest you. I'm going to help them with a plan to build their business. I'll do market research to identify their target market. It will position them better. Then I'll do a competitive analysis, develop a strategy, look at their budget and define some metrics and...'

Ned's eyes glazed over.

'Being able to put into practice the knowledge from my marketing course will give me confidence that I can help you take the import–export business to a new level. Also, if this goes well, I can earn some money.'

Ned leaned back, sizing up Harry. 'I'll tell you what, if you turn this cafe business round and make it successful and I mean really successful, then I'll get you to look at expanding the import-export business. If it doesn't work, you accept whichever job I decide. Agreed?'

'Agreed.'

Harry lived in a council house Ned had bought through the Right to Buy scheme. Harry and his cousin Reg shared the house, paying rent to Ned. Reg was five years older than Harry. After escaping from the Children of Gliese 581c sect, Harry had gone to Ned for help. Ned had asked Reg to look after him. Reg enjoyed Harry's company but couldn't understand why he was wasting his time at college.

Harry pored over research data on fast food chains through white papers he found on the Internet. He examined the rise of the brunch phenomenon and researched major food players, developing profiles on each one. He identified the market segments that each successful food chain targeted. He examined the demographic of the

Starlight Cafe's location and the proximity of competing businesses.

Harry trekked the streets to give himself a user experience. His feet blistered from the extra walking and after a week he'd drunk coffee at most of Starlight cafe's competitors. Despite feeling jittery from so much caffeine, he started to form a plan. He worked through the early hours of each morning looking at options and narrowed down factors like cost, location and number of tables. In the end he developed a radical solution but it was going to be a tough sell.

Jack found Harry sitting on the steps of Starlight Cafe's door, huddled in his brown overcoat. A battered briefcase rested on his knees.

'Morning Harry, your eye looks a lot better.' Jack unlocked the door.

'Thanks, how's business been?'

'Crap, a few extra portions of chips and that's about all. I keep checking Anton's Deli and it's always packed with people.'

Jack was curious about Harry's plans and watched as he unfastened his briefcase. The failed robber took out a folder boldly marked 'Starlight—in confidence'.

It was a thick-looking plan and Harry turned immediately to the second page, headed:

"Situation Analysis:

- Investment capital—low

- Local competition—strong
- Ranking in area—last
- Current returns—less than break-even"

The list went on. Harry read each section of the report describing Starlight Cafe's business, the food they sold, the types of customers by age, group and profession, socio-economic groupings and return on investments. 'That's impressive,' Jack said, flicking through the report.

'As you can see,' Harry continued, 'you attract a small section of the community. They are mainly office staff, five days a week between 7.30 a.m. and 3 p.m. The cafe is in an excellent inner-city location with a large population of residents. It's close to cinemas and nightclubs. But you miss a lot of people because you shut at three and only open during the week.'

'That's easy to fix, I'll open in the evening and weekends.'

Harry shook his head. 'No. You might get a few more customers but this place isn't attractive enough. They will still go elsewhere.'

'So, you're saying I'm stuffed, no matter what I do?'

'If you leave the place the same, that's right but that's not what you're going to do. I read some interesting stuff about the way fast food chains operate. The secret is establishing a brand. You also need to keep things simple and consistent with a fast turnaround. I'm not suggesting that you copy a chain like Burger-a-Day but we can apply the same principles.

'For a start, think about sandwiches, the number of ingredients you need and how long it takes to prepare them. Think about how you organise your time. All those dim sims, hash browns, onion rings, hot dogs and so on. You should cut out everything except the burgers, chips and drinks. Put all the effort into these. Develop the best burgers in town with good variety and make them trendy and unique.'

Jack listened intently.

'The other major change is the look of this place. It needs to appeal to a different market. Younger people with more disposable income. You can't compete with someone like Burger-a-Day or Anton's Deli head-on, so you need to be more upmarket, trendier. Offer better quality but with similar convenience and consistency.'

'But I haven't got loads of money to change this place, I'd need new everything. The equipment here is at least thirty years old.'

'I've thought of that. You won't have to change any of the furniture. The Laminex stuff's back in fashion, given the right setting. I know someone with a bit of flair who can paint the window and walls to give you more atmosphere. We'd need to rip up the lino and polish the floorboards and after that you won't recognise the place. We can get rid of the sandwich area and extend the grill for more burgers.

'You looked worried Jack. I promise it won't cost a fortune.'

'It's not that Harry, it all makes sense. I'm determined to make the cafe a success but it's such a major change. I need to think it over.'

Harry's heart sank. 'Well, I'll leave you the report and if you want to go through it again, give me a call.'

Harry wrote his number on the front cover and handed his report over.

'Here's your driving licence,' Jack pulled it out of his wallet. 'Thanks for all the work you put into this.'

Harry took back his licence, closed his briefcase and left the cafe. He felt miserable. His only prospect now was joining the family 'firm'.

'Hi Jack,' Ben arrived at eleven for his lunch shift. 'You OK?'

'I'm fine. Met Harry this morning and he's come up with some ideas. Wouldn't mind getting your opinion this afternoon.'

Ben read the report and looked up at Jack. 'It's a big change but makes sense.'

Jack paced the floor and turned to Ben. 'Some of Stan's regulars have been getting lunch from Starlight Cafe for thirty years. It's an institution around here. I used to come here after school for milkshakes and vanilla slices. Sat at that table over there. Stan would be shocked if I turned it into a burger cafe.'

'Well, Jack, it's going nowhere as it is. Your uncle let the place go and you're never going to compete with places like Anton's. He should have retired years ago instead of poisoning half the district.'

Jack bristled. 'He ran this place for years without any trouble. He made one mistake, that's all.'

'Pretty big mistake poisoning a load of senior citizens and that's the ones you know about. The place was a health hazard before you cleaned it up. He was lucky not to have killed someone,' Ben shot back.

'Stan started this cafe from scratch and everyone loves him round here.'

'Don't think they love him that much Jack. His so-called regulars have gone off to Anton's. Truth is, this place might have been here a long time but you can't eat history.'

'Well, why don't you bugger off like the regulars then?' Jack snapped.

'Suits me.' Ben grabbed his coat and left.

Ben walked along a bike path beside the old outer circle railway, kicking at stones as he walked, chin down on his chest. He kept his fists deep in his pockets; he was frightened they would lash out on their own if he released them.

Jack threw his cup in the sink, smashing it into pieces. He cleaned up the cafe, deep in thought and drove home.

'How did it go with Harry?' Julie asked, peering up from the television.

'He thinks I should completely demolish the place and turn it into a place that only sells burgers. He's right but Stan will hate it.' Jack threw himself onto the couch.

'What did Ben think?'

'We had a row. He said Stan was a danger and should have retired years ago. That he was lucky not to have killed someone. I love that place Julie, so many good memories. If I ever got worried or frightened, Uncle Stan or Aunty Ruby would look after me. They'd cheer me up and make me laugh. I hate Ben going on about Stan.'

Julie picked up Harry's report and started reading.

'Do you think Harry's plan is any good Jack?'

Jack re-arranged the couch cushions to make himself more comfortable. 'I'm not a marketing genius but his ideas make a lot more sense than what I'm doing now. If you can believe the figures, there's room in the area for a quality fast burger-style business. Mack 'n' Morti's is the nearest fast-food place and as we know, it's booming. There's no other local competition. It's a good idea and maybe it won't cost as much as I think. We could probably work with the existing cooking equipment for a while.'

The scene with Ben kept repeating over and over in Jack's head. He couldn't help feeling defensive about the Starlight but Ben saw it for what it was: a rundown old cafe. He realised it wasn't Stan he was defending but his own childhood.

He turned to Julie. 'I shouldn't let my childhood memories hold us back. I'll give Harry's plan a go. Shit, I wish I hadn't fired off at Ben so fast. What can I do about him?'

'You know the answer to that.'

The following morning, Jack drove to Ben's flat in the Towers. He trudged up the concrete stairs to Ben's door and pressed the buzzer. From inside, he could hear the muffled commentary of the cricket. Ben opened the door in his pyjamas.

'I'm sorry mate. I don't know what got into me. I talked a lot of crap yesterday. I've been a complete dickhead.'

Ben motioned Jack to come in. Jack slumped into one of the old armchairs Ben had bought at the second-hand furniture shop.

'Julie's read the report and agrees Harry's onto something. If it hadn't been Uncle Stan's cafe, I wouldn't have gotten so worked up. What you said was right Ben. I've got to make the Starlight the best place to get burgers in London. I'd like you to be part of it, what do you say?'

Ben was wary.

'I can't keep going part time, I need you to offer full-time work and not for a couple of weeks. If the revamp doesn't work though, I'll understand.'

'Yes, I agree, full time, no recriminations. Are we back in business?'

'Yes, as long as you don't throw a fit when we gut the place.'

'I promise I'll behave. We need to see Harry pretty quick before he stuffs up another holdup and gets stuck behind bars.'

A sense of excitement grew in Jack as he made his way home.

'How did it go with Ben?' Julie asked.

'He's short of money and needs full-time work. I can't do this on my own and I trust him. I know he's going for interviews, so I agreed to hire him full time.'

'How? We don't have enough savings. How are you going to pay him and renovate the cafe?'

'I'll show you.'

Jack went into their bedroom and came back with a small suitcase. He pressed the locks and lifted the lid, then gently lifted out an original Luke Skywalker action figure with telescoping lightsabre in its original box. 'It's a collector's item and I checked the latest sale price last night after you went to bed. I couldn't believe it. In mint condition like mine, they sell for around twelve thousand pounds. Funny really, I bought this with my paper-round money when I was eleven. It took me months to save up but I knew I had to have Luke. He was special so I kept him in the box on a shelf away from my other toys.'

Julie looked shocked. 'Jack, are you sure you want to sell it?'

'Taking over the Starlight was exciting at first but the more time I spend making sandwiches the more I feel like a clone of Stan. I've copied what he's done without thinking. Harry's report opened my eyes. I love Stan but the Starlight is our future, Julie and I want to make it into something we can be proud of. I have to make this work.'

CHAPTER 14
CASSIE

'What did you say? You want me to meet you at the cafe?' Harry asked in surprise. 'Can't hear what you're saying, what's that banging noise?'

'That's Ben ripping the sandwich cabinet off the wall. Come over quick, before he destroys the place. We've got work to do.'

When Harry arrived, Jack and Ben were unscrewing the crockery cabinets.

'You don't hang around, do you? Taking the place apart already!'

Standing on the countertop, Jack unscrewed the last bracket from the cabinet.

'Yeah, we thought we'd see how hard it was.'

Ben brushed the dust from his jeans and spoke to Harry. 'Have a look over in that corner. I ripped up some of the lino and the floorboards look in good condition.'

With help from Harry, they lifted the cabinet onto the floor, then settled around a table to discuss the report.

'I had a look at a couple of cafes near where I live,' Jack said. 'One had similar furniture to ours. They decorated it with big green plants in tubs and lined the walls with corrugated-iron sheets. Looked great and the place was busy.'

Jack looked at the bright yellow walls of the Starlight.

'This whole place needs a re-design with a strong theme, something fresh to attract younger customers. We need to decide on that before we go much further. First thing is to find a good, creative painter.'

Harry smiled. 'You need to meet my cousin Cassie. She's fantastic and not too expensive.'

'Great! When can we meet her?'

'I'm seeing her in the next hour or so. I'll ask her what she thinks, I've told her about the Starlight.'

'Ben and I can go with you?'

'Don't worry, I'll bring her here.'

'The van's outside, we can go together,' Jack insisted. 'Save you a walk.'

Harry's heart sank. He wasn't sure it was a good idea taking them to where Cassie worked but he didn't want to cause an argument.

They measured out the cafe. The removal of the cabinets allowed extra space for customers. They tore down the partition hiding the deep-fat fryer and grill to free up more space, then measured out space for a larger grill and bigger coffee machine.

On the way to Cassie, Harry crouched in the back of the van behind the two cabin seats and gave directions.

Jack slowed down as they approached a railway station.

'Keep going Jack, past the station and turn right up the alley.'

Harry pointed to a set of large, half-open iron gates at the entrance of a cobbled alley. The alley ran between two derelict red brick shunting sheds.

The van squeezed through the gates. Jack looked at the

faded sign, hanging at a drunken angle from the left gate: *Private Property—Trespassers prosecuted.*

'You sure this is OK, Harry?'

'Yeah, no one comes here, we'll be fine. Cassie's around here somewhere.'

They drove to the end of the sheds. Harry directed them past a rusty disused railway line. They reached another big red brick shed and parked the van. Jack and Ben followed Harry past rusted machinery and areas overgrown with tall weeds. They came to a padlocked entrance in front of another brick building. The heavy wooden doors were big enough for a train to go through but there was no sign of a door handle or access door. Harry produced a penknife and started working on a small panel in the right-hand corner. The panel swung open and they squeezed through.

'Been here before then, Harry?' Jack closed the panel behind him.

'A few times, follow me and watch your step.'

The interior of the shed was dark and cold. Light filtered through dirty windows set high in the walls. They walked in silence, single file between rusty rail lines. Light peered through the cracks in a door at the far end. The shed was empty apart from piles of dust-covered crates. Wooden slats were strewn all over the floor.

Suddenly, a raging, snarling ball of fur launched itself from the top of the crates and crashed into Harry. It sent him flying to the floor in a cloud of dust. Jack and Ben were several steps behind and only caught a glimpse of whatever landed on Harry. The snarling noise was terrifying and echoed around the empty shed. Jack grabbed a wooden slat and ran towards Harry, tripping and stumbling in the dark.

'You stupid fat mongrel, Colin!' Harry yelled.

He clambered to his feet, brushing down his jacket.

'This is Colin, Cassie's dog. He's pretending to be a guard dog but he's too old and fat to hurt anyone, aren't you, fatso?'

Harry patted Colin and the dog rolled onto its back, waiting for Harry to scratch his stomach.

'Sounded bloody dangerous to me,' Ben said, keeping a close watch on Colin.

'You sure he's OK?' Jack asked.

Harry grabbed a handful of fur on each side of Colin's head and shook him. 'Stop frightening my friends, you stupid dog.'

Colin wagged his tail and lolled on his back again.

'Where's Cassie, Colin? You go find her,' commanded Harry.

Jack and Ben followed Harry and the dog to a door hidden by a crate. The door led to a large courtyard, surrounded by walls from other shunting sheds. Tarmac covered the ground but long cracks broke its surface like a network of veins. The cracks grew clumps of stringy grass broken up by tall thistles.

Jack squinted as they left the shed. He saw Colin walk toward a bucket next to a battered rucksack. The dog settled next to the bucket and barked. Now Jack and Ben could see him in daylight, it was clear that he was a mixture of Border Collie and Labrador. An overweight, black and white mixture.

'What was all that row?' came a female voice. It sounded like it came from the roof.

'Bloody Colin playing attack dog again,' Harry replied, shielding his eyes from the sun. 'That dog will have a heart attack one day.'

'He was being playful, wanted to surprise you Harry!' the voice shouted back.

'I'll kick him in the balls if he does that again. Then he'll get a surprise.'

'Don't be a misery Harry, you know he loves you.'

A minute later, the end of a rope dropped to the ground beside the rucksack. Ben was transfixed watching a small figure bathed in sunlight gracefully abseil down the side of the shunting shed.

'How are ya, Harry?' Cassie unhitched her rope.

Cassie was nineteen. Ben felt self-conscience as he dusted off his jeans and pushed his hair away from his eyes. He felt the colour rising in his cheeks as he was drawn into the gaze of her big brown eyes. Cassie smiled at Ben, showing a glimpse of perfect white teeth set against the brown of her skin. Her patched khaki cargo pants and shirt were covered in paint and pockets. Out of the bottom of the pants protruded black lace-up boots.

'Cassie, this is Jack and Ben, they're interested in your artwork.'

'Sure thing, I can show you some of my stuff if you like. Follow me.'

'Not up the rope?' asked Ben.

Cassie laughed.

'No, I was working on a second-storey wall, so we can walk to where we're going.'

They followed Cassie through a narrow alleyway that led to the other side of the sheds. Ten-feet-high graffiti featured the length of its wall. It showed three distorted people swirling through a multicoloured whirlpool. The whole piece was overlaid with a series of indecipherable letters.

'Did you do this?' Jack asked Cassie.

'Sure did.'

'This is fantastic. I've never thought much about graffiti before but this is amazing. The more you look at it, the more detail shows up.'

He turned to Cassie. 'Has Harry told you what we need?'

'A bit. You want to jazz up some old dive and turn it into a burger joint.'

Harry winced.

Jack looked back at the wall. 'We hadn't thought about graffiti. I mean, the cafe isn't big like this. Have you done murals and sign-writing inside buildings?'

'It's a matter of scale. Trust me, I'll show you some designs to make your joint look wicked, it won't frighten you.'

'She's good,' Harry said, 'you gotta trust me on this one Jack.'

'Your work is beautiful Cassie. Let me think on it for a day or so.'

'Sure.' Cassie shrugged. 'Hey Harry, can your mates give me and Colin a lift to Uncle Ned's? I promised I'd drop in this afternoon.'

'That all right with you, Jack?'

Jack nodded.

Cassie emptied her pockets of spray cans and put them in her rucksack. As she went to pick up the bag, Ben bent over and grabbed it, carrying it back to the van.

She took the bag from Ben. 'Move over Harry, I'll get in the back with you.'

'No, no, no.' Ben guided Cassie to the front passenger seat.

Ben climbed in the back with Harry and Colin jumped up after them. The dog placed his head between the two front seats and drooled on the handbrake. A pungent smell filled the van.

'You dirty bastard Colin,' Harry choked and coughed, covering his nose. 'Quick, open the windows or we're all going to die.'

The odour reached Jack in an instant. 'Smells like someone's died,' he spluttered, winding down the window fast.

Ben's eyes started to water. 'Hope the paintwork hasn't peeled off the van.'

Colin wagged his tail, looking pleased.

'Thanks for the lift Jack,' Harry said as they pulled up at Ned's house. Ben handed Cassie her rucksack. She smiled. 'Thanks Ben, hope the cafe goes well.' Cassie followed Harry up Ned's driveway with Colin by her side. Ben stood on the pavement watching her go before he returned to the van.

'Come to dinner tonight Ben. Let's talk things over with Julie.'

Jack and Julie's small glass-topped dining table sat at the far end of the kitchen. The kitchen led through to a comfortable sitting-room furnished with a leather three-piece suite. A door led upstairs to the bathroom and two bedrooms. Jack poured out beers for he and Ben and a glass of chardonnay for Julie.

'How are the burger recipes coming along Ben?'

'I've been following chefs on YouTube to find ideas. They say to make the perfect burger you can't use any old cheap mince. We must use lean ground beef and fresh ingredients. It will cost more but we'll sell the best burgers in town.'

'Great, we'll come up with some clever names after we try them.'

Julie poured a second chardonnay. 'Jack told me you were at school together and shared a passion for *Star Wars*. But he hasn't told me how you became friends.'

Ben smiled. 'We were about ten when Miss Pennyfeather started at our school as a student teacher. So, Jack is obsessed and follows her everywhere.

'Well, the Bromley brothers live on our council estate. They were nasty bastards bashing up and stealing from the younger kids at school. Jack sees Eric Bromley scratching the door of Miss Pennyfeather's red Mini with a compass in the school car park.

'I'm on my way home and I see Jack launching himself at Eric. Eric falls over and Jack starts pummelling him. Trouble is, he hasn't noticed Reggie Bromley stealing the hubcaps on the other side of the Mini. Reggie gets Jack in a headlock and Eric recovers and starts punching Jack.

'Well Jack's in my class and I like him. I run over and swing my satchel at Eric. Inside is a metal bowl I made in metalwork. There's a loud dong as it hits Eric's head and he falls across the bonnet of the Mini, snapping the aerial. I grab Reggie around the neck, trying to release the headlock on Jack. We shuffle and push each other, bending the wing mirror of the Mini against the window.'

'That's right,' Jack said. 'Then Eric Bromley grabs you in a headlock. We're all-in headlocks. We stagger, swear and kick at each other, sometimes connecting with the sides of the Mini trying to get an advantage.

'Two teachers prise us apart and promise us a bollocking from the headmaster the next morning. So, then I talked Ben into going to his house because he tells me he has a new *Star Wars* poster.' Ben felt a wave of embarrassment remembering Jack's face as they entered the neglected kitchen,

'That's very funny,' Julie laughed. 'You know, Jack is still a bit fiery.'

'Yes, I know.'

'Ben,' Jack said, suddenly looking uncomfortable. 'We haven't spoken about this but I need to tell you something.'

'I remember going into your house the first time. It was so cold and gloomy. You told me you looked after yourself. Your dad had left a long time ago and your mum usually stayed at her boyfriend's house. At first, I thought you were lucky but the more I looked around the empty rooms, the more I realised how lonely you must have been. It made me sad to see only one breakfast bowl on the table. I saw the pile of coins near the sink your mother left you for food. As a child, I didn't realise how wrong it was. Child Services should have been there to help you. I feel so guilty I didn't tell my parents.'

'That's in the past mate.' His brown eyes watered. 'We were just kids. I understand why dad left; my mother was a real bitch. She never wanted me; I think I was an accident. She met some bloke at a pub and started spending nights at his place. I was scared to say anything, or she'd start yelling. That's when Dodger offered me a way to make money.'

'Is that why you left school Ben?' Julie asked. 'Did you have to move away with Dodger for work?'

Ben felt an icy hand crawl up the back of his neck. He cursed himself for mentioning Dodger. He looked up at Julie's gentle face, he couldn't hide hist past from his friends any longer. Ben took a deep breath.

'I got sent to juvie for nicking cars. They call it the Young Offender Institution training program. Mum moved in with that bloke permanently and she kept forgetting to leave me money. A mate of Dad's called Dodger gave me a few quid to act as a lookout. He used to steal cars, deliver them to another bloke who stripped them and sold off the parts. We got caught on CCTV. It was scary at first but I got regular meals and my roommates never gave me trouble. They kept us busy with classes and training, so we always had something to do. I did a stint at Burger-a-Day. It was part of a government initiative with the Burger-a-Day corporate responsibility program to rehabilitate young offenders.

My case manager at juvie helped me get a job in a meat-packing place in Aylesbury. The place closed so I came back here.'

Jack poured Ben another beer. 'That sucks, why didn't you tell me? My mum and dad would have looked out for you.'

Ben shrugged. 'I don't know. I just got angry and it seemed an easy way out.'

Julie laid her hand on Ben's shoulder. 'That's terrible Ben, I can't imagine how hard it was. I'm glad you and Jack have caught up after all these years.'

Beeping from the oven broke the silence.

'I'll go.' Jack stood up and went to the kitchen.

The beeping stopped. 'It's ready,' he shouted from the kitchen.

Julie and Ben sat at the dining table. Jack carved roasted chicken onto a platter and placed it on the table next to bowls of salad and boiled potatoes. They started talking about the visit to Cassie.

'I don't know about using a graffiti artist,' Julie said, handing Ben the salad.

'Cassie is brilliant,' Ben enthused. 'She's got real talent. The work we saw today was fantastic; her colours have a life of their own.'

Jack passed Julie the chicken. 'Ben's right, her work is great and would make us stand out.'

Julie frowned. 'Are you sure you want to get involved with Harry's family? It's already a risk using him. It's illegal to graffiti private property; she may have been in trouble with the police.'

Ben shook his head. 'I don't think so.'

'Why are you so certain Ben?'

'She's cute,' Jack winked at Julie.

'Oh, I see, I may not have an impartial witness here.'

Ben blushed. 'The potatoes are great.' Ben placed several onto his plate.

Jack laughed. 'I'll give Harry a call after dinner and find

out the cost for both to help renovate the cafe. Worst case is we paint over it if we hate it.'

Later that night, Jack phoned Harry. 'Hi, Harry, it's Jack. We've had a talk about your plan and decided to go ahead. But I need to get an idea of what it's going to cost for you and Cassie.'

Jack waited in silence. 'Are you there Harry?'

'Y-Yes, I'm here. I didn't expect to hear from you. I mean so soon,' he stammered.

'How about we work on an hourly rate Jack. What does ten quid an hour each sound like?'

'That's fair enough. Can you and Cassie come to the cafe tomorrow? We want to start planning our next steps.'

'I'll check with Cassie but I'm sure that will be okay. You won't regret this Jack. The Starlight Cafe is going to be the greatest place to buy a burger in London.'

After the phone call Harry was overcome with relief. *You've done it, Harry, you've done it.* He saw a faint glimmer of hope in avoiding a life of crime.

'Slow down Harry, slow down. What's that about the cafe?'

'They want to go ahead Cassie; we've got the job. Ten quid an hour. Can you meet me at the cafe at ten tomorrow?'

'Well done Harry, I could do with the money and those two seem like nice guys. Looks like you won't have to rob a bank after all,' she laughed.

Harry opened the fridge, grabbing a beer and a slice of

cold pizza. He collapsed on the couch next to his housemate. 'I've got a job Reg, a legit one at the cafe.'

CHAPTER 15
END OF AN ERA

Jack woke up early, excited by the prospect of starting work on the new Starlight. He grabbed his jacket, kissed Julie goodbye and swallowed his last mouthful of tea.

'Don't forget to talk to Mrs Edgecombe and Henry at the neighbouring shops. Do it before you start changing everything!' Julie shouted as Jack climbed into the van.

'I don't want a burger place next to my florist,' Mrs Edgecombe moaned. 'My clients are professionals. I'll complain to council the minute I see kids with those silly baseball caps racing up and down on skateboards. And there better not be any mess left near my lilium and gazania display buckets. I don't understand why you want to go changing things. Your uncle had a good business selling sandwiches every day to people with proper jobs.'

Henry the tobacconist, was more receptive.

'You need to make changes. To be honest, my business has gotten quieter too. If you manage to get a new set of customers, it might rub off on me.'

Jack and Ben were moving furniture into a storage shed at the back of the cafe when Harry and Cassie arrived.

Cassie wore bright-yellow jeans with frayed patches sewn over the knees and a red knitted sleeveless top. She carried a large sketchbook.

Ben wondered if she was seeing anyone.

He showed her around the cafe, telling her about the recipes he planned for the burgers. 'We're going to sell the best burgers in town using good-quality meat. They won't be anything like the rubbishy burgers you get from fast food places.' Ben stopped and apologised. 'Sorry, Cassie, this must be boring for you, don't know why I'm rabbiting on.' Cassie smiled.

'No Ben, it's great that you're having a go at this. Have you thought of having a vegan option for your burgers? I'm sure they would help bring in a younger crowd.'

'I don't know much about vegan food Cassie. Sounds like a great idea. Do you know where I can find out?'

Cassie smiled. 'I'll write down a few suggestions for you when I'm in next.'

She started unpacking her rucksack and pulled out a round green container that held chalk and sharpeners. As she started to unscrew the two halves, Jack shouted, 'Stop! That's it! Genius. I've been trying to work out how we can package Ben's burgers. I want to be environmental and stylish. Not like Burger-a-Day with so much waste.' Jack took Cassie's green container and examined it carefully. It was in two halves, joined by a screwed thread. The top half had five small, round holes. 'We can wash this and customers can use it like they do with a recyclable coffee cup. Where did you get this one, Cassie?'

'They have them in all colours at the Emporium on Cecil Street.'

Jack returned the container. 'It's great, the holes in the lid will let out some heat and stop the burgers going soggy. We could charge extra for the containers and give a discount each time they bring it back for another burger.'

'I like that,' Harry said. 'The first reusable fast-food container. Let's see, how about we call it the "Burger Bin"; it's great branding.'

Ben examined the container, turning it over in his hand. 'But what if people bring them back for a refill dirty? they'll accuse us of poisoning them.'

'We'll offer a service to clean them,' Jack said. 'Can't use a dishwasher and handwashing will be too slow when we're busy. I'll chat to Magpie; he might come up with something.'

'Who's Magpie?' Cassie asked.

'He's an old mate of my dad. He calls him Magpie because he never throws anything away. I was only about ten the first-time dad took me to his workshop. He scared the life out of me. He had these thick, black-rimmed glasses held together with gaffer tape and big tufts of curly black hair poking out of a tea cosy. His overalls were full of holes and covered in grease. He'd made me a fantastic soapbox cart that even had suspension. We became good mates after that and he let me help him sometimes in his workshop.

'He still runs a small engineering shop near the airport. The place is filled with stuff he reckons might come in handy. Magpie is clever, a great inventor. Also, the world's greatest optimist; he reckons he's going to crack the big time and make his fortune one day. Trouble is, he gets distracted and things go wrong. I'm sure he'll invent a great cleaning machine for us but we'll have to make sure it doesn't kill anyone. I'll go and see him tomorrow.'

Harry looked around the cafe. *I still can't believe Jack's accepted my ideas. I've got to make it work.* He turned to Jack. 'How's the new layout going, Jack?'

'I've sourced two counters from Crusty's reclamation yard that sound the right size. I'll have a look at them tomorrow after I've seen Magpie. I've also spoken to a mate I used to work with who can sand and polish the floorboards if we get rid of the lino.

'Funny, the Starlight has been here thirty years and always looked the same. It's the end of an era.'

'It's still got the same name,' Ben said, 'all you're doing is updating it.

Jack looked around the cafe. It's got to make money to keep going.'

'But I want to keep the spirit of Stan's cafe alive and work his legacy into your design Cassie.'

'I can do that, it's a beautiful idea Jack,' Cassie said.

She leaped up and did a star jump in the middle of the shop.

'I'm so excited! Starlight Cafe will be fabulous.'

Ben couldn't stop staring as Cassie jumped about the shop. She was the most wonderful girl he'd ever seen.

CHAPTER 16
SECOND THOUGHTS

Stan sat at the breakfast table, carefully picking out pumpkin seeds from his toast. 'What are you doing Stan?' Mary asked in an exasperated voice.

'This stupid bread has got bird seed in it. Gets stuck under my dentures.'

Stan flicked out one obstinate seed that flew in the air and landed in Mary's tea.

'For goodness' sake, Stan. Go and get some plain toast.'

Stan looked towards the toaster where two people were waiting.

'Can't be bothered, there's a queue. I tried the other bread yesterday; it gave me indigestion. It's that sourdough rubbish.'

Mary sighed. 'We thought we'd visit the animal sanctuary today. They've got two of those beautiful Jerusalem Donkeys.'

'I don't want to go to a sanctuary. Anyway, donkeys bite if you get too close.'

Mary felt her blood pressure rise. 'You moaned on our walk around Harfield Castle yesterday. Then you complained to that nice waitress about the scones in the tea-room.'

'Well, they were stale.'

'And I bet you haven't apologised to that poor little girl, have you?'

'It wasn't my fault,' Stan said sulkily.

'Stan, you agreed to look after her little dog while she bought an ice cream.'

'I did look after it. She took too long, so I tied the dog up. I wanted to read the paper.'

'Why the bloody hell did you tie it to the boom gate?'

'I was trying to read; I didn't look properly. If that car hadn't turned up, it would have been fine. It was just bad luck she came out of the shop as the boom gate went up. It just hung there and whined a bit. I waved the driver through and the boom gate came down.'

'I've had just about enough of you Stan. You've been nothing but a misery this holiday. George and I are going to the sanctuary, we'll see you tonight. Don't forget to apologise.'

As children, Stan and Mary were discouraged from expressing their feelings. *Just get on with it*, their father used to say. He felt terrible when the little girl saw her dog in the air but his embarrassment stopped him from comforting her.

He couldn't shake his melancholy; no matter how hard he tried, he kept thinking about the Starlight Cafe.

He'd endured sleepless nights since the start of his holiday and spent the early hours wandering around the resort waiting for breakfast to start. He avoided the family accommodation area with its playground and paddling pools. It reminded him of Ruby and the girls in happier times. It also brought memories of regret for not listening to the girls as they grew into teenagers.

Mary and George left for the animal sanctuary. Stan wandered to the river with his rod but the fish weren't biting. The sun glinted through the trees on the bank of the slow-moving river that ran through the resort. Stan's bright-orange float drifted slowly towards a large eddy where he was convinced a fish was waiting. He sat forward on his stool, elbows on his knees, feeling the warm sun on his back.

Stan and Ruby had bought their semi-detached house fifty-two years ago in Palmers Green, in the borough of Enfield. Money was tight for the young couple and Ruby's father had loaned them the deposit. Stan worked in the kitchen at the local hospital; he was famous for his lumpy mashed potatoes and mushy carrots and peas. Ruby worked on the counter at Sainsbury's until she was eight months' pregnant. They hadn't expected twin girls. Raising them was hard and Ruby, constantly tired, couldn't return to work. Without Ruby's income they scrimped and saved paying back the loan and mortgage. Over the years, the tranquillity of the countryside gave way to housing developments. New roads appeared and shopping centres sprung up. They spread like oil slicks, devouring the surrounding apple orchards and market gardens.

Stan was happy in the hospital kitchen but dreamed of buying his own cafe. He and Ruby became regulars at the Willow Coffee House in Bowes Road. Stan marvelled at Carlos as he chatted to his regulars and worked the coffee machine, all the while making sandwiches. When

Stan told him about his dream, he offered to help. He sat with Stan and Ruby, telling them how he ran the Willow Coffee House. One Saturday Carlos waved to Stan to meet him behind the counter. 'Stan, my cousin Matias told me about a cafe that's for sale. It's in a good location and has been established for over twenty years. It's got a steady turnover but needs updating. Here's the address if you want to have a look.'

Stan showed Ruby the scrap of paper. 'That's only about five miles away on the way to London, Stan. We can have look next week.'

Stan stirred his tea distractedly, slopping it into the saucer. 'Dad, that's the fifth sugar you've put in your tea,' his daughter Ginny said, nudging her sister in amusement.

Rebecca made her move. 'Dad, can we have your vanilla slice?' Stan's mind was elsewhere, he gave a faint nod and continued stirring his tea. Rebecca carefully slid the slice away.

Ruby smiled as the girls devoured the slice. She nudged Stan. 'I know you're not going to rest until we see this place. How about we have a quick look now?'

'That's a great idea.' Stan looked at his empty plate. 'Where's my vanilla slice?'

The Starlight Cafe sat between a betting shop and tobacconist. The cafe closed on Saturdays but they were excited at what they saw through the window. He and Ruby had a little money saved but not enough to buy the business.

Ruby's father was generous and helped them out with another loan.

Night after night, when the girls were in bed, Stan and Ruby sat at the kitchen table talking plans. They wanted to bring it into the seventies and cover the wooden floors and heavy panelling. They traded in the old furniture for new, vinyl-upholstered chrome chairs and Formica-topped tables. With help from Stan's parents, they stripped the walls and painted the whole place bright yellow. Then they laid light-grey, marble-effect lino on the floor.

The cost of the renovation and loan weighed heavily upon them. The couple spent long hours at the cafe to pay off their debts. They were busy from 6am getting ready for work and preparing the girls for school. By 7am, deliveries started to arrive and they began making food for the day ahead.

The Starlight opened at 7.30 for the first wave of customers on their way to work. A second, larger wave came at noon for lunch. Initially they sold only sandwiches and cakes but Ruby convinced Stan to buy a griller. The burgers and chips were a success and the cafe flourished. Ordering from suppliers and accounting tasks became a regular evening job once the dinner table was cleared.

It meant less time to spend with Ginny and Rebecca. Through their school years, the girls had breakfast next door with the neighbour's children. After school they went to the Starlight to do their homework where Stan served up their tea and a favourite drink.

The girls' cousin, Jack, frequently visited the cafe after school. He loved being in the cafe, taking in the comforting atmosphere and the warm smell of food and hot drinks. He'd watch the steady stream of people placing their orders at the counter. On rainy days he peered out at people walking past, bowed over, clutching their umbrellas. He felt cosy as he saw cars and buses go by with headlights blazing through the late afternoon winter gloom.

At sixteen, both girls left school. Ginny enrolled at the London College of Beauty Therapy to become a hairdresser. Rebecca applied for a job as a library assistant. Stan was disappointed. 'I can't understand why you won't work at the Starlight. Your mother and I have built a great business and I want you to be part of it.'

'I'm not working in the cafe Dad,' Ginny said. 'After I get my diploma, I'm going to save up and open my own salon.'

Stan looked at Rebecca. 'Sorry Dad, I don't want to work there either. I love the library and want to be a librarian.'

Stan was hurt. 'If the cafe's good enough for us, I can't see why being a hairdresser or librarian is any better. The Starlight's our family business and you should be proud to be part of it. We did this for you. You can't turn your backs on it as if it's nothing.'

Ginny snapped. 'Don't try and shame us. It wasn't for our benefit. Mum told us you always wanted a cafe, Christ knows why.'

Rebecca spoke more calmly. 'The cafe is *your* dream Dad, it's not ours. We don't want to be on our feet all day serving people, then catching up on paperwork at night. When was the last time we spent time together as a family?'

Stan clutched the back of the kitchen chair, his knuckles turning white. He spoke slowly, deliberately, as his face reddened. 'We've worked our fingers to the bone to support you two. Other children would give their eye teeth to be given this opportunity. But it's not good enough for both of you. You are just a couple of selfish brats.'

An uncomfortable silence hung over the house. Ruby couldn't find out what had happened. The girls left three days later. Their note to Ruby said they wouldn't be back. No forwarding address.

Ruby had been the unflappable one in their marriage but when the girls left, she broke down and sobbed uncontrollably.

At first Stan tried to justify his confrontation with the girls but seeing Ruby so distraught made him realise the true extent of his actions.

Ruby blamed Stan entirely.

'Stan, I don't care what you have to do but I'm begging you to find them.'

Stan tried to find his daughters. Their friends either didn't know where they'd gone or weren't talking. The house grew silent without the animated chatter between Ruby and the girls. Stan tortured himself reliving his last conversation with Ginny and Rebecca. Ruby spent less time at the cafe, away from Stan. At home, their conversations became stilted. She couldn't forgive Stan and distracted herself by spending time alone in the garden.

In later years, both girls married and had children. There was a kind of reconciliation, with Ginny and Rebecca returning home from time to time to see Ruby. After Ruby died, they rarely came. Stan spent his time in the house and tending the garden. He thought of the girls all the time and displayed their photos in pride of place on the sideboard. But Stan hadn't seen either daughter for over a year. He rang them but they seldom answered. If they answered, the conversation was short and strained. He invited them over but they either had children's parties or trips away planned.

Stan discouraged other family and friends. Apart from the BBC news his house was silent. He preferred living alone with all his memories and swore he'd never live anywhere else. 'I want to be carried out in a box, not a wheelchair,' he told Mary.

Mary was four years younger than Stan. She rang him every week to make sure he was coping. Since Ruby had died, Stan had settled into a fixed routine. Work all week at the cafe, Saturday morning he would go shopping at Tesco's. Saturday afternoon was hoovering and dusting. Sunday morning, he washed and ironed and gardened in the afternoon. Stan loved his roses and the garden was alive with their colour and scent. He had a small square of lawn but rose beds took up most of the space. Stan maintained it as Ruby laid it out when they first bought the house.

The fish still weren't biting and Stan's mind drifted. He was back unlocking the Starlight, jiggling the key in the stubborn lock. Turning on the tap and filling the kettle. The gas ignited on the hob and blue flames lit the underside of the kettle. Stan fed the toaster with two slices of bread, then placed his cup of tea on a cafe table, unscrewing the lid from the raspberry jam. He went through the motions of taking sandwich ingredients out of the fridge and putting them out on the counter. He wondered how many sandwiches he'd made over the years. Half a million was his guess. Maybe he deserved an entry in the *Guinness Book of Records*. His fingers moved slowly across his knee as if spreading the butter. The doorbell jingled. Andrew James came in wanting his usual, a toasted ham and cheese sandwich with white coffee. They'd have their usual grumble about the weather as he paid. Stan fast forwarded to lunchtime and saw his regulars sitting at tables reading newspapers and eating his food. Fast forward to the end of the day. He turned the sign from *Open* to *Closed,* cleaned the cafe and adjusted the chairs around the tables. Stan could see himself turning off the lights and jiggling the key once more to lock the cafe. He said goodnight to the Starlight, gently patted the old door and left. He was looking forward to getting into his slippers to relieve his aching feet.

The line jerked and he sat up with a start as his elbow slipped off his knee and he nearly toppled off his stool.

He thought about what life would be like when he got home. Weekends were always lonely but at least he had the company of strangers from Monday to Friday. The thought of being home all week depressed him. He just didn't know how to fill the hours. Apart from his garden, he had no other interests and few friends.

His stomach still churned, thinking about the Under New Management sign.

What if Jack's caught the chip pan alight and burnt the place down? It's easily done. I had a few near-misses myself.

And I bet he's stuffing those sandwiches with too much filling. He won't listen.

No, he wasn't ready for retirement. What was he thinking? Jack simply didn't have the experience. He just needed a holiday. When he was back home, he would take the cafe back and make some improvements: new sandwich fillings, fancy cakes. Check out the competition, spend a bit of time sampling their bestsellers.

The idea grew bigger in Stan's mind; he couldn't think why he hadn't thought of it before. The dark cloud around him began to lift.

His fishing line yanked again and he leaped up, ready to reel in fast. This was the big one, he knew it.

CHAPTER 17
MAGPIE

Turning into an industrial estate, Jack arrived at Magpie's workshop. A rusted sign hung above the roller door entry, Unit 23, Apex Engineering. Jack ducked under the half-open roller door and paused, adjusting to the dark brick interior. He peered into the corner office looking for Magpie.

The sound of a grinder reached him from the far end of the workshop. 'Magpie, you down there?' The sound of the grinder continued. He saw sparks flying from underneath an overgrown lawn mower. Jack carefully picked his way through several large piles of metal sheeting, stepping over old rusty pipes. Three half-dismantled Land Rovers blocked his progress until he found a gap and made his way past, pressed against the wall. He walked alongside a long steel workbench covered in a jumble of spanners and power tools. He loved the familiar smell of oil and grease in Magpie's workshop. Jack spotted him under a large machine. It had circular brushes protruding from the sides that reached to the floor. 'Magpie, it's Jack!' he shouted over the sound of the grinder.

'Hi, Jack,' Magpie crawled out from under the machine and wiped his oily hands on an even oilier rag. He stood up, scratching his grey, unkempt hair. Jack caught the familiar rich, dank smell of motor oil from his overalls.

'What's this Magpie? A mechanical centipede?'

'You'll be sorry when you read about my Turf-O-Matic in the *Financial Times*. It will change the world of tennis courts. You'll eat your words then.'

'Tried it yet?'

'Ah well, I've had teething problems. 'The first attempt created difficulties and the client over-reacted. I must go back when they get their tennis court repaired.'

Jack told Magpie about the cafe and their plans to turn it into a burger place.

'I'm thinking of using these containers. We need to clean them quickly with minimal manual labour.'

'Hm.' Magpie examined a container, turning it over and over in his greasy hands.

'Shouldn't be too hard,' he said. 'I've got a few bits and pieces that I could put together.'

He waved his hand vaguely at the piles of junk lining the workshop. 'Leave me with a few samples and I'll see what I can do. Give me a week.'

Jack's next stop was Crusty's Reclamation Yard in Enfield. The yard had been around since Jack was a child. An elderly man in a boiler suit was sticking price tags on old doors.

'What are you looking for mate?'

'I rang you about a shop counter for my cafe.'

'Try the aisle over there, near the black hob.'

Jack found three counters and checked their dimensions. The second one he looked at had a black marble effect but was too long.

'Can you cut the length down by eighteen inches?' he asked the man in the boiler suit.

'Sure, it'll cost you an extra fiver.'

Hunger pangs gnawed at Jack's stomach as he drove back to the Starlight. He smiled when he remembered Ben was preparing samples of burgers ready for the opening.

Ben had asked Harry and Julie to come along to give their opinion.

Ben experimented for hours with meat and seasonings and finally settled on a combination using mild herbs for the basic lean burger. He found the buns hard to find; most were too big or chewy but then he found a baker who made a slim muffin-style white bun.

He added salad, additional ingredients and sauces to complete the range of burgers.

They sat around a table as Ben brought out the first samples, cut into bite-size pieces.

'Do you think we should chew a few times and spit out the bits in a bin?' Jack suggested.

'Don't you dare!' Julie warned. 'It's not a wine tasting; swallow it and don't push your luck. Let's try Ben's first one, the basic burger.'

Ben looked expectantly from face to face while they finished off their samples. 'So, what do you think?'

Jack swallowed. 'Not bad Ben, meat's not too dry or chewy. A good squirt of ketchup and it'd be perfect.'

Ben's eyes narrowed.

Julie laughed.

'Ignore him Ben. He's teasing. It's absolutely delicious.'

Harry swallowed the last piece of the burger. 'This is so much better than Mack 'n' Morti's. It's a winner.'

Ben smiled in relief. 'The next one has a mild green curry and yogurt sauce with cucumber slice. I love the combination but it might be a bit hot,' he explained, removing a tray of samples from the oven.

'Hmmm,' murmured Harry. 'Fantastic, this is going to kill 'em. How about we call it the Bombay burger.'

They started the third sample. Jack swallowed and grabbed a glass of water. 'What the hell was that?' he spluttered as his eyes started to water.

'Chilli sauce special,' Ben said with a laugh.

Jack dabbed his eyes. 'Let's give it a trial period and call it the Blaster burger.'

'Next is your classic cheeseburger but we're not using those plasticky cheese slices. They're convenient but they taste like plasticine. And they're full of chemicals and colourings.'

There was a unanimous chorus of approval.

The last burger Ben presented was one with bacon and a fried egg.

Julie sniffed the burger. 'A breakfast burger!' 'Nothing better than the smell of bacon and eggs in the morning. Great selection, Ben! Now you have to practice making them in bulk and fast.'

Ben showed them how the bun he'd sourced from the bakery fitted snugly in the container they'd bought from the emporium.

'Jack will demonstrate.'

Jack stood back from the table and started with a flourish, 'Ladies and gentlemen, I give you a world first, the reusable bin burger. Not only are our burgers the finest and healthiest burgers in existence, they are also the most ecologically responsible. Now, while you're admiring the containers, I would also like to suggest that we call the plain burger Ben created, the Stan burger. It's a classic.'

'Nice idea, Jack,' Julie clapped, 'nice idea.'

Julie smiled at Ben. She thought back to the beginning. *So much has happened since Stan offered the cafe to Jack. Jacks relished the challenge to make the Starlight a success. I was wrong about Ben. He's good company. I don't think we could do this without him.*

CHAPTER 18
TRANSFORMATION

Jack arrived early, placing a notice in the window. *Closed—Re-Opening next Saturday*. Ben and Harry arrived shortly after Jack. A hiss of airbrakes signalled the arrival of the van from the demolition yard with the marble countertop.

The three worked at a rapid pace removing the faded lino and installing the new counter.

Jack hitched his trailer filled with lino to his van and headed to the tip.

He returned in time to meet Gary, who ran a floor polishing business. Gary was in his fifties and prided himself on keeping fit. He wore a black tight-fitting t-shirt printed with Aristocrat Floor Polishers on the back complimented with slim fitting jeans and black trainers. He'd worked with Jack before, restoring gymnasium floors at the schools.

'Cutting it a bit fine aren't you Jack?'

'Sorry mate, ripping up the lino took longer than I thought.'

Gary wheeled his sander into the cafe. 'I'll finish sanding this afternoon and put the first coat of polish on tonight. Don't walk on it for a couple of days.'

Thursday arrived. The floors shone with new life and everything was ready for Cassie to begin. She arrived with her sketchpad and a large bag of paints, brushes and spray cans. She spread protective sheeting over the newly polished floorboards and then presented Ben with a parcel.

'Hope you like it,' she said.

She'd been thinking a lot about Ben since they met and was nervous that he might not like her ideas. The parcel contained a thick wad of printed greaseproof paper. In the centre of each sheet was a design—a faded fifties-style picture of a tasty-looking burger. Around the outside in lettering: 'Starlight—Best burgers in the Universe'.

'Cassie, these are brilliant. People will buy our burgers for the wrappers alone. How did you do them?'

Cassie breathed out hard.

'A friend of mines at art college, so we printed them there last night. We can do more if you like them.'

'Like them! They're fantastic. The burgers will look brilliant.'

Cassie beamed with pride. 'I'd better make a start.'

She started mixing up Polyfilla in a plastic container.

'Let me help you with that,'

'That would be great Ben. Here's a scraper. We need to make small repairs on the worst of the cracks and dents in the walls and skirting boards. This stuff dries fast, so, once it starts to set, smooth it over with a damp cloth.'

They stood side by side, working their way around the room.

'Do you get on with your Uncle Ned?'

'Yeah, he always looks out for me, why do you ask?'

'Harry says he's a big crime boss.'

Cassie laughed, turning to Ben. 'He's more Arthur Daley than the Kray brothers.'

Ben filled the high sections while Cassie concentrated on the lower half. They looked around the cafe walls covered in white blotches. 'Looks like it's got measles,' Ben said.

Cassie handed him a sheet of sandpaper. 'OK, let's go around the room and smooth out any bumpy bits.'

'What's next, Cassie?'

'Grab that cloth and wipe off the dust where we've sanded.'

Ben turned around after wiping the walls. He burst out laughing.

'What's so funny?' Cassie asked in a muffled voice.

'Sorry Cassie, I can't help it,' Ben tried to suppress another fit of laughter. Cassie had changed into a set of lime-green plastic overalls. She wore a pair of welder's goggles and a half-mask painter's respirator. Her hair was covered by a paint-splattered woollen beanie.

'Out of my way you.' She gave Ben a playful punch in the ribs. 'I've got work to do.' She loaded her pockets with cans of spray paint and ushered Ben from the room.

The smell of acrylic paint was overwhelming. Cassie kept painting through the rest of the day. Ben insisted she stop for short breaks.

As night fell, her vision started to form. She'd created a night sky effect on the ceiling with stars and a moon. Arching across the whole ceiling were the words Starlight:

Out of this World. She made the letters look like tiny stars spread out in a Milky Way effect.

The wall colour descended from the ceiling into a softer tone, ending at mid-blue near the floor.

Jack wanted the bins and burger names to be highlighted, so she included them in the design.

Each wall displayed plastic burger containers looking like comets. Around them was graffiti writing in vivid colours of red, yellow and green. Bold lettering spelt out 'Starlight burgers—Only the leanest beef'. 'Try a Stan burger for a meal to remember' and 'Blaster burger—Big, Bad and Beefy'.

Cassie painted the largest window with the same design as the greaseproof wrappers. The hoarding above the cafe changed from Starlight Cafe to Starlight Burgers in white letters on a dark-blue background.

Jack and Harry arrived back at the Starlight to find Cassie standing in the middle of the cafe, covered in paint.

Ben turned to Jack, 'It's spectacular isn't it Jack. Cassie's a genius.'

'Not bad, is it?' Cassie said with a broad grin.

Harry looked around the walls. 'Knew you'd do it Cuz.'

'Stan will have a heart attack,' Jack said, 'but wow, it's amazing. Let's grab a celebration drink. I'll give Julie a ring and we can meet her at the Pickwick.'

The Pickwick was a small pub dating from the eighteenth century. One of the few pubs not owned by large brewery conglomerates, it retained its old-world charm. It was a favourite of Jack and Julie's, specialising in locally produced craft beers. They found a quiet corner in the welcoming snug next to the open fire. They settled into some well-used armchairs and a small settee.

Jack ordered the first round and packets of crisps. Ben squeezed in next to Cassie on the settee. They sat squashed together, sharing warmth from their bodies. A faint whiff of midnight-blue acrylic paint from Cassie's hair reached Ben's nostrils. She laid her head on his shoulder, exhausted. He never realised the smell of acrylic paint could be so lovely.

'I hear the transformation is remarkable,' Julie smiled at Cassie. 'Cheers Cassie and you too Harry. Jack is always telling me how glad he is to have you on the team.'

Jack brushed chip crumbs from his mouth with the back of his hand. 'I thought we should have some sort of official re-opening of the Starlight. I'm not sure how social media works but I reckon it's the way to go.'

'I can help with that,' Harry chimed in. 'We can advertise on Facebook, Instagram and Twitter. I'll set up the accounts and do a basic Facebook page to get you started.'

'Thanks Harry,' Jack raised his glass.

'By the way,' Harry said. 'I told my Uncle Ned about the cafe and I'm sure he'd like to drop by with a few friends if you have an opening night.'

Jack coughed and looked across at Ben. 'Er, sounds great.'

Harry looked up at the clock over the bar. 'Christ, it's ten o'clock. Reg will kill me. I promised to get his car back by 7.30. I'll drop you off Cassie.'

Harry held out his hand, helping Cassie to her feet. Ben stood up, not wanting her to leave. 'Night Cassie.' Cassie gave him a small wave as she left the bar.

Jack stood and laid his hand on Ben's shoulder. 'Come on Ben, we'll give you a lift.'

Julie picked up her backpack turning to Ben. 'Cassie wasn't what I was expecting, she's gorgeous and so talented.'

'Yes, she is.'

'And she seems pretty keen on you Ben.'

Ben's face flushed, 'I hope so, I can't stop thinking about her.'

CHAPTER 19
THE OPENING

'I can't believe we're doing this Julie.' Jack held Julie in his arms as they lay in bed. 'This is the most exciting thing I've ever done in my life.'

'You're not missing the handyman work then!'

'Not in the slightest. This is a chance to build our future. The handyman trade was hard. I was out in all weathers and regular work was hard to find. I'm starting to see why Stan loved the old place so much.'

He glanced at the bedside clock. 'Maybe I should go in now, there's a lot to set up for tonight.'

'It's six thirty in the morning Jack, you don't open till tonight.'

'But what if I've missed something?'

'When are you meeting Ben?'

'He'll be there at ten. I'll set up and help him to prep. I hope opening at six o'clock isn't too late; we should be able to catch people going home from work.'

'You've got plenty of time before you meet Ben.' Julie pulled Jack closer. She whispered in his ear. 'Give me a cuddle and I might even make you breakfast.'

Jack put the key in the lock to Starlight and gave it the customary shove but it remained stubbornly shut. He took the key out, checked he had the right one, reinserted it and gave another push. 'Shit,' he said under his breath. He saw Ben get off the bus and walk across the road toward him.

'What's up, Jack?'

'The lock's buggered and I can't get the bloody door open,' Jack said with a rising sense of panic.

Ben took the keys from Jack and began jiggling. The door remained stuck fast.

'What am I going to do, we've got to open at six?'

'Let's try the back door,' Ben said. They ran past the tobacconist and up an alleyway leading to the rear of the cafe. Jack tried putting the key in the lock but it wouldn't fit. Jack then remembered what Stan told him. 'Stan said he didn't have the key to this door, he only opened it from inside.'

'Fuck! I'm going to have to smash the door in. Stand back, Ben.'

'Hold on, I've got a pla—'

Too late. Jack was running at full pelt, leaping in the air and smashing into the door with his shoulder. He collapsed in a heap on the ground, clutching his arm. 'Ow, fuck! Ow, fuck!' He stood up and kicked the door. 'Ow, ow!'

The door hadn't moved. He hobbled back, preparing for a longer run up. Ben held up his hand.

'Let me try something.'

Ben scrutinised the lock. 'Give me your credit card and hand me that piece of wire by the fence.'

Ben slid the credit card in the crack of the door next

to the lock. He pushed the wire into the keyhole and wiggled it while sliding the credit card up and down. A sudden click and the door opened.

Jack slowly lowered his arms from his running position. 'What the? How did you?' he spluttered.

Ben looked embarrassed. 'I didn't get all my training at juvie from the teachers.'

They went inside and Jack undid the snib on the front door. 'Thanks, Ben, don't know what I would have done without you. Why didn't you open this one?'

Ben twisted the lock mechanism. 'This is a more secure lock, harder to open. The back door has an older style of lock. My roommate taught me the difference.'

Jack turned on the lights. 'We'd better get to work.'

Six o'clock came and Jack turned the sign over to *Open*. He turned on all the lights and Starlight Burgers opened for business. Within a minute a young couple strolled in.

'Can you change a five-pound note, mate?'

Ben saw the flash of disappointment on Jack's face. 'Sorry, we're short of change.' The couple left again.

'Not the best start in the world,' Ben said, smiling at Jack.

Jack shrugged his shoulders. 'Gotta start somewhere!'

'At least we got someone in the door!' Ben laughed.

Six-thirty came and went and still nobody. Jack stood by the espresso machine, tapping his fingers on the counter. Ben re-arranged his spatulas next to the grill.

'Not looking good, is it?' Jack said.

'Bit quiet. Bound to pick up soon,' Ben answered without conviction.

At seven o'clock the street started to buzz. Jack stood

by the Eftpos terminal next to the espresso machine, ready to take orders. Ben stood nervously behind the grill, ready to go.

A family of four walked in.

The mother grasped the hand of a small girl picking her nose. 'What have you got that's quick?'

'Best burgers in town,' Jack said, 'you'll get them quick as a flash.'

'Don't like burgers, thought we were having fish and chips,' the father said, pulling his son away as he aimed a crafty kick at his sister.

His wife sighed. 'Well, you'll have to put up with a burger if you want to catch the movie.'

Jack took their order for three cheeseburgers, a Bombay burger, chips and coffee. Ben started cooking while Jack prepared the coffee.

'How long has this place been here?' the father asked, looking at Cassie's work on the ceiling.

'First night,' Jack said.

'Wasn't it an old cafe before? I remember the place being here for years. Shame these old places get taken over by fast food restaurants.'

Ben fought back a desire to slip extra chilli hot sauce into the man's Bombay burger. He passed over their food, maintaining a smile.

The father kept grumbling. 'I hate burgers; no real meat, limp salad, it's not a proper meal. I bet the coffee's crap as well.'

'Shut up Tom, you're always whining about something,' his wife snapped. The children giggled and started eating.

The father finished his burger, picking at the crumbs.

'You going to finish that?' he asked, looking at his wife's burger.

'Every bit. Order another one if you're still hungry.'

He returned to the counter and ordered a second Bombay burger.

'Pretty good burgers, hey Dad?' said the youngest son through a mouthful of chips.

'Just a better class of cat; the Bombay curry takes the taste away.'

Cassie's painting on the window attracted people to come into the Starlight and try a burger on their way home.

As the night continued, Ben's grill became jam-packed with burgers. Orders were coming in thick and fast and Ben started getting the orders confused.

Jack saw the look of rising panic on Ben's face and dashed over from the counter. 'Concentrate on the burgers Ben. I'll sort out the orders.'

Jack checked each order with the waiting customers, apologising for the delay. He came out in a cold sweat. *Why didn't I take their name or put the table number on the order*? Seated customers and the growing take-away queue were getting impatient.

'Sorry folks,' Jack stammered. 'First day. I'll be as quick as I can.'

Jack felt sick as a couple left their table and walked out the door.

'These burgers are great,' a hipster sporting a deerstalker said. 'Give me a cheeseburger and I'll have it on the way home. The containers are a great idea by the way.'

'Thanks!' Ben beamed.

Julie arrived by bus later in the evening. She held onto the rail by the exit doors as the bus pulled up near the coffee shop. Yellow street lighting shone down on the pavement. She stood back as people pushed past on their way home. Across the road she saw the Starlight lighting up the pavement. *Wow*, she thought *look at all those people, what a difference.* A young couple stood back from the Starlight windows admiring Cassie's artwork. Several people were crowded around the door waiting patiently to get inside. She saw a break in the stream of cars and hurried across the road. Julie found Jack looking flustered behind the counter.

'Sorry I'm late, want a hand?'

'You're not kidding, it's been crazy busy. We're nearly out of drinks.'

Julie had been dealing with an elderly client in her office at Brascoe's Solicitors. She had planned to go home early and change but the client insisted on telling her life story.

She moved behind the counter.

Julie hung up the jacket from her slim fitting navy blue business suit and grabbed an apron to cover her white blouse. 'It's okay Jack, I'll take the orders.'

He glanced at Julie as she spoke to the next customer. Jack couldn't imagine life without her, she gave him the confidence he needed to succeed.

A line of black cars pulled up outside, dropping off passengers and leaving again to find parking spaces. Uncle Ned entered, followed by Harry and a throng of relatives. Ned wore a dark-grey double-breasted suit with yellow silk tie and his signature handmade Hockerty black brogues.

Harry made his way through the crowd with Ned to the counter. 'Ned, this is Jack and that's Ben over on the grill.' Ben waved his spatula.

'I tried to get him to come casual,' Harry whispered to Jack, 'but you can't change him.'

Ned looked over at Ben before meeting Jack's glaze. 'Nice to meet you Jack, how's your opening going?'

'We've been flat-out, I don't where they've all come from. Harry's done a great job advertising the place.'

Ned was half listening, eyeing the wine bottles. 'Sell a bit of wine, do you, Jack?'

'Yes, it's been outselling the beer.'

'Interesting. I can do you a favour here. I've got a nice line of Spanish red wine, top shelf stuff. Five quid a bottle, family rate. Let Harry know how many cases you want.' He winked at Jack and wandered over to meet Cassie as she entered the cafe.

Cassie had dyed her hair and nails dark blue for the occasion. She wore a bright-yellow jumpsuit tied at the waist with a dark-blue cord, accentuating her slender figure. A Stan burger fell off the end of Ben's spatula and flopped on the floor as Ben's attention focused on Cassie. She waved at him.

'Ben, the burgers,' hissed Julie over the counter. Ben looked down and saw the burger he'd trodden on.

'Bugger,' he mumbled, slinging it in the bin.

'What do you think, Uncle Ned?' Cassie asked.

'You're a good painter Cassie. You should give up graffiti and become a decorator. Then you'd make some real money.'

'Graffiti is art Uncle Ned, you need the right medium to exploit it. Big brick walls and industrial landscapes.'

'Bollocks,' Ned said.

By ten o'clock, the Starlight was starting to empty. Ben whispered to Jack, 'We've run out of burgers, what should I do?'

'Apologise and offer extra chips.'

'Two cheeseburgers, two colas and make it snappy,' drawled a young man holding hands with his girlfriend. He looked about nineteen, his hair thick with gel. He sported two days' stubble and dark glasses. His tight black jeans restricted his blood flow.

'Sorry mate. We've run out of burgers but we've got chips. Apologies, it's our opening night.'

Theo's night was going badly. Apart from his jeans squashing his scrotum, his car wouldn't start. He was driving his brother's Volvo on condition that he filled it up with petrol. The movie "Romulus and Scaticus" wasn't a graphic film about sex and violence in Roman times as his friend promised. Instead, it was a children's cartoon about a bulldog and a cat. Romulus and Scaticus joined forces to rescue their kidnapped master. Theo's new girlfriend hated the movie. He wanted to kill his friend, his plans for a night of unbridled sex evaporating fast.

'What kind of place is this? You're supposed to sell burgers and you don't have any sodding burgers? Is this some kind of joke? You can stuff your chips—I want a burger!' he yelled.

The cafe went silent.

'Vincent,' Ned pointed his finger.

Ned's right-hand man was Vincent. He had a face like

a robber's dog, weighed over twenty stone and he 'sorted things' for Ned. One of Ned's early enterprises had been as a boxing promoter. He had high hopes for his rising young star, Vincent. Ned trained him up to be the next heavyweight champion of Great Britain. Vincent was strong and fast but suffered from a lazy eye. If the fight went on for too long, his double vision worsened and he found it exhausting fighting twins. He retired in his late thirties after winning a few minor championships. His prospects were poor but Ned needed some 'muscle' in his expanding business, so Vincent became his minder.

Vincent walked up behind Theo, who continued to tell Ben what he could do with his chips.

Vincent silently picked the man up by the waist of his skin-tight jeans and the collar of his jacket and threw him into the street. His girlfriend shrugged and ordered an Uber.

Everyone in the cafe cheered.

'Let's go Vincent,' Ned said.

Vincent swallowed the remains of his beer and followed Ned. 'Come with us Cassie, we'll drop you home.' Cassie looked across at Ben. His head was down cleaning the grill. Cassie tried to catch his attention but he didn't see her. Ned waved his hand impatiently for her to leave.

Jack closed the Starlight at eleven.

'Think we deserve a drink,' he said, collapsing at a table.

'What a night. I can't believe the number of people who came,' Julie said. Harry offered to help clean up.

'What did Ned think of the burgers, Harry,' Jack asked.

Harry smiled. 'He said they'd go great with a glass of Spanish red wine.'

Jack laughed. 'Great job Harry, you really delivered the goods.'

As Harry basked in the glow of success, a small, niggly voice haunted him: *Well Harry, what's next? Import–Export?*

Ben brought a tray of beers to the table and sat down.

'Great job with the burgers tonight Ben. Well done mate,' Jack said.

Julie looked across at Ben. 'They were a huge success Ben. You look a bit down, everything OK?'

'I'm tired, that's all.'

Ben hadn't been able to leave the grill all evening and had hoped to see Cassie after closing. He felt a lump in his throat when he saw her leave with Ned without saying goodbye.

Jack and Julie split the cash and receipts to count the evening's takings. They looked at each other in delight. Jack put some money in an envelope and handed it to Harry. 'I think this covers your hours and there's something extra for your help and the report.'

Harry looked surprised. 'I wasn't expecting this.' He hugged Jack. 'Thank you Jack, it means more than you know.'

CHAPTER 20
THE BIN-O-MATIC

'Jack, get up, you're late.' Julie patted him on the chest.

'I'm so tired, let me have a few more minutes,' yawned Jack.

Julie dragged the bedcovers off and shook him. 'Hurry up, the cafe won't open by itself.'

Jack dragged himself out of bed. He reflected on the opening night as the hot water poured over him in the shower. *A few teething problems to iron out but a great start. I wonder if Ned was serious about his cheap Spanish wine. Can't wait to open today.* Jack dressed quickly and ran downstairs, joining Julie in the kitchen.

'You're a slave driver,' he said, yawning widely as he finished his toast. 'Do you want to come in tonight and give us a hand?'

'Sorry, Jack, I haven't got time. Mr Brascoe gave me a pile of new cases to review and I'll be up half the night.'

'OK, I'm sure tonight will be easier.'

'Why can't you make my curried egg and lettuce sandwich?' Mrs Lohning complained. 'Stan never let me down in thirty years, always had it ready for me, he did. I don't know what's happened to this place. Looks like someone spilt a bucket of blue paint all over and then scrawled the walls with crazy writing. Did vandals break in?'

Jack tried to explain but Mrs Lohning wasn't interested. 'I want the place back as it was.'

'Would you consider trying a curried burger?' suggested Jack.

'Won't get me eating those things,' she said. 'You wait till I see Stan; he'll sort you out.'

She marched out the door.

The cafe had a mixed morning. Regulars wanted their sandwich back. A few tried the breakfast burger but said it wasn't the same.

'We need a different clientele,' Jack said. 'Stan's regulars aren't interested in burgers. They like their sandwiches and cakes; we won't change them.'

'I think we need to advertise a lunch time special but I don't know how. What do you think, Ben?'

'Let's call Harry. He's the one with the marketing background.'

Loud banging at the back door interrupted the conversation. Ben opened the door to an excited Magpie.

'I've finished your cleaning machine, it's in the van. One of my best, works like a dream. You'll do.' Magpie grabbed Ben with a greasy hand. 'Give me a hand to carry it in.'

He rushed Ben off and they reappeared, carrying a small silver box in the shape of a coffin.

'Mind out the way!' Magpie shouted as they staggered to the counter and slid the box up one end. The box's sides contained stickers which read: 'Starlight Bin-O-Matic'.

'Have a look inside.' He lifted a hinged panel on the back. Everyone peered in at a jumble of wires, pipes and brushes.

'Looks like a car wash for garden gnomes,' Ben said. Magpie pushed him aside to start the machine.

The machine whirred into life with an ominous throb.

'Keep all the switches in the same position. Whatever you do, don't alter the knob settings. They need fine-tuning and any alterations bugger things up.'

Magpie flicked the switches on and the machine whirred louder. A strong sucking noise filled the room as the conveyer belt jerked into motion. Magpie put two burger containers onto orange rubber suckers. The suckers gripped them tight.

They disappeared into the bowels of the machine. A blast of steam emerged as brushes whirred away at high speed. Dirt flew out in all directions.

After several seconds of furious spinning, the brushes retracted and bins clattered into the tray.

Magpie gave Jack a gentle punch. 'I know, it's bloody brilliant. Go on, admit it.'

'You're right, Magpie, it is brilliant and we'd love to try it out.'

Magpie patted the Bin-O-Matic and left.

'Shit,' Jack stared at the machine. 'What are we going to do with this coffin thing? We can't keep it on the counter. People will think we've gone mad.'

'Why don't we give it a week?' Ben said. 'It can't do any harm and, by the noises it makes, it won't last long anyway.'

'How did it go today?' Julie asked.

Jack grabbed a beer from the fridge and joined Julie on the couch. 'Great, we had a steady stream of customers over lunchtime and we got busy again in the evening. The main bottleneck is the size of the griller. Think we'll have to get something bigger if this keeps up. I'm knackered. Can't believe Stan's gave me this chance; he's the greatest.'

'Once Stan returns from holiday, we can talk to him about paying him instalments as part of a purchase agreement,' Julie said.

'Yeah, I'm sure Stan would be pleased and I'd feel we'd own it more. Can't wait for tomorrow.'

CHAPTER 21
CHAOS

Ben finished prepping the burgers ready for the coming lunchtime crowd. He was carrying trays to the storeroom when he heard a familiar voice.

'Hi Jack, thanks for the call,' Harry said. 'Cassie wanted to come along too. Help with the marketing designs.'

'Is Ben about?' Cassie asked.

Ben bounded out of the storeroom, stumbling into a chair. 'Cassie!'

'Hey Ben, good to see you.'

Harry pulled out a notebook from his briefcase. 'Now tell me what you need Jack and I'll update the social media outlets. Cassie's offered to design the paper flyers you asked for.'

'Sounds like a plan. We've got a couple of hours before the lunchtime crowd arrives. Jack cleared a space on the counter to work on.

Cassie found a table in the far corner of the cafe, opened her bag and took out a sketchpad and pencils.

'Can I get you a drink or something?'

'No thanks Ben. You can help me with the flyers though.'

Ben drew up a chair, tidying his crumpled shirt.

'Great opening night Ben, the burgers were perfect.'

'Thanks! Yeah, we were flat-out all night. Ran out of burgers around ten.'

'I saw the queue, so didn't want to disturb you,' Cassie said. I was going to help clean up but Uncle Ned insisted on giving me a lift home because it was pouring with rain.'

Cassie opened her sketchbook. 'This is the design I thought might work for the flyer,' she slid the sketchbook towards Ben. Ben moved his chair closer to Cassie; he could feel her warm breath on his face as she spoke. 'I've added small sketches of the burgers but can't remember their names.'

Ben took Cassie's hand and counted the burgers off on her fingers. 'We have the Stan burger, Bombay burger, Blaster burger, Cheeseburger and the Bacon and Egg burger,' Ben said proudly.

Cassie laughed and opened a roll of oil pastels. She began adding the names to the design.

'Hey Ben,' Jack said. 'It's almost twelve.'

The social media posts and leaflets promoting Starlight Burgers lunchtime specials drew a new crowd. The Starlight became busier than Jack ever remembered.

He started to think about other ways to deliver the burgers.

The Friday evening queue built up so quickly customers started getting impatient. Jack called Julie. 'Sorry Jack, I really can't. I've got to be in court on Monday and I'm nowhere near ready. Why don't you give Cassie or Harry a call?'

'Sure,' Cassie said, 'I could do with the cash. I'll be there in twenty.'

Cassie arrived with her dog, Colin.

Jack looked down at Colin. 'He's not going to attack anyone, is he?'

'Not a chance,' Cassie crossed her fingers.

'He's not allowed in the food preparation area but he can hang out near the back door,' Jack said.

'Colin, go and lie down.' Cassie pointed to the back of the cafe. Colin's nose sniffed towards the grill but he reluctantly wandered to the corner and slumped down with a groan against the back door.

'Thanks Cassie.' Jack gave her the list of customer names and orders. 'Unless they're at a table, package up their order, call their name and hand it out.'

The queue started to dissipate at 9.30. Ben took off his apron. He felt nervous but this was a now-or-never moment.

He straightened his shirt, 'Cassie, I want to ask you...'

Cassie was looking at the box on the counter, covered by a tablecloth and didn't seem to hear Ben. 'What's under the cloth Ben?'

'It's the new reusable burger bin washer, one of Magpie's inventions but we're not sure what to do with it.'

Cassie removed the tablecloth to see the silver coffin shaped box. She burst into laughter. The remaining customers started to gather, asking questions about the machine. Ben sighed at his lost moment and unscrewed a bin into the two halves to wash. He followed Magpie's instructions and the Bin-O-Matic whirred into life, whining and shuddering. The crowd stood back in alarm but in a matter of seconds, the bins reappeared at the other end of the machine, sparkling clean.

Silence fell on the Starlight, then the crowd broke out

into applause. Everyone wanted a bin so they could watch the Bin-O-Matic in action again.

'More bins!' they shouted, 'who's got bins?'

A small girl pushed to the front holding two bins and Ben loaded them in. Her father lifted her up to get a better look. As she leaned forward, she knocked the setting on the suction switch.

The Bin-O-Matic was in its drying phase. With the sudden loss of suction, the brushes spun the bins faster and faster. The Bin-O-Matic developed a high-pitched scream and a red bin top came flying out of the machine at high speed. It ricocheted off the wall and headed straight for Jack. He ducked and it hit the espresso machine with a crack, then went spinning towards the retreating crowd. The top bounced off the elbow of an elderly man before crashing to the floor. Panic set in as the second, third and fourth missile followed. It started to look like an alien invasion from a B-grade movie. Bins clattered around the cafe as people dodged to miss them. The last one gave a final wobble and fell to the floor.

'What a disaster,' Jack gasped.

People lay on the floor, chairs turned over, coffee and burgers spilt across the cafe.

The commotion woke up Cassie's dog. He struggled to his feet and his nose picked up the smell of squashed burgers. Colin slunk along the wall like a fox until he reached the dining area. A middle-aged woman lay on the floor, a cheeseburger squashed under her elbow. Colin seized his chance and greedily gobbled the burger, licking the woman's elbow. She shrieked in surprise, staggering to her feet. Colin spotted a Stan burger on the floor between the legs of a smart businessman recovering on a chair. He threw himself at the Stan burger, upending the chair and sending the man to the floor. Colin spotted another Stan burger dangling from a sobbing girl. As he prepared himself to launch again, Cassie grabbed his collar.

'Sorry folks!' Jack shouted, as he helped people to their feet. 'Slight technical hitch. On behalf of Starlight Burgers, please accept a free burger and coffee.'

'I could sue you for emotional stress,' the businessman said, wiping Colin's slobber and burger from his trousers. 'I've got a good mind to go to Creeper and Arnold.'

Jack offered to pay dry-cleaning bills for several irate customers. He hoped they wouldn't gang up and bring a class action against the cafe.

Ben loaded the griller with the free replacement burgers, while Cassie tied a contented Colin up to the door handle on the back door.

'Sorry Ben,' Cassie said. 'I didn't know that thing was so dangerous.'

Jack locked the door behind the last customer. 'What a night, I'm shattered.'

'Good move, offering free burgers to calm the crowd though,' Cassie said.

Jack was deep in thought. 'You know, the Bin-O-Matic was a big hit with the crowd, we should give it another go.'

'You're joking,' cried Ben, 'the bloody thing almost decapitated half our customers.'

'Trust me,' Jack said, 'it's a great novelty item. We should give it another chance. Magpie needs to make it a bit safer though.'

Ben shook his head. 'We were lucky no one lost an eye.'

CHAPTER 22
GOING MOBILE

'Jack, we need to talk,' Ben sat down next to him. 'When it gets busy, I can't keep up with the orders. The grill isn't big enough to get all the burgers on. People are complaining about the wait time.'

'Yeah, I know. It's fantastic, I never dreamed we'd be so successful. We'll need more space for seating if the business keeps expanding at this rate.

'But you're right. People won't wait around. I've got a brilliant idea. We know that the peaks occur when people are on their way to or from movies or concerts. Rather than us waiting for them to come to the cafe, we should go to them.'

'What? Home delivery, like Dial-a-Starlight?' Ben looked worried. 'I'm not making deliveries on a pushbike.'

'Of course not Ben. How about we fill a van with burgers and wait outside cinemas or wherever at closing time. People can buy straightaway. And if we only sell Stan burgers, that keeps it simple.'

'That's not bad,' Ben said, 'but we'll have to find some way of keeping them hot. What sort of van were you thinking of?'

Jack raised an eyebrow and slowly turned, looking at his van parked in the street.

'You don't mean your van Jack? Julie won't want your van smelling of burgers.'

'It would only be for a short time; Julie will be fine. If it's successful we can buy another one.'

Ben looked warily at Jack. 'It's worth a try but you'd better check with Julie.'

'You want to do what?' Julie cried in horror.

'It's only for a trial month,' pleaded Jack.

'You won't know the difference and I'll scrub it out every night to make sure it doesn't smell. The business is going better than we ever imagined and this is a chance to expand in a new direction. If the trial goes well, we can buy another van and hire extra help.'

Julie poured herself a glass of wine and sat on the couch. 'OK, I'll agree on one condition.'

'Anything.'

'If the trial is successful after one month, we buy a proper car and not another bloody van.'

'OK, agreed.'

'And to be clear,' pressed Julie. 'A car that's reliable, easy to drive, with real seats in the back.'

'Agreed.'

Jack arranged a meeting with Harry and Cassie to discuss the van venture.

'Thanks for coming Harry, I'll make you a coffee.'

Ben whistled. 'Nice jacket.'

Harry looked embarrassed. 'I bought it as a twenty-fifth birthday present to myself.'

'You should have told us it was your birthday,' Jack said. He felt the leather. 'That's really nice, love the dark green.'

Cassie arrived. 'Wow, so you bought the bomber jacket. Looks great with those jeans.'

'Thanks Cassie. Ned's mate Fish Fingers runs a stall on Broadway Market, he gave me a good deal.'

'Let's sit down,' Jack said. 'Firstly, I want to say thank you for making the Starlight so successful. I couldn't have done any of this without you. When Stan first offered to sell the Starlight to me, I wasn't sure I wanted to do it. But now I'm totally committed and would love you all to be part of it.'

Jack ran through his concept for the take-away van.

'I know we're flat-out running the Starlight but I'm hoping you can help get this off the ground. We'll use my van to trial it for a month.'

'I can do the signage,' offered Cassie. She smiled at Ben.

'Fantastic!' Ben said. 'We'll make the van the star of the show.'

'But who's going in the van?' Harry asked. 'Everyone's busy in here.'

'Let's all help out and see how it goes. If it's a success, we can hire extra help,' Jack said.

CHAPTER 23
ALARM BELLS

Chuck Adams sat in his chair fuming. His mind was elsewhere as he half listened to the monthly reports. Vine Tobacco's corporate newsletter from head office had sent him into a rage. 'The Executive of Vine Tobacco is pleased to announce the promotion of Miriam Fox to Junior Vice President, Franchising Operations. Miriam will take up her position in New York, effective 1ST July.'

You conniving bitch, that's my promotion. I'll watch your back while you're away, you said in bed at the Sheraton.

Chuck tried to concentrate on the meeting. Frank Wilson, one of Chuck's ambitious young up and coming lieutenants, read out his report. The last section covered new franchises and single enterprises. 'Our market intelligence tells us that no new franchises have opened during the last month. Also, there are no new solo operators opening competitive burger restaurants. I should mention there's a small cafe near one of our franchises that's converted to selling burgers only. I don't consider them a threat. That's the end of my report, all looking good.'

Frank sank back in his chair, hands at the back of his head.

'Wait, go back,' Chuck said, 'what's that about a cafe near one of our franchises?'

Frank hurriedly re-opened his report searching for information.

'It's nothing Chuck, a rundown cafe called the Starlight selling burgers, nothing to worry about. As a matter of fact,' he continued, 'we ran an impact assessment on the place. The risk rating came back as 3.6. As we all know that rating means we keep a watching brief but take no competitive action. Anything that scores over six means we go into an actionable marketing plan to preserve Mack 'n' Morti's position. So, at this stage, we do nothing.'

'How did this new place get started?' asked Pete Crabshaw. 'Our health inspector friend usually gives us a tip off; we haven't heard about this place.'

Chuck threw his pen on the table. 'How did we let this one open right under our noses?'

Frank glared at Pete.

'Well,' Frank said, 'in this case it used to be a mixed business. Sold sandwiches and burgers but now they've gone all burgers.'

'It was owned by some geriatric called Stan Morrison. Now a young guy is running it with some friends. Very low-cost operation, minimal advertising, open six days a week. The only thing the report mentions of interest is the product itself. The burgers are unusual, nothing like ours, so we checked them out. They use extra-lean beef, fresh salad and sugar-free rolls.'

Frank passed a sheet of paper from the report around. It showed the results of a detailed analysis of a Starlight burger and chips.

	Mack 'n' Morti's	Starlight
Calorie Count	>1200	<400
Fat Content	>60mg	<15mg
Cholesterol	>160mg	<30mg
Sodium	>2400mg	<600mg

Chuck stood up and paced the room.

After a short silence, he said, 'If there's one thing that could endanger our operation, what do you think it might be?

'C'mon, boys, think about it.'

No one spoke. Chuck gazed around at the team.

'Tell 'em Chris.'

Chris Atkins was a small, chubby, balding man in his early fifties from Boston. He was sent over by Vine Tobacco to be Mack 'n' Morti's company secretary. He'd been with Chuck from the beginning and was one of the architects of the Hook 'em Early campaign.

'Well Frank,' he said in a condescending tone. 'The answer is healthy burgers, goddam healthy burgers.

'Our entire profit structure depends on low-cost ingredients and an addictive taste. Doesn't matter which of our competitors you choose, the taste is the same. Making healthy burgers is bad for our profit margin. The Starlight operators might be deadshits but we don't want some smart-arsed, do-gooder son-of-a-bitch journalist doing the sort of comparison you've reported. And we don't want them writing that you can buy burgers that are healthy.'

Frank turned to Chuck. 'These guys will go broke in a couple of months. I can't see them being a threat.'

Chuck glared at Frank. 'Look, the tobacco industry thought it was invincible once. Vine Tobacco is sensitive to anything that might cause our products to be compared unfavourably. Particularly when we know our burgers are full of fat, salt, sugar and chemicals. The bottom line for you Frank, is that this operation, no matter how small, has the potential to get out of hand.'

'I just don't see how we can stop this size operation,' Frank said, throwing his report on the table.

'Hey Chuck, this place is near our outlet that sells the trial toddler burgers. We shouldn't be letting any competition into our trial zone, even if it's tiny,' Craig Robinson said, barely disguising his glee. 'Geez Frank, reckon you should've got onto this one sooner.'

The veins in Chuck's temples started pulsing.

'How could you let this happen Frank? Something that could endanger our entire Hook 'Em Early campaign? You need to shut this cafe down or blow it up, I don't give a shit. Fix it now. Or I'll get someone to do it for you.'

Frank's face went red and he felt a sickening rumble in his stomach.

'Er, of course Chuck, I'll get right onto it. Starlight Burgers will be a dead comet in a couple of weeks at the most,' he stammered.

'See that it is Frank,' Chuck said. 'Meeting over, see you all in a month.'

Frank drove away from Mack 'n' Morti's in despair. He'd gone to Craig Robinson's office after the meeting but Craig shut the door as he approached. Craig pointed to his phone, pretending to be on a call. Then Frank caught up with Mike Binks in the corridor. 'Sorry Frank, love to talk but I'm late for a meeting.'

This was Frank's first black mark and he needed to get rid of the healthy burger cafe. He thought through his options. *I need a fool proof plan that doesn't link back to Mack 'n' Morti's and damage the corporate reputation. How can I get a small, growing business to fold without direct intervention?*

Frank opened the door to his apartment. A notice from the finance company was a reminder to pay the overdue payment on his Audi. His body churned at the prospect of losing his job. Warming yesterday's fish pie, he grabbed a beer from the fridge, threw himself on the couch and played his favourite album, *Adele 25*, on Spotify. He turned up the volume, closed his eyes and added his toneless voice to duet with Adele. A minute into the song the most heart rendering line arrived. He raised his arms and blasted out the words with tears in his eyes. A loud banging on his ceiling brought Frank's rendition to a close. He felt emotionally drained but calmer. Frank turned his mind to the Starlight. The solution didn't come to him until later that night when he was in bed dozing off to sleep. He sat up and almost laughed aloud. His idea was brilliant.

'Gotcha,' he said to himself before falling back into a contented sleep.

CHAPTER 24
DRESS TO IMPRESS

Cassie fished her phone out from her back pocket as she got on the bus from art class. 'Cassie here.'

'Cassie, it's Jack. I'm going to see Magpie about the van tomorrow. Could you come over and give Ben a hand over lunchtime?'

'Sure, I'll be in by ten-thirty.'

On the bus home, Ben worked through the limited options in his wardrobe. *I've got nothing decent to wear. I can't work with Cassie looking like this.* He stared down at his jeans, baggy at the knees with flecks of cooking oil stains. Then he put his finger through the hole in his shirt sleeve. He got off the bus two stops earlier than his home stop.

'Can I help you?' asked the young saleswoman in Marks & Spencer.

She found Ben a pair of deep-brown moleskin jeans and a dark-green shirt.

'They are a great fit, perfect,' she said.

Ben tossed and turned all night, thinking about being alone with Cassie. His last attempt to ask her out had been ruined by the Bin-O-Matic. He got up early, dressing carefully in his new clothes.

'You going somewhere special?' asked Jack when Ben arrived at the cafe. 'You're all dressed up.'

'Thought I'd have a change, that's all.'

'The shirt's good value for nine ninety-nine,' Jack said.

'How do you know that smart arse?'

'Could be something to do with this price label.' Jack tugged the label hanging out the back of Ben's shirt.

'Quick, cut it off,' Ben said in a panic.

'Okay, stand still.'

'Swear there's a whiff of aftershave in the air.'

'Aren't you meant to be going over to Magpie's?'

Ben helped Jack carry the Bin-O-Matic outside to the van, then returned inside.

The sound of the cafe door opening brought Ben out of the storeroom.

'Hi Cassie.' Ben tried to sound casual. 'Jack said you'd be coming in to give a hand. No Colin today?'

'I don't think Colin's welcome anymore.'

Cassie had changed her hair colour to a light pink and wore a short cotton summer dress in pale blue.

Ben planned the right moment to ask Cassie out. He calculated they would be too busy getting the cafe ready for lunchtime. Lunchtime was out of the question, too many customers. He'd do it after the rush and before Jack got back. Ben wasn't feeling confident, so, if Cassie turned him down, he only had a short time before closing to feel awkward.

Lunchtime brought a steady stream of customers.

'You're getting flash flipping those burgers Ben,' Cassie gave him a thumbs up.

'That's nothing, watch this.' Ben slid a burger onto the spatula and flipped it high in the air. 'Double somersault.'

'Bet you can't do a triple.'

Ben flipped the burger higher into the air. Cassie coughed.

'Oh, so close,' Cassie giggled as half the burger landed on the floor.

'That's cheating.' Ben laughed as his confidence rose. They were interrupted by the sound of the cafe door opening.

A tall man stood in the doorway and looked across at Cassie.

'Hey, haven't I seen you at college?'

'Yes, we're in the same Art History class,' Cassie replied. 'It's Neville, isn't it?'

Ben hated men like Neville. Neville reminded him of men from underwear adverts. Chiselled face, shiny hair and straight white teeth. His tanned chest gleamed through a loosely buttoned, crisp white shirt. The buttock-hugging jeans led to fine Italian shoes worn without socks.

'Love your hair colour Cassie, Lace Pink if I'm not mistaken.'

'Wow, Neville, you're good on shades.'

'Are you going to the Arts in the Dark party on Saturday?' Neville asked.

'Maybe,' replied Cassie.

'Let's hook up if you do,' he said.

Ben felt his world crumbling around him. Cassie passed Neville his burger.

Neville threw his Ted Baker leather satchel over his shoulder. 'See you Saturday, Cassie.'

The rush of lunchtime customers dwindled at one-thirty and by two o'clock the cafe was empty. Ben started cleaning up in silence.

'What's up Ben?' Cassie asked.

'Nothing, I'm preparing for tonight.'

'Do you want some help?'

'No, it's okay.'

Cassie picked up her rucksack and left, feeling confused. Ben found a scourer and began furious scrubbing.

CHAPTER 25
VAN WITH A VIEW

Jack found Magpie reading the paper in his office, an asbestos-lined cubicle built into a corner of the workshop. It contained a small brown desk piled high with paper and unopened envelopes. Four upturned oil drums served as seats. The greasy walls were covered in old posters from car manufacturers.

Jack explained what happened the night the Bin-O-Matic went wild and Magpie scratched his head.

'Wonder what speed they were doing when they came out of the machine? Bet they would have gone a long way and—.'

'Magpie,' interrupted Jack. 'We need a cover over the switches.'

'That's easy, follow me. I've got something that will fix it.'

Jack told him about his idea of selling burgers from the van. 'We need to keep them hot and have some sort of sign on the roof.'

'You've come to the right place.'

Magpie climbed over a pile of twisted metal and rummaged through an old cupboard. He produced a long, thin box with Perspex sides that said Ambulance in big red letters.

'It plugs into a twelve-volt system and lights up well. All you have to do is get someone to replace Ambulance with new Perspex sides saying Starlight Burgers. Keeping the burgers hot is a different matter. That will need a lot more power and we'll have to put in an extra heavy-duty battery. You will need to store the burgers in a warming chest to keep the heat in.'

'How can we serve the burgers?' Jack said. 'We don't want to pass them out the window. We need a proper counter and space to spread out.'

Magpie stroked his chin, leaving greasy streaks on his skin.

'This calls for some serious thinking, we'd better adjourn to the pub. Come on, we can walk from here.'

'Same as usual, Magpie?' Smithy the barman offered, more of a statement than a question.

Jack pulled his wallet from his pocket but Magpie held up his hand as if he were stopping traffic.

'Hang on Magpie, we haven't paid you for the Bin-O-Matic yet.'

'My treat. Couple of beers Smithy.'

The bar was long, thin and smelled of stale beer. Apart from the crash of balls from men playing billiards, it was quiet. They sat in small green vinyl armchairs that creaked with every movement.

'Nice place,' Jack said, as he looked around.

'Yeah, used to be a real dive till Smithy cleaned it up. He's got a new cook and is going to advertise it as a gas-tropub.'

Jack choked on a mouthful of beer. He could see that Magpie was serious.

'You all right Jack? I should have got you a bitter instead.'

'No, it just went down the wrong way. Had any thoughts on the van?'

'Best thing is if we cut out a panel in the side. I can build a metal flap that's hinged at the bottom to fold down outside the van and make a counter. Then you can sit inside and hand out burgers from the heated trays.'

Jack nodded. 'Sounds good to me.'

'Not sure that Julie will like a big hole in the side of our van though. I had enough trouble getting her to agree to using it.'

'She'll be fine. I can return the van to its original condition if needed,' Magpie said, waving his hand in the air. 'She won't remember the hole existed. I better get back to the workshop Jack. My Turf-O-Matic suction is still too strong. I turned it on and half my spanners got sucked into the workings.'

'See you Magpie.' Jack walked to the van.

Back at the Starlight Jack told Ben about the proposed changes to the van.

'You know Julie's going to kill you, don't you?'

'Best not to think about it,' Jack said.

CHAPTER 26
A MISUNDERSTANDING

'Hi Cassie, It's Jack. Sorry for the late call but the last few days have been crazy at the cafe. I meant to thank you for helping Ben. I've got the ambulance sign I told you about. I was hoping you could paint some new Perspex sides to say Starlight Burgers.'

'Sure, I'll be over tomorrow. Is Ben OK?'

'He's been a bit quiet this week but I think he's fine.'

Cassie arrived at the Starlight the following morning. 'OK, show me the sign.'

Jack placed the ambulance sign and a selection of screwdrivers on a table in front of her. 'Like a coffee?'

'Yes, flat white please Jack.' Cassie examined the sign and unscrewed the casing. She removed the Perspex ambulance sides and fluorescent tube.

'The only tricky bit is the lettering. Looks best painted on the inside of the box and reversing the letters takes some time. I can have it done by Monday but I'll need new Perspex.'

'They sell it at Krampits,' Jack said. 'Hey Ben, take the van and drive Cassie over to Krampits. I want to tell Harry about Magpie's van ideas.'

'How far is the hardware shop?' asked Cassie as they climbed into the van.

'About ten minutes,' replied Ben in a monotone voice.

Krampits hardware shop was on St John Street in Islington. Cassie stared out the window as Ben drove along City Road. She saw thousands of identical, soulless apartments under construction in new high-rise buildings dotting the skyline. Occasional relief came as they passed ornate three-story pre-war shops and cafes filled with people.

'What's wrong, have I done something to upset you Ben?'

'No. Did you have a good time at your Arts in the Dark party,' Ben said, sulkily.

'What are you talking about Ben?'

'I heard you talking to Neville. He said you were going to hook up with him at the party.'

'You prat Ben. I'm not interested in that tosser. Do you think I'm that shallow?'

'Er, well... He knew the colour shade of your hair. And you didn't say no to the party.'

'I didn't agree to anything. I wanted to get rid of him. He spends his time hitting on my friends at college. He acts so superior with his flash clothes and Porsche. His parents are loaded so he thinks he can get whatever he wants.'

'Oh, you didn't go to the party then.'

Cassie punched Ben playfully in the arm. 'Ow, you punched me.'

'Ben, you're an idiot.'

They arrived at Krampits. Krampits had been in business for over fifty years. Its dark interior hid a treasure trove of items dating back many years. Ted Krampit Senior took the Perspex ambulance sign from Cassie. He disappeared into a small workshop to cut the new pieces.

'I've been an idiot,' Ben confessed to Cassie. 'I had this great idea until Neville showed up.'

'What idea Ben?'

'I hoped you might go on a date with me.'

'Oh, is that why you dressed up?' Cassie teased, smiling at Ben.

'Yes,' confessed Ben, blushing.

'Well then.'

'Well what?' Ben replied, looking confused.

Cassie smiled again, put her hands on her hips and waited. Ted Krampit laid the Perspex on the counter. 'That'll be twelve pounds.' He turned to Ben. 'And for goodness' sake, ask the girl out.'

On the way back to the cafe Ben said, 'How about tonight? We could go for a drink?'

'Sounds great.'

'I'll pick you up on my motorbike.'

'That would be fun. I didn't know you had a motorbike.'

'I got fed up with the bus. Dodger, an old friend of mine was selling a Triumph. I liked the idea of being out in the elements. Pick you up at seven?'

'Okay.'

'How did you get on at Krampits Cassie?' Jack asked.

'Fine.' Cassie held up the Perspex sheets. 'I'll head off now and be back Monday to fit them.'

'I'm looking forward to an evening at home,' Jack said. 'A movie, a few beers and takeaway. How about you Ben, any plans?'

'Taking Cassie for drink at the Cat and The Fiddle,' replied Ben, unable to hide his excitement.

'That's great. How are you getting there?'

'We're going on my motorbike.'

'Do you want to take the van instead?'

'No, but thanks for the offer.'

Cassie was the first passenger Ben had taken on his motorbike; he borrowed a helmet for her.

He rode slowly down Darling Road counting down the numbers until he arrived at 32. The house was a rundown council home in an ugly street. Cassie opened the door. Ben had a glimpse of threadbare carpet on the stairs and a waft of stale cigarette smoke.

Colin wagged his tail and tried to slip through the door as Cassie left. 'Inside, Colin, go on.' He lowered his head and slunk inside. 'Bye Mum.'

A couple of kicks and the Triumph roared into life. Cassie climbed on the back and tapped Ben's helmet to say she was ready. When they hit the main road, Ben opened the throttle and the Triumph hit sixty miles an hour. Cassie wrapped her arms tightly around Ben. She felt intoxicated by the wind through her clothes and the noise of the engine as they flew along the road. The cool evening air brushed her legs as she snuggled closer, feeling the warmth of Ben's body.

They pulled into the car park of the Cat and the Fiddle. Ben switched off the engine, removing his helmet. 'How did you like the ride? Great to feel the wind and being in the open air.'

Cassie climbed off the Triumph; the vibration of the engine through the footrests had given her pins and needles. She clung to Ben's arm as they walked into the bar. The cosy pub had four low-ceilinged, small rooms. On every wall there were shelves full of porcelain cats. The back of the bar had sketches of cats in various poses and dress. On the bar was a picture frame with a sketch of Trevor the barman as a Burmese cat. 'This place is crazy,' Cassie said. 'I love it.'

She examined the sketches on the wall while Ben ordered the drinks. 'Lager and lime and a pint of London Pride bitter please.' Ben handed Cassie her lager and lime.

'Was that your parents' place where I picked you up?' Ben asked.

'I stay there sometimes to keep Mum company but mostly live with three friends in a shared house.

'Dad left when I was five. I remember him as always being happy and he loved Reggae. We'd dance around the living room singing Peter Tosh songs like Maga Dog. He'd tell me funny stories about growing up in Jamaica.

'A vacuum salesman turned up at the door one day and dad bought a new cleaner. Mum got angry as we already had one. The salesman kept coming back. He and dad spent a lot of time together, even going away for fishing weekends. Mum and dad started to argue a lot about the salesman; I didn't know why. The last memory I have was him sitting on the back of the salesman's motorbike disappearing up Old Kent Road.

'Mum went to pieces and Uncle Ned became like a father to me. He helped us out when we were short of money.'

'That's tough Cassie, have you heard from your dad since?'

'Yeh, we keep in touch. He's still with the salesman, he's not a bad bloke and Dad's happy.'

'Mum refuses to see him though. It's awkward. As a kid I didn't understand what he had to put up with when he first came here. He couldn't get any work when he first arrived but got a job on the buses a few months later. There was so much racism at the time. I know mum's family were dead against them getting married. I think it's getting better for my generation and I don't put up with any crap if it comes my way.'

'I'll order the food, same again?' Ben said pointing to Cassie's glass.

'Thanks.'

Ben stood at the bar, happier than he could ever remember. 'Lager and lime, pint of London pride, Chicken salad and Chicken Tikka Masala please.' He returned to the table.

'How about you Ben? Do you see your family much?'

'No, my father left when I was young and Mum didn't have much interest in me. She got a new boyfriend when I was at school and I lived by myself most of the time. I met Jack at school and he became my best mate until I screwed up.'

'What do mean?' asked Cassie.

Ben looked away.

'Ben, there are things I've done that I regret but it's what you learn from it that's important.'

He took a deep breath.

'I don't want to hide anything from you Cassie. I got expelled from school. Mum had left and I didn't know what to do. I should have told the school I lived alone but a mate of my father's said he'd pay me for helping him. He nicked cars and I was the lookout. We got caught and I went to juvie. The main things I learned was how to cook and pick locks. After juvie they got me a job at a meat processing plant about forty miles away in Aylesbury. I liked living there but the meat works closed, so I moved back here. I met up with Jack and he's been a real mate. Gave me the job at the Starlight.'

Ben felt wretched. *That's that, finished before it starts.*

Cassie reached over and took his hand.

'Don't worry Ben, we've both had to deal with shit in our lives. We can't change it, so we have to move on.'

Ben looked at Cassie. She had the sweetest smile. He felt wary but for first time in many years, dared to believe someone loved him.

'Chicken Masala and Chicken salad,' the waiter announced.

'Great salad,' Cassie said, finishing off the last dried tomato. Ben sat back in his chair. 'I didn't realise I was so hungry, that was the best.'

'We'd better get on the road Ben; it's starting to rain.'

They walked through the car park in darkness. A light drizzle cooled the night air. Ben wiped the motorbike seat with the sleeve of his shirt and with three kicks of the starter, it burst into life.

'Better turn the lights on Ben!' shouted Cassie above the noise of the engine.

'They are on!' shouted Ben as he joined the traffic. Cassie hugged Ben tightly to keep warm. Ben gritted his teeth as the drizzle soaked his shirt. The night air made him shiver. Cassie's calves and feet were numb from the cold and vibration of the motorbike when they arrived at her house. Ben helped her inside.

Cassie's mother glanced up from the television.

'You're soaked Cassie. Dry your hair, there's a clean towel in the kitchen. You'll catch your death of cold.'

Ben saw the cold white fluorescent light flicker into the life in the kitchen.

'Hello Mrs Hugget,' Ben said, dripping water on her carpet.

'Who are you?'

'I'm Ben, a friend of your daughter.'

Cassie's mother sighed. She tapped ash off her cigarette into an ashtray that rested on the arm of her well-worn sofa. Colin lay asleep in front of the gas fire. 'Well, you're shivering too, how about a hot drink?'

'No thank you, I've got to get up early.'

Cassie wrapped the towel around her shoulders and walked with Ben to the front door. 'I've had a great night, thank you Ben.'

'Even though I've given you pneumonia?'

Cassie laughed. She reached up and kissed him lightly on the cheek. 'Goodnight Ben.'

Ben rode away feeling his heart was about to burst. He

opened the throttle of the Triumph and raced home. *I'll ring Dodger first thing and see if he's got a car for sale.*

CHAPTER 27
BOOZY SECRETS

Craig Robinson drove slowly along the busy high street looking for number 312, the swish of windscreen wipers the only sound. A wide variety of well-maintained shops extended for half a mile on both sides. Several coffee shops spilled tables and umbrellas onto the generous pavements. Craig's sweaty palms gripped the steering wheel. *I hope this bastard doesn't give me any trouble. I can't go to the next monthly review without a result.*

The numbers on the shops ticked down until, at last, he reached 312: Sid Slater Real Estate. He stared at the window filled with house pictures displayed with glowing descriptions. In pride of place sat a large artist's sketch of the Bueno Vista housing development project.

Sid sat in a coffee bar opposite his office. *I wonder what Mack 'n' Morti's have got to offer. Craig sounded like he was under pressure when he rang to meet me. I'll play him along and see what I can get.*

He saw Craig pull up and get out of his car. He had Craig in his sights like a sniper eyeing his victim. He looked at his watch.

'Dead on time, Mr Mack 'n' Morti. Let's annoy you a little; fifteen minutes should do it.'

A buzzer rang as Craig opened the door. He

approached Sharon, Sid's twenty-five-year-old receptionist. She was planning a holiday on the Costa del Sol after reading her horoscope. 'Libra: Sudden financial opportunities emerge now, so don't hold back.'

'Craig Robinson, I've got an appointment with Sid Slater.'

She looked up at Craig, a hint of annoyance on her face. 'He's out, back soon. Take a seat.'

Her eyes immediately flicked back to the Costa del Sol brochure. Craig sat in an armchair in the waiting area. The office was painted stark white with black leather furniture and chrome light fittings. He started reading a brochure on the Bueno Vista housing development. Craig wondered if Sid kept all his clients waiting.

The minutes ticked by and Sid rushed through the door. He thrust out his hand with a broad smile.

'You must be Craig Robinson. Sorry I'm late, got held up in traffic. Tea or coffee?'

He ushered Craig into his office, offering him a low chair. Sid slid into the expensive Italian-style leather armchair behind his desk. He gestured to Craig to start.

'Vine Tobacco is a global company,' Craig began. 'Our strategy is clear. While we want to be fair and reasonable, any divergence from that strategy is taken seriously.'

Craig sat forward in his chair. 'Frankly Sid, it would be in your best interests to accommodate a Mack 'n' Morti's franchise at Bueno Vista. I don't want any unforeseen difficulties for you as other, less-cooperative people have experienced. I can tell you are a good bloke and I want to help you.'

Sid studied the man sitting opposite him. Craig

couldn't look him in the eye. He looked like he hadn't slept for a while. There were beads of sweat on his face and his shirt collar looked damp. Craig unconsciously played with the buttons on his jacket and fidgeted in his seat. *You're in trouble Craig. I'll bet your jobs on the line if you don't get my agreement to the franchise deal.*

Sid played him along. He objected to the outrageous demands that Craig put forward while confiding his fear of big companies. They talked on and finally Sid threw up his hands. 'I'm starting to see where you're coming from Craig. Let me think about your proposal.'

The tension left Craig's face immediately and he upped the charm. 'Sid, you're making the right decision. Let me take you to lunch and we can discuss the deal in detail.'

They sat at Sid's favourite table in Mamma in Cucina. They both ordered salad followed by lasagne. 'How about a drink Craig?'

Three bottles of Chianti Classico Reserve later, Craig had trouble keeping Sid in focus.

'Craig my friend, I want to thank you for explaining this opportunity to me. I think we understand each other better now. I'm excited about working with you and the team. I've got loads of opportunities on the horizon and you can look forward to more deals in the future with Sid Slater Real Estate.'

'You're a bloody good bloke Sid,' Craig slurred. 'You've made the right decision. I don't want you ending up like the poor bastards they're closing down on Saturday.'

Sid threw his arm around Craig.

'Thanks Craig. I've always admired Mack 'n' Morti's and it's gonna be fantastic working with you. Hope you can come skiing with me next winter. I've got access to a private lodge next to the chair lift.'

Sid continued. 'Any losers you're gonna shut down deserve all they get. They should work with a great company like ours— oops, sorry, I'm being premature. The deal isn't signed off yet.'

Craig and Sid laughed loudly, slapping each other on the back.

Sid was curious. 'So, how are you going to close them down?'

Craig laughed aloud.

'Best part is they don't even know it's happening.'

Craig pulled Sid closer, the effort almost pulling him off his chair. 'The boss is pissed off because these bastards are selling healthy burgers. They make ours look and taste like shit. We're gonna close them in case they become a nuisance.'

'How can you close them if you don't own their business?'

'We've got the health inspector on the payroll,' said Craig, attempting to tap the side of his nose.

Sid leaned in towards Craig. 'Love the way you operate Craig. Look, don't feel you have to but what's the name of the place?'

Craig beckoned Sid closer. A warm blast of Chianti Classico and garlic wafted over Sid.

'It's a place called Starlight Burgers. We'll have it locked up tight by Saturday night. But mate, not a word to anyone.'

'Course, mate.' Sid smiled.

CHAPTER 28
A NERVOUS WAIT

'Jack!' Magpie yelled down the phone. 'I'm at an auction. They've got a load of commercial cooking stuff, including pie warmers and chip fryers. Best of all, a big griller that's perfect for your burgers. Even got warming ovens underneath. I reckon I can get this lot cheap. Interested?'

'Sounds great, get what you think's best. I'll pay you when we bring the van over. Thanks!'

Ben sat in his flat looking at his phone. He picked it up then put it back down on the table. *I'll have a cup of tea.* Ben added water to the kettle and switched it on. He leaned against the bench staring at the kettle. As it started to boil, he switched it off and sat down again. The phone stared back at him. *Come on Ben you can do this, don't be scared. The worst that can happen is she'll say no.*

The phone was in his hand. He found Cassie's number, hesitated as his finger hovered over the phone icon. *Maybe I should text instead. Give her time to think of an excuse to say no.* Ben composed his message 'Hi Cassie, hope you have recovered from the motorbike ride. I should have checked the weather and I'm sorry for getting you so wet. I was wondering if you would like to go and see a movie at the Odeon in Holloway Road this week? I'm sure you are busy so understand if you can't make it.'

Ben checked the message carefully for spelling mistakes. He looked at his options. Send or Discard. A flash of panic hit him as the message displayed SENT. He checked his volume was turned up and re-boiled the kettle. Cradling the hot cup in his hands, Ben stared at the phone willing it to ding. *That's it then, she's hit Delete. What was I thinking? I'll have to play it cool when we are at the Starlight next.*

Ben packed his laundry bag ready for a trip to the launderette. DING. He threw the bag down and rushed to the phone. A message from Cassie. 'Love to Ben, sounds great. I've dried out. How about Thursday night?' Ben quickly replied. 'Perfect, I'll come to your place at seven and we can take the bus to the Odeon.' Ben dropped the phone on the chair, turned up the music and danced around the flat in joy.

The laundry bag lay near the door. *Can't be bothered with the launderette today, I'll go and see Jack instead.*

Ben met Jack at the entrance to Magpie's workshop. They found Magpie in his office reading the *Sunday People*.

'How are you boys? That griller I picked up is out back.'

They followed Magpie past the piles of metal sheeting, Land Rovers and work benches to the rear roller door. He pressed the open button and the roller door screeched and clanged. Outside was a large griller.

'This is perfect Magpie,' Ben said. 'Look at the size of the grill, it's twice as big. And in great condition. Good job, Magpie.'

'Now boys, you leave the van with me and I'll have it ready to go by tomorrow. Have you got the new Starlight Burger signs for the light box?'

Ben held up the signs. 'Cassie's done a great job. I can't wait to see them lit up Magpie.'

'You can borrow my van if you like,' Magpie dangled the keys.

His green battered van sat in the yard near the griller. Jack sat in the driver's seat and wound down the window.

'How do you adjust the seat? My knees are under my chin.'

'You can't, I welded the seat to the floor when the seat rails broke. I didn't get the position quite right. You get used to it.'

A car jack, several spanners, screwdrivers, pliers and hammers lay on the floor.

Jack looked up at Magpie. 'Ever thought of putting these in a toolbox?'

'Nah, this is my horizontal toolbox. Don't brake too hard or you'll get the jack stuck under the brake pedal. And don't pull too hard on the gear lever. It can fall out.'

Jack and Ben drove back to the Starlight, blue smoke belching out the back of the van. Jack had arranged to meet Julie at the cafe after she visited a new gallery around the corner.

Julie was already waiting for them when they pulled up. They kissed.

'How was the gallery?'

'They had some great still-life watercolours by local artists. I'd like to get something for our living room.'

Ben wandered over to the old griller with a tape measure as they entered the cafe.

'Come and sit down Jack. I went through the figures this morning.'

Julie powered up her laptop and opened an Excel spreadsheet titled Starlight Accounts.

'Good news,' Julie said, scrolling through the P&L. 'At this rate you can start paying yourself a wage and make a small profit.'

'What a relief.'

'And you can start paying back Stan.'

'That's brilliant Julie, I can't believe it. This calls for a celebration.'

Jack handed out beers from the fridge and Ben grabbed packets of crisps.

'Fancy another beer,' Jack said, pointing to the empty bottles.

'Why not,' Julie said. He went to fetch the drinks.

'So how are things going with Cassie, Ben?' asked Julie.

'OK, I think. We're going to the cinema to see *The World's Fastest Indian* with Anthony Hopkins.'

'That's great, I heard it got good reviews.'

'I want to buy her a present but don't know what to get.'

'How about a book?' suggested Julie. 'Cassie's interested in graffiti art, so maybe something like that?'

'You're brilliant Julie, that sounds perfect.'

CHAPTER 29
HOLE IN A VAN

'This van's never going to make it back to Magpie's,' Jack said as it came to another stop in Archway Road.

The 263-bus pulled up behind with a hiss of air brakes. Ben held his hand up in apology and pushed the van into the bus lane.

'This is the third time today,' Ben said, perspiring from the effort.

They opened the bonnet and poured more water into the radiator.

'Once it starts, you have to keep moving Jack.'

Jack put the van in second gear. 'I'll wait for a decent gap and go for it.'

'Left, left!' Ben shouted.

Jack screeched the van left up a side road as a long line of stationary traffic appeared ahead. The female voice from Google maps directed them on a circuitous route back to Magpie's yard. As they drove onto the forecourt, they saw Jack's van.

'My van!' Jack gulped. 'Look at that big hole in the side.'

Magpie leaned out of the long opening in the side of the van.

'Cup of tea, bag of chips, ice cream? Brilliant job, don't you think, boys?'

'Very funny, look at my van. How am I going to explain this to Julie?'

'Don't worry about it Jack. With all the gadgets inside, you could be the James Bond of fast food. Come and have a look.'

They entered through the rear doors. Along the side Magpie had installed racks of warming trays for the burgers.

'These trays warm up using small heaters located above and below the racks. They run off auxiliary batteries located in that box against the back wall. Charging is from an extra alternator fitted into the engine bay. The cash tin is here on the floor and switches for the lights are along this panel.'

'Explain the switches to me.'

'It's all very sophisticated Jack. Now, this switch is for interior lights, this one is for the lights on the roof and the signage. Music here and this one is for the tray heaters.'

'Hang on, what do you mean, music?'

Magpie flicked the third switch. The William Tell Overture blared out from a megaphone on the roof of the van.

'It's like ice cream vans. You have to let the customers know you're coming.'

'We'll frighten the life out of them with that noise,' Ben said.

Magpie ignored him.

'This switch is for resetting the counter. This one is for

turning on the counting light and this big button is for registering the sales.'

'Back up a bit, what's the counting stuff about?' Jack looked confused.

'Oh, I thought Harry must have told you. He said you needed a display on the roof showing people the number of burgers you have left to sell. Saves them queuing if you are about to run out. You hit this button every time you make a sale and the sign on the roof counts down the number. I bolted on the "burgers to go" part and a friend of Harry's got the counting sign and logic processor.

'See under this lid?' Magpie lifted a small steel lid exposing computer logic boards. 'You can even display messages but you need to plug in a laptop through this USB port.'

'You've done a great job Magpie,' Jack admitted. 'We'll give it a run tonight. Thought we'd test it at the *Vue Cinema* in Hornsey at closing time. We can set up nearby and grab people on their way home.'

Magpie closed the flap over the opening and left the van. 'I'll load this griller on later and drop it off.'

Jack fished in his jacket pocket and handed Magpie an envelope full of cash. 'Thanks Magpie, you've done a brilliant job.'

As Jack and Ben parked outside the Starlight, Harry came running out. He circled the van twice.

'This is great. Wow! I can see you'll have a fleet of them in a few months.'

'That would be nice if Julie doesn't kill me first,' Jack said.

Harry tried the switches. 'What do you think of the "burgers to go" display? Rather good if I say so myself. We need a "back in ten minutes" message when we run out of burgers. Must find someone to program that. By the way, Cassie is really excited about being in the burger van tonight.'

'Glad she can make it, we are a bit stretched now,' Jack said. 'Thanks for looking after the cafe this morning.'

'No problem, it wasn't busy. Mainly coffees and danishes.'

Ben signalled impatiently to Harry. 'Come on Harry, the lunchtime rush will start soon and we need to get the burgers ready.' They made their way inside.

'No problem, I've got everything prepared. I really appreciate you trusting me tonight.'

'It's great to have back-up Harry. You can do all the cooking today and I'll just look on.'

Harry checked the temperature of the griller and tightened the Starlight Burger apron around his waist. 'Are you sure you want to go in the van tonight Ben? It's just a matter of handing out pre-cooked burgers.'

'Yes, yes. It's important I see the reaction from the customers and make sure everything goes smoothly.'

Jack was at the espresso machine. He looked at Harry and silently mouthed.

'*CASSIE*.'

'What are you smiling at, Harry?'

'Nothing Ben, just pleased to be here.'

Ben turned around, looking suspiciously at Jack—who was cleaning the espresso machine with gusto.

The Starlight door opened. A steady stream of customers built over the next two hours.

Magpie's van crawled over the brow of the hill. His face peered through the spokes of the steering wheel. He turned the van down the cobbled alley behind the Starlight.

'The griller's a bit heavy!' he shouted, 'but between us we should get it in.'

'Bloody hell, this thing weighs a ton. Mind your fingers Ben,' Jack said.

'That's it, boys, slide it, just a bit more, stop. Lower your end on the ground. Jack, you push the trolley underneath. Me and Ben will lower this end.'

Ben and Magpie grabbed each side of the griller and eased it away from the van.

'Easy,' Jack said. 'Nice and slow.'

Magpie grasped the front of the griller. 'I'll guide it into the kitchen and you two can push.'

They maneuvered the griller until it sat alongside the old one.

'How did you get this on your van in the first place?' asked Jack, stretching his back.

'Oh, that bit was easy; I used a hoist. Didn't know it was going to be quite so heavy though. It was touch and go up some of those hills.'

'Plumber will be here later this afternoon so it will be in action for tonight,' Jack said.

The griller dominated the kitchen with its large stainless-steel front and heavy-duty grilling plates.

Ben ran his hand along the top. 'Looks fantastic, I'll give it a polish.'

'Oh, I almost forgot,' Jack disappeared into the storeroom. He leaped out with a loud, 'Surprise!' He stood in the middle of the kitchen and flung open his arms. He wore a dark-blue T-shirt with 'Starlight Burgers Out of this World' in bright red.

Magpie whistled. 'I love it Jack, can I have one?'

'Of course, as inventor of the famous Bin-O-Matic and mobile burger van, you must have a T-shirt.'

Magpie put it on over his grimy shirt and went to his van.

Jack and Ben watched him drive slowly up the cobblestoned alley leading from the back of the cafe to the main road. A puff of blue smoke appeared as he changed gears.

'Hey Jack, do you need some sort of permit to sell food in a van?' Ben asked.

'I don't think so. We've done the Level 2 Food & Hygiene course, got a premises licence and Public Liability Insurance.'

Jack took out his phone and Googled.

'Oh shit. It says I'm supposed to register with our local authority, have some sort of hazard plan and get a risk assessment.'

'What? But we've got everything ready Jack.'

'I know, how about we take a chance and do one run

tonight? What can go wrong? It's down to me if there's a problem. I'll get onto it tomorrow.'

'Okay, let's chance it,' Ben agreed.

Standing in the street, they stared at the modified van in silence. Jack wondered how long it would take before Julie forgave him.

CHAPTER 30
SECOND THOUGHTS

Jack looked around the Starlight. It was buzzing and packed. *We got that griller just in time.* He handed change to a young girl and the next customer stepped forward.

'Two Stan burgers and chips to take away.'

More people came through the door, forming a queue.

Jack gave Ben the latest orders. 'It's really busy tonight. How's the new griller going?'

'Brilliant, couldn't be better.'

Jack went back to the counter just as Julie rushed through the door.

'Jack, I need to talk to you urgently.'

'We're flat-out, can't it wait?'

Julie went around the counter and whispered in his ear.

'I had a call from your mum, they're back from holiday. Stan as well.'

'I thought they had another week?'

Julie waited while Jack took the next order.

'No, she's angry with Stan. He talked about nothing but the cafe the whole time. He told them he wants Starlight back; misses his regulars. Your mum said Stan's already worked out what he's going to do. He's planning to get someone in to re-decorate. Apparently, he visited several cafes while he was away and is going to update his menu.'

Jack took the next order.

'What about us?' Jack whispered in alarm. 'He told me he was retiring. We just had to organise contracts of sale when he got back.'

'He seems to have forgotten that. Thinks you are only looking after it while he's away.'

'But that's crap, he said the business was mine. He never mentioned anything about coming back.'

'That's what your mum told him. They got into a blazing row and haven't spoken since.'

'Tell me exactly what Mum said Julie, I can't believe what I'm hearing. Stan can't come back and take away our cafe.'

Julie looked at the growing queue. Jack didn't move. He felt the room start to spin as he slumped against the wall, holding his head in his hands. His dreams for the Starlight evaporated.

Ben rushed over.

'You look as if you've seen a ghost.' Ben put his hand on his shoulder. 'What's wrong?'

'Stan's back early from holiday Ben,' Julie said. 'He wants the cafe back.'

'You've got to be joking, he retired and sold the cafe to Jack.'

Julie turned to Jack. 'We need to think this through but right now you've got a place full of hungry people. I'll stay and give you a hand and we can talk after you close.'

CHAPTER 31
SIGN OF TROUBLE

'Keys are near the toaster, don't forget to fill her up before you get back,' Reg yelled.

Harry grabbed the keys. Reg was Harry's cousin. He lived alone but when Ned told him about Harry's escape from the cult, he offered him a room. Reg let Harry borrow his car on the condition he filled it with petrol. 'Thanks Reg, I owe you one.' Reg looked up from *Match of the Day*. 'See you Harry, say hello to Cassie for me.'

Harry pulled up outside Cassie's mother's house and rang the doorbell.

'Hi Harry, come in. Thanks for picking me up. Can't wait to try out the burger van tonight.'

Colin jumped off the couch and ran to meet Harry. After a short wrestle, the dog left a trail of slobber on Harry's jeans.

They arrived at the Starlight to a subdued mood. Ben looked up from the grill. He smiled and waved weakly to Cassie.

'What's going on Ben?'

'Think there's going to be a problem with Jack's uncle.'

Harry threw Cassie a Starlight T-shirt.

Ben placed cooked meat patties in stainless-steel covered trays. The unopened buns were packed in a plastic box. Harry put on the Starlight Burger apron and positioned himself behind the griller.

'See you guys later.'

Ben and Cassie carried out the trays and slid them into the warming oven in the van, parked in the alley at the back of the cafe.

'What's going on with Jack's uncle?' Cassie asked as they drove onto the main road.

'It looks like his uncle wants the cafe back,' Ben replied.

'I can't believe his uncle would do that to him.'

They arrived outside the cinema in time to see crowds pouring out the doors. Ben switched the lights and music on and released the flap to reveal the counter.

Cassie felt the burgers. 'The burgers are still hot; the warming oven works well.'

Ben set the counter display to 90. The van became a lighthouse; its bright-orange paintwork shone out below the lights positioned around the roof. A warm glow came through the counter opening.

A group walked straight toward them.

'What have you got?' asked a woman with two teenage daughters.

'The Stan burger—a classic burger,' Ben said, flashing his best smile.

'I'll have two for me and one each for these two,' pointing to her daughters.

The crowd grew and the burgers sold quickly. 'Only two left,' Cassie said. The queue dispersed when 2 clicked over on the counter display.

A middle-aged man with his daughter peered through the hatch. 'We've been to your cafe; great burgers. We'll grab the last two.' Ben took the money and thumped the button twice to register the sales.

Cassie passed out the burgers.

The man glanced up at their sign on the roof in confusion.

'Um, you might want to turn off your sign.'

Ben was curious and went out to check.

'Oh shit.'

'What is it?' Cassie said.

In flashing red lights their sign now scrolled "Smith's Parking—Car Park Full".

'Look over there,' Cassie nudged Ben. 'At the car park entrance, where the entrance sign is.'

'Oh, double shit.' Ben stared at a gaping hole with wires poking out. Next to the hole a display showed the words 'spaces left'.

'Quick Ben! Get in the van and turn the sign off.'

Ben quickly took off from the car park, crunching the gears. 'Harry organised the sign. He promised us it was legal. Jack will be pissed if the cops turn up. He'll never trust him again.'

Cassie sighed. 'Harry never learns. I bet he got it from Sammy. He's family but you can't trust him. If the police ever raided his lockup, they'd have a field day.'

They walked into a miserable atmosphere at the cafe. Jack and Harry were cleaning up in slow motion.

'Let's not mention the sign right now,' Ben whispered to Cassie.

CHAPTER 32
UNDER SUSPICION

'We need to talk,' Jack said, motioning everyone to a table. Together, he and Julie told them his mother's news.

'So, you think Stan's pretty definite about wanting Starlight back?' Harry asked Jack.

'He's been missing it and wants the cafe back. Reckons he's worked out new sandwich combinations.'

'I told Jack's mum about the changes to the cafe and she said he's going to have a fit,' Julie added. 'The business is still in his name.'

'You mean you didn't get anything in writing?' Harry asked. 'First rule of business is to have a formal agreement, Jack.'

'I know that but he's my uncle, I've known him all my life and I convinced Julie it would all be fine because he's family. We planned to formalise everything when he got back from his holiday. I never dreamed he'd do this to me.'

'You've all put in so much hard work and now it's going to be a crappy old cafe again,' Cassie said. 'Why don't you look for somewhere else to set up? I'd be happy to decorate and give a hand again.'

Jack shook his head. 'It costs a fortune to set up a cafe from scratch. You need to buy all the kitchen equipment and furniture. Then go through all the health compliance rubbish. Not to mention obtaining a business licence. The other choice is to buy an existing business but we don't have that sort of cash.'

'Don't suppose we could get Uncle Ned to have a word with Stan?' Harry suggested.

'Harry,' said Cassie, looking shocked, 'what are you talking about? He's Jack's uncle. Even if he is an old bastard, he's flesh and blood.'

'Sorry, I wasn't thinking.'

'How about you offer to buy him out so he can start up another place?' Ben suggested.

Jack shook his head. 'He's been here for thirty years, can't see him going anywhere.'

'Stan told you he was retiring and wanted to sell you the business. That must count for something in law?' Ben said. 'He can't change his mind after you've turned it round and started making a profit. The courts wouldn't.......'

Julie interrupted Ben. 'We can't afford to go to court over this. The only people that will make money will be the lawyers and we'd end up broke.'

'Would we have to return the place back to what it was?' Ben asked.

'Don't think you could find that much grime,' Harry chimed in.

A loud knock on the door interrupted the conversation.

'We're closed!' Jack yelled.

The knocking intensified. Harry opened the door to a tall, middle-aged police sergeant. Harry froze.

'Good evening, sir, are you the proprietor of this establishment?'

'N-no.' Harry stood aside as the sergeant brushed past him.

'Earlier this evening, a serious crime occurred at the Smith's Parking premises. We have it on good authority that a gang removed a valuable display sign and associated equipment.

'The sign has been reported as being spotted on top of a light-coloured van in the vicinity of the crime scene. The occupants of the van were selling burgers.'

The policeman looked around the walls at Cassie's paintings of Starlight burgers.

'I've been in the force for many years and have seen some pretty stupid criminals. I find it difficult to comprehend the stupidity of displaying stolen goods within twenty yards from the crime scene.'

No one spoke.

The policeman gave a thin smile.

'Don't suppose anyone minds if I have a look around?'

Cassie stepped forward. 'Of course not, where do you want to start?'

She led him through the cafe to the back door and out to the back alley. Jack's eyes widened as the policeman disappeared. When they returned, the sergeant turned to Harry.

'Don't suppose you know anything about stolen signs or vans with bright lights on the roof do you, sir?'

Harry felt uncomfortable around police; he'd seen so many at Uncle Ned's house over the years. He shook his head and cleared his throat.

'About to say something, sir?' pressed the policeman.

'No, no.'

'Well, I may be back. As you can imagine, I need to get to the bottom of this.'

No one spoke. The sergeant turned and left the cafe. They heard his squad car cruise off into the night. Harry collapsed into a chair.

Jack turned on Harry. 'You bloody idiot! What the hell do you think you were doing using stolen goods for our business? It's bad enough Stan wanting the cafe back without going to jail for receiving stolen goods. What were you thinking? I know your families got a proud tradition of thieving but you're supposed to be the straight one. Christ, why did we ever let you in?'

Cassie shot to her feet.

'Don't you ever talk to my cousin like that! He didn't know it was bent gear until tonight. Our cousin Sammy promised it was straight. Harry's only mistake was being a halfwit for trusting him. Harry's done heaps for this cafe, put his heart and soul into making it work. You should give him more credit.'

Jack was about to launch into another attack when Ben spoke.

'You can argue all night but that signs on your van Jack and the copper didn't believe a word Harry said. I'll dismantle it right away.'

Jack turned to Cassie. 'Is the van parked out the back?'

'Well of course not. Or else he would have seen it. We parked it behind the tobacconist, in case someone dobbed us in.'

Ben grabbed a torch from a cupboard and disappeared outside.

'I'll help you, Ben,' Cassie said.

Ben undid the nuts holding the counting display to the roof. He pulled the stolen sign away from the roof while Cassie cut the wires. He placed the sign inside the van. Cassie unscrewed the box containing the logic boards. He and Cassie removed the switches from the control panel, wrapping everything in a towel.

'Thanks Cassie, Magpie can strip everything back and patch up the holes.'

Ben took Cassie's hand as she climbed out the back of the van. He held her gently and felt her warm breath and soft touch of her lips on his. 'Oh Cassie, I'm so glad you are here.'

Cassie laid her head on Ben's shoulder. 'Shame about the sign Ben, we sold the burgers without trying. I got the fright of my life when I saw the "Car Park Full" sign on the roof. I guess someone dobbed us in. Poor Harry would never have thought the sign was stolen.'

'He seems a bit lost. Did you ever meet his parents?'

'I can't remember them very well. I was young when they joined the cult. I used to play with Harry before they took him away. We caught up again after he escaped. Since then, we've become good mates and look out for each other. You and Jack were so cool to give him a job after he tried to rob you. He'd do anything for the Starlight.'

'That sergeant tonight wasn't stupid,' Ben said, 'he knew it was us but couldn't prove it. How did you know we needed to hide the van like that?'

Cassie smiled. 'If you grow up in the Cleghorn family,

you have a sixth sense for trouble. People love calling the cops; I knew we were at risk.'

They returned inside and found Jack, Harry and Julie still sitting around the table deep in conversation.

'Your mum thinks Stan's planning to come here on Monday to deliver the bad news,' Julie said to Jack.

'It can't wait that long. I'm going round to see Stan and sort this out. I hope I keep my temper when I see him. In the meantime, let's keep at it, we need all the money we can earn. But we need to ditch the car park gear. I don't want it anywhere near this place.'

Harry held up his hand. 'I'll look after that, it's my mess to fix.' He carried the sign back from the van and left with Cassie.

'See you in the morning,' Jack said as Ben picked up his bike helmet. 'Things can only get better.'

'Yeah, sure but I've heard bad luck comes in threes?'

Jack drove the van around to the front of the cafe. Under the cold glare of the fluorescent streetlight, it looked battered, a gaping mouth for the counter and holes for the signs and equipment. He put his head on the steering wheel while he waited for Julie.

How could Uncle Stan do this to me? The Starlight is going so well. I love the crowds of customers chatting and laughing as they wait for food. They're my regulars now. Ben's cooking great burgers and Cassie's artwork has transformed the place. This is our cafe, our future.

He seethed with anger. I'm not going to let that old bastard get away with it.

Julie got in and sat next to him and laid her head on his shoulder.

'Sorry about the van, Julie. I should have told you.'

'Don't worry, Jack, it's only a van.'

'I've really stuffed up. I'm so sorry to put you through this. It was all going so well. For the first time in my life, I couldn't wait to go to work. I've been so excited about building this business for our future.'

'It's not your fault. Harry was right. I'm a solicitor and should have drawn up an agreement before Stan left on holiday. I guess we were both too trusting.'

'I don't want to go back to being a handyman Julie but it's the only thing I'm good at.'

'That's wrong, Jack, you've turned the Starlight into a great business. I'm proud of what you've done. You've done it once so I know you can do it again. I'm sure we'll come up with something. My salary will cover our expenses, so you've got time to think things through.'

Jack looked embarrassed. 'But I should be the main breadwinner, what about when we have kids.'

'You sound like my father, Jack! Women are breadwinners too. I love being a solicitor. I want to continue my career even when we have children.'

Jack started van. 'I need to tackle Stan; he needs to keep to our agreement.'

CHAPTER 33
UNWELCOME EXTRA

Reg heard a key in the front door. 'Is that you, Harry?'

'Won't be a minute.' Harry ran up the stairs to his bedroom with the car park sign.

'What's up Harry, you look like shit. What's happened?'

'That sign for the van I told you about: Sammy nicked it from the car park. The police paid a visit to the cafe.'

'Sammy's a dick Harry, you can't trust him. I don't know what you were thinking. Was that what you were carrying upstairs?'

'It's in my bedroom.'

'I don't want it in the house Harry. I don't care what you do but get rid of it first thing tomorrow. You can take my car.'

Harry stared at the car park sign.

How am I going to get rid of this thing? I could slip over to the carpark now but they'll see me on CCTV. I'll have to wait till the streets get more crowded.

He tossed and turned as the hours ticked by.

If I leave it somewhere in the car park and disappear, they'll find it and that will be the end of it. Then again, if someone finds it and takes it away, the sergeant will think we've still got it. How about I tell the car park I found it by the side of the road? But if they still get the cops in, they'll know my name and think I stole it for sure. I don't reckon the old 'bought it from a man in the pub' routine will work either. And who buys car park signage in pubs? It would be different if it were a hi fi system or a watch.

Harry felt a cold sweat coat his body.

I'm going to jail, for sure. The family will know I'm a complete failure. I can't even receive stolen goods without stuffing it up. Jack won't want to know me after this. I'll spend years staring at the sky through the bars of a prison cell. No one will want to visit me and I won't have any friends when I get out.

Harry hadn't slept as dawn approached. He stumbled out of bed in the half-light, tripping over the car park sign.

A cold wind added to the air of gloom as Jack opened Starlight Burgers the following morning. Jack had tried to contact Stan but he wasn't answering the phone. He went around to his house but he wasn't home.

Ben arrived for work but he and Jack barely spoke. A stream of breakfast customers kept them too busy to discuss their woes.

'Arrrgh!' A man sitting alone stood up suddenly, spitting out burger over his table. His chair crashed to the floor.

'Look at this,' he spluttered, spewing burger on the floor. He ran around the room, thrusting his burger contents at customers who drew back in revulsion. Jack ran around the counter, followed by Ben. The man thrust the burger at them. In the middle of the meat sat a big, fat, brown cockroach. It lay on its back, legs wriggling in the air, long feelers dabbing at the burger.

'This place needs condemning!' he shouted at Jack. 'You wait till the health inspector hears about this. He'll shut you down, I swear. Oh, I feel sick,' he moaned. Clutching his stomach, he rushed out the door and ran up the road, disappearing from sight.

'I feel sick,' said a young hipster gagging on a Stan burger. Other customers started to feel sick and wanted their money back. They headed for the exit, leaving the Starlight empty. Jack looked around at the tables containing half-eaten burgers. He slammed the door shut and put up the Closed sign.

'This is the last bloody straw! How did a cockroach get in the burger? What were you doing, for Christ's sake?'

'Don't blame me, there's no way a cockroach could get in. I would have seen it. Did you see the size of that thing? Must have been when you served it to him.'

'That's stupid Ben, cockroaches don't crawl on top of hot meat. It was on the bun and you didn't see it.'

'Look, I would've seen it when I put the burgers together. Unless it's Houdini, it couldn't have gotten on the bun. This one's down to you, Jack.'

Harry's heart pounded as he approached the car park. After a sleepless night and thumping headache, he'd decided against South America. He would throw himself at the mercy of the courts. He held the sign and logic boards under his arm and approached the car park attendant.

'Excuse me mate, can you tell me the way to the manager's office?'

'Yeah but it won't do you no good, they're off till Monday.'

Now what'll I do?

'What's your problem? I look after most things when they're not here.'

'I don't know what to do. I've got your missing car park sign and wanted to return it and explain what happened.'

The car park attendant studied Harry. 'Where did you get it?'

'It's a long story. I want them to have it back.'

'Where exactly did you get this sign, or, should I say, who gave it to you?'

'That's not important, it's back now.'

'What's your name?'

'Harry Cleghorn, why?'

'You're not related to Sammy, are you?'

'He's my cousin, what's it to you?' Harry replied.

The attendant looked over his shoulder. He beckoned Harry closer and whispered, 'Are you bloody nuts? Don't bring that thing back here. I sold it to Sammy a few days ago. If you don't want it, go chuck it in the river or burn it for all I care.'

'Can't do that, the cops already suspect I've got it. My only chance is giving it back and they might let me off for good behaviour.'

'You sure you're a Cleghorn? Never heard of them giving anything back.'

The attendant thought for a while. 'The only other way is if I say I found it behind a pillar, get the on-call sparky to re-install it. Then the owners might not pursue it with the cops.'

'Worth a try. It's all there.'

'Mind you,' the attendant said, with a sly look at Harry. 'I'm not giving any of the money back and it'll cost you another twenty for the trouble.'

Harry handed over the equipment and twenty pounds.

'Thanks, mate, you've saved my life.'

'Take my tip,' the attendant laughed, 'get another occupation. You're not cut out for a Cleghorn life of crime.'

CHAPTER 34
THE INSPECTOR

Harry looked at the closed sign on the door in surprise. He peered through the window and could make out Jack and Ben standing at the counter. They appeared to be arguing. *I'll cheer them up with news.*

Harry banged on the door. Jack looked up and let him in without speaking.

'I've fixed the problem with the police,' Harry said. 'I spoke to the car park attendant and the sign's going back up without any fuss.'

Ben and Jack ignored him.

'What's up with you two? Has Stan been in?'

'Ask Jack, he's the one making all the accusations.'

'Well what else could have happened?' Jack snapped. 'You're the one that cooked it.'

'Can somebody please tell me what's going on?'

Jack told Harry about the cockroach and closing the cafe in case they had an infestation.

'You know,' Harry said, 'all the time you've been open, I haven't seen any insects. If you had cockroaches, you'd see a lot more around. Believe me, I've lived in some real dives and know about cockroaches.'

Jack looked around at the spotless cafe. 'You might be

right, Harry. When we pulled this place apart, I didn't come across any insects.'

He began opening cupboards and examining them inside. 'Let's split up and see if we can hunt down any vermin.'

Ben fiddled with the espresso machine. 'What's the point? If we find one or a hundred, we can't escape the fact that we saw a cockroach in the burger with our own eyes.'

'Come on Ben,' Jack said. 'When the food inspector arrives, I want to make sure there aren't any more. I know this looks bad but as I always say, know when to jab and know when to duck.'

Ben laughed. 'Christ, you talk a load of shit, Jack.'

'We've torn this place apart and there's no evidence of an infestation,' Ben said. 'I thought it may have come from the new counter,' Jack nodded. 'I've been over every inch of it and it's as clean as a whistle.'

Ben agreed. 'I've taken the cooking equipment apart bit by bit and not a sign of an insect. I've been through the whole kitchen area and nothing.'

Harry joined them at the counter. 'No sign of roaches in the toilets, store or seating area.'

Jack began pacing the floor. 'We've been at this for two hours, there's nothing here.'

'I don't understand,' Harry said. 'Did you get the man's name and phone number? We can talk to him and get more information.'

Jack shook his head. 'No, he ran out the door before we had a chance.'

'Well, what should we do? Open tonight or wait until we hear from the health inspector?' Harry asked.

'That decision may be made for us,' Ben pointed to the front door. Outside stood a thin man bent over like a question mark. He had greying hair, a long grey coat and grey complexion. He stared at his clipboard, then knocked. Harry opened the door. The man held out an identity card. 'My name is Winston Fagg. I am the food safety inspector for the borough. We have received a complaint about contaminated food being served at this establishment. It is my duty to serve an order preventing you from serving food until further notice. Also, you must place this notice on the entrance informing the public.'

They read the notice:

> *"These premises are closed until further notice. In due course an inspection of the premises will occur".*

'There are no cockroaches on these premises,' Jack said. 'Check the place over now so we can get this over with.'

'An examination of your premises will occur at the appropriate time,' the inspector said, ignoring Jack. 'You must close these premises until then.'

He snapped his briefcase closed and left.

Jack slammed the door after him. 'How can they shut us down without some sort of inspection? That can't be legal.'

'Guess it must be. The inspector would know,' replied Ben.

'But Uncle Stan didn't get shut down after the senior citizens' incident,' Jack said. 'We need to get this nonsense sorted out as fast as we can. I want to see the evidence. There's something suspicious going on.'

A silver 850 BMW drew up to the kerb.

Sid Slater read the notice and entered the Starlight.

'Do you work here?'

Harry nodded.

'I've got a couple of questions if you're the proprietor. My name's Sid Slater.'

Jack recognised the silver BMW. 'Sid, what are you doing here?'

A flash of recognition registered on Sid's face. He searched his memory, then remembered and went red. 'I know you. You lost me valuable clients. I should sue you for impersonating a real estate agent.'

'Come off it Sid, who ever heard of anyone wanting to impersonate an estate agent?'

'Cut the crap and tell me who owns this place,' Sid said with an impatient glare.

'What's it to you?'

Sid shrugged and left.

Jack watched as the silver BMW merged into the traffic. 'We need to find out what's going on, this whole thing stinks.'

'I'll talk to Uncle Ned,' Harry offered.

'He's got contacts everywhere.'

Jack turned to Harry in alarm. 'We don't want to end up as accessories to murder.'

'Don't be stupid; he's not a murderer. He's a networker. He's the best bet to trace that creep with the cockroach.'

CHAPTER 35
TALKING IT OVER

Stan looked at the clock radio. 6 a.m. He turned over, willing himself back to sleep. He forced his mind back to the river and tried to imagine himself catching a large trout. The river faded. Frustrated, he lay on his back, arms crossed on his chest. His thoughts darted about, as if his brain was trapped in a pinball machine.

6.10 a.m. Stan gave up and turned on the radio news.

'Breaking: catastrophe strikes Bridlington Rovers. Roddy McFee sent off during the second quarter final after an altercation with the goalkeeper. This is a major blow for the Rovers, said a spokesman for the team. In another breaking story, relief as Timmy the cat found by...'

Stan rubbed his eyes and went to the kitchen. He sat shivering in his pyjamas waiting for the kettle to boil. It was 6.20 a.m.

He wished he hadn't asked his neighbour Brian to look after the place while he was away. Brian was a keen gardener and liked helping Stan out. He had cut the grass and weeded the garden so there was nothing left for Stan to do.

Stan warmed his hands on the mug of tea and his thoughts turned to the Starlight. He recalled the excitement when he and Ruby first signed the lease. The regulars he'd got to know over the years and their kindness when

Ruby died. He felt scared the connection to all those memories was being torn away. A lump in his throat rose, followed by an uncontrollable sob. He could taste the salty tears that ran down his cheek. So many memories.

Pull yourself together Stan, he wiped away the tears. He finished his tea and went upstairs to get dressed. On the bedroom floor lay his half-emptied suitcase from the holiday.

It had been his first holiday without Ruby. He emptied the rest of the suitcase and slid it back next to Ruby's in the wardrobe. Stan fought the rising lump in his throat as he looked at the tag on her suitcase showing her name and address.

He heard the newspaper being pushed into the letterbox and returned to the kitchen. The headline story was an in-depth article on the Bridlington Rovers catastrophe. Stan swore and pushed the paper away.

His mind went back to the argument with his sister and her reaction to him wanting the Starlight back. She'd confused him. He thought Jack would be like his girls, who had no interest in running the cafe. He never thought Jack would stick at it. He seemed hopeless when he was showing him the ropes.

A cat slipped over Stan's fence and carefully worked its way through the roses towards the bird table.

'You bastard.'

He crept outside and turned on the cold water tap at full force. As the pressure built, Stan turned the hose towards the cat, taking it by surprise. Levitating, it let out a screech before landing and tearing off across the garden and back over the fence. Stan spun around, clapping his hands in glee. He scratched his backside and went back to the kitchen. He heard a knock at the door.

'That was quick, must be the neighbour about the cat.'

It was Jack.

'Hello Stan, thought I'd come by and see how you are.'

Jack thought Stan looked relaxed after his holiday. He'd put on some weight and got some colour in his face.

'This is a surprise. Come in the kitchen Jack. I'll make a cup of tea. I've been meaning to call you all week.'

Stan put the kettle on and told him about his latest skirmish with the neighbour's cat. 'Only good cat is a flat cat. It's always killing the birds. It killed all the chicks from a nest in the rafters of my garage. I'm going to buy an air gun. That way it gets more than water up its bum.'

Jack listened to Stan rave on about the cat. During a pause Jack managed to ask him about the holiday.

'The fishing was great and we met a good bunch of people on the coach tour. Hope to keep in touch with a few of them. Mind you, it was too long; I started to miss the house and cafe.'

As Stan poured the tea, Jack said, 'Mum mentioned you want the cafe back Stan. That's a surprise. Is it true?'

Stan finished pouring and joined Jack at the kitchen table.

'Well, Jack, the holiday gave me time to think. I know Mary thinks I should retire but after a couple of weeks away I started to miss it. I have some ideas to revitalise the old place.

'I know it's a bit run-down but it's like a second home to me. It gets lonely here on my own. At the cafe I meet my regulars who are like old friends. I've been to a couple of senior citizens' events but they make me depressed. One old geezer spent an hour and a half telling me about his hip replacement. I got caught by an ancient bird who told me about her husband's hernia operation. They're all so old; they're just waiting to die. That's why I'm afraid to retire. The cafe gives me purpose.'

Stan offered Jack a biscuit.

'I was upset when I saw the Under New Management sign before I left for holiday. I don't understand why you had to do that Jack. But Mary tells me you've started to make a go of the place. Perhaps we could share it. Roster the days and split the workload. I don't need the money but it would be great to see the regulars again and have a bit of a chat.'

'I don't know the best way to say this Stan but the cafe has changed. We've attracted a different set of customers. It can't go back to the way it was.'

Stan smiled. 'Oh, I suppose you've added the pastrami and those fancy breads you talked about. That's great, I was thinking along those lines myself.'

'Not exactly. Tell you what, how about we take a ride and you can have a look for yourself?'

'Why not? I can't wait.'

CHAPTER 36
WHERE'S THE CAFE

Jack opened the passenger door for Stan. 'What happened to your van?' Stan stared at the racks in the back and flap on the side.

'Long story Stan, I'll tell you later.' He parked outside Mrs Edgecombe's florist shop. Stan walked straight past the Starlight. He stopped outside Henry's tobacco shop and scratched his head. He turned round and walked back to stand outside the cafe. He peered in the window, took four steps back towards the kerb, then three steps forward.

'Where's the cafe?'

He turned to Jack but no words came out of his mouth. His mouth opened as his head turned slowly from side to side. Jack thought of the fairground amusement where balls were rolled into revolving clown's mouths.

Jack unlocked the door and Stan went inside.

'Where's the cafe? It's gone!'

Stan moved his hands over the surfaces, trying to find something familiar.

'I know you said you'd made changes Jack but I don't recognise anything. Where's the section for the sandwich ingredients? Where's the display cabinet?'

He staggered slightly.

'Sit down and I'll make you a coffee Stan.'

Jack put two flat whites on the table. 'Stan, I tried to run it your way but I couldn't make it work. I tried bringing it back to the same condition as when you first opened but that didn't work either. Anton's Deli was killing us.'

'In the end Harry came up with the idea of trying it as a specialist burger place. I only sell a limited range which keeps my overheads down and Ben makes the best burgers in town. They're completely different to your average burger.'

'You know, your aunty Ruby tried to convince me we should do something like this. I said it was too risky and we should stick to the things we know. Maybe I was wrong.'

Jack showed Stan the accounts on the laptop. Stan's eyes widened as he ran his finger down the numbers. He could see the increase in income compared to when he ran the cafe was dramatic.

'These profit margins are impressive,' he admitted.

'I'm sorry about the refurbishment Stan but you said you'd sell me the business and retire. This is the report from a friend of mine, Harry. He came up with the business plan. I love you Stan but I need certainty for me and Julie's future. Please tell me straight if you're not going to sell me the business. Otherwise, I want to sign a formal contract to buy it as we agreed. You can come here whenever you want but it's a different business now.'

'I'm surprised, I didn't think you'd make a go of it like this.'

He looked around at the bones of his old cafe dressed up in its new suit. Underneath all the paint his cafe still existed. He saw Jack as a small schoolboy sitting near the window, slurping his milkshake.

He remembered his regulars lining up at the counter with their latest family news.

'I don't know Jack, I had second thoughts on holiday. It's a big decision letting go of the Starlight. Let me think about it, maybe we could come to some sort of arrangement.'

'It's all or nothing Stan. I need an answer so I can work out what I'm going to do next.'

'Why has the health department closed you down?'

The question took Jack by surprise. He didn't think Stan had read the sign on the way in; he seemed too shocked to notice.

Jack explained about the mystery cockroach. Then he told Stan about Winston Fagg, the health inspector and the visit from Sid.

Stan's eyes narrowed. 'Winston Fagg, that slimy little toad is the one who tried to close me down last time.'

'Well, you did poison the Edgeware senior citizens on their bingo outing.'

'Yes but he tried to get five hundred quid from me. He threatened to close Starlight down for three months. He was an assistant then and I told him to piss off or I'd report him to the press. He soon backed off.'

Stan sipped the last of his coffee.

'Show me the report he left you, ordering you to close.'

'He didn't give us one, just made us stick the notice in the window. I asked him to check the place out but he wasn't interested.'

'Sounds to me as though Winston's strings are being

pulled by someone with interests other than health. You need to find the man shouting about the cockroach. Do you know his name?'

'That's the mystery Stan. He ran out the door and we've no idea who he is. I think I'd recognise him. Harry has an uncle who seems to have ways of finding people.'

'We need to visit Fagg,' Stan said. 'I'd like to know why you don't have a detailed report and see some evidence of the claim. They can't keep the Starlight closed without a good reason. I've never seen a cockroach here. Mark my words, you'll be open again in no time.'

They sat in silence as Jack drove his uncle home. Stan felt a strange gnawing feeling in the pit of his stomach. He tried to ignore it by looking out the window as shoppers crowded the pavements along the shopping strips. Visions of Ruby behind the counter of the Starlight flashed before his eyes. His promise to sell the Starlight to Jack began to haunt him.

CHAPTER 37
BAD PRESS

Frank Wilson paced his apartment in his maroon tracksuit, waiting for the call. His two-bedroom apartment was on the third floor of the new CityViews complex. Frank had furnished the apartment with white Ikea furniture. He felt it gave the apartment the *Grand Designs*, minimalist feel. He'd set up his second bedroom as a home office and gym. He trained on his treadmill if the weather was bad to beat his colleagues at Chuck's lunchtime runs.

The phone rang.

'Ah, Mr Wilson, Winston Fagg calling. Thought you'd like to know that the mission is accomplished. Had to cut corners, so I don't know how long we can keep them closed. But the press coverage tomorrow should finish them off,' he sniggered.

'Thanks Winston, you're a master craftsman. I owe you for this. The boss will be extremely pleased.'

'Always happy to help. Please send my fondest regards to Mr Adams.'

'Of course Winston, your fee will be transferred to your usual account.'

Frank hung up the phone and breathed a sigh of relief. *Mission accomplished. Winston's slimy manner makes my skin crawl but the creeps reliable and efficient.* Frank looked forward to crowing about his masterful stroke at the next meeting. He imagined Chuck shaking his hand, slapping him on the back and telling him what a great job he'd done.

Jack ran his fingers gently down Julie's spine and kissed her neck. She stirred, still half asleep. He slid his hand under her thin shirt, feeling the warmth of her skin. Julie turned over and kissed him deeply on the lips.

The front doorbell rang. 'Shush,' whispered Jack. 'They'll go away.' They kissed again and Julie removed her shirt. Someone started banging on the door and ringing the bell at the same time.

This was their first lie-in for weeks.

'You'd better go,' Julie sighed, 'it sounds urgent.'

Jack lay on his back. 'I don't believe it.'

The banging continued while Jack threw on his jeans and a top. 'I'm coming!' he yelled as he raced down the stairs.

'Stan, what are you doing here this time of morning, it's only seven-thirty?'

'Never mind that.' Stan barged past. 'Put the kettle on then sit down and read this.'

Gone off his rocker, thought Jack as he yawned. He switched on the kettle and slumped in a chair.

Stan handed Jack the *Hackney Gazette* and Jack stared at the front page. There in huge letters, was the headline screaming: Starlight Burgers—Health Hazard. It sat above a colour photograph of a burger with a huge, fat cockroach lying in the middle. The caption underneath joked about the latest fashion. 'Try the cockie burger for extra crunch'. The article advised only going to fast food outlets with a proven health track record, such as Mack 'n' Morti's. Jack read and re-read the article.

Julie came into the kitchen in a hastily wrapped dressing gown. She'd heard Stan's voice in the kitchen and come to see why he'd turned up.

'What are you doing here this early Stan, is someone hurt?'

'Have a look at the paper.' She stood behind Jack and read the article over his shoulder.

'My God, how did they get this story Stan?'

'It's a set-up Julie and that creep Winston Fagg has his fingerprints all over it. Whoever's behind this has got some clout and Fagg is in their pocket.'

CHAPTER 38
BREAKFAST BRIEFING

'What a right old cock up,' Ned said. 'I heard about the cops visit to the Starlight. Who sold you get the carpark sign?'

Harry watched Ned stir his tea from across the dining table. He rubbed his sweaty palms together. 'I paid twenty-five quid for it. I thought it was legit.'

'I didn't ask you that. Who sold you the sign?'

Harry's lip started to quiver. 'I don't want to say Ned.'

Ned stared intently at Harry. 'Who are you protecting Harry? Let me guess. Sammy.'

Harry gave an involuntary nod.

'He's a little turd. I've told him before not to flog bent gear to family. I'll sort him out later. It's a good job Cassie was there to save your arse. She's a good kid.'

'Cassie told me about the health inspector closing the Starlight,' Ned continued. 'From what she said, it looks like a set-up. She wants me to find the bloke with the cockroach. I told her to bring Jack here this morning and I'll work out a plan.'

Harry felt the colour returning to his face.

Jack was surprised when he and Cassie arrived at Ned's house in Stoke Newington. He thought the imposing double-story Edwardian building was more like a bank manager's house.

'Come in Jack, Harry and Cassie tell me you're in a spot of bother. Have a seat.'

The dining room was tastefully decorated with striped wallpaper and plush curtains. The long, polished walnut dining table accommodated eight chairs. A chocolate-coloured Burmese cat stretched itself on the windowsill.

Ned's wife brought in a breakfast tray of eggs, toast and jams.

Ned cracked open a boiled egg and topped up his tea.

'Come on you three, have something to eat. The most important meal of the day is breakfast.' Ned scooped out the remains of his egg and reached for the toast.

Ned's large, sausage-sized fingers held the delicate teacup to his lips. His greying Brylcreemed hair was neatly combed back in even lines and he wore a dark-blue double-breasted suit and yellow tie. The tie stood out against his crisp white shirt. His breast pocket held a matching folded handkerchief.

Jack sat in silence, confused by what appeared to be a comfortable middle-class family having breakfast. Ned flicked crumbs of toast from his tie. He slowly made a fist in one hand and tightly clenched the other around it. His knuckles cracked, giving Jack a start.

'Tell me what you know so far.'

Jack pushed the front page of the paper across the table to him. 'Why would anyone do this to us?'

Ned read the article and pushed the paper back to Jack. 'What did the man with the cockroach look like?'

'He was about forty, thin, maybe five foot ten. Short-cropped mousey-brown hair. He wore a brown tweed jacket and grey trousers.'

'What did he sound like, did he have an accent?'

'He was a bit whiny, high-pitched and extremely dramatic. The weasel ran around the cafe showing the other customers the cockroach.'

Ned's phone rang. He looked at the number. 'Won't be a minute.' Ned stood up and walked to the window. He stared out the window listening to the caller. 'Pickles, I've told you before don't get the labels from Toenails, they're crap.' Ned listened again; his voice rose. 'I don't care if Puddyfoots are more expensive, they've got to look right. We can't flog premium gin with dodgy labels. Tell me when they're ready.'

Ned ended the call and returned to his seat. 'Now, where were we Jack?

'Did you catch his name?' Ned reached for more toast.

'No, he ran out of the shop before we could ask for his details. We were so shocked we didn't think to run after him.'

Ned reached for more toast. 'I'll put out some feelers around the pubs and clubs. With a bit of luck, we should hear something on the grapevine. We should also lean on your health inspector friend. Vincent can persuade him.'

'Can we find the cockroach man first Ned?' Jack said. 'We must clear Starlight's name so we can reopen. There's a bigger story going on with Fagg. My uncle's had run-ins with him before and thinks he's working for someone else.'

'OK, we'll start with Mr Cockroach.'

CHAPTER 39
THE PLAYGROUND

Chuck Adams felt good. He sat at the head of the table in the plush wood-panelled boardroom. In the distance he could see the Skyline residential tower in Hackney, shrouded in low-level smog. The expansive full-length windows gave a clear view of the car park and Barry's gatehouse.

The monthly figures were ahead of target. With further fine-tuning they could maintain the increase next month. He listened as Pete Crabshaw, his marketing manager, presented the next phase of the Hook 'Em Early campaign.

'We've got a new range of plastic toy ready for distribution as part of the toddler burger meal. It's a miniature pinball game. The meals are selling well but the toys will give them a further boost. There's one glitch. Our overseas outlets tell us toddlers keep swallowing the little plastic balls when the game breaks. Happens if they pull the lever too hard.'

Chuck leaned back in his chair. 'Look Pete, we've saved costs by making the burgers smaller for toddlers. I'm sure as hell not going to lose any margin by re-issuing the game. Put a sticker on the bottom in a small font warning that any liability will be down to the parents. Write that they should supervise the game, therefore it's not our fault. A damn two-year-old kid should be smart enough not to eat plastic. It's hardly our problem.'

Chuck's intercom buzzed. 'What is it Sal.'

'There's a Mr Slater on the line Chuck.'

'What does he want?'

'Something about a franchise arrangement with his development called the Bueno Vista.'

'That's Craig's area, put him through to Craig or take a message.'

'I tried that but he says he either speaks to you or the newspapers.'

'OK, put him through.'

Chuck waved at Pete Crabshaw to leave and waited on the phone, tapping his pen on the table.

'Hullo Mr Slater, Chuck Adams here, how may I help you?'

'Hi Chuck. A Craig Robinson from your office approached me recently about setting up a Mack 'n' Morti's franchise at my new Bueno Vista development. I told Craig I already have an exclusive arrangement with another fast-food outlet but he threatened to make life awkward if I don't play ball. But Craig is such a chatty fellow, don't you think? He told me about the way you dealt with Starlight Burgers. Nice touch putting the cockroach in the burger and letting the newspaper journalist do the rest.'

Chuck's face muscles hardened as Sid continued.

'I know the guys that run Starlight, so I paid them a visit. They have no idea how the cockroach got there. So, I thought I'd have a chat to you before I tell them. Now Chuck, how much would a scam like that cost? I'm wondering to myself, who would you need to have in your pocket to make it work?'

'Look, Mr Slater,' Chuck replied, keeping his voice under control. 'I don't know why Mr Robinson gave you the impression that we have anything to do with Starlight Burgers. We at Mack 'n' Morti's pride ourselves on our professional conduct. I'm shocked that you think we would involve ourselves in the type of incident you're describing.'

Sid's voice stayed icy calm. 'Was it something to do with the fact that Starlight's burgers are healthy? Yours are full of fat, sugar and salt, I believe; at least that's what Craig told me.'

'Mr Slater, I assure you that Mack 'n' Morti's use only the finest ingredients. Our own tests show that they are high in nutritional value. If it was Craig Robinson you really talked to, then I can only think he's on some sort of medication. Or else you misheard him. Your claims are unbelievable tales.'

'If you call three bottles of wine a medication, then I'd have to agree with you Chuck.'

Foul expletives crashed around Chuck's head at atomic speed. He fought to keep his voice steady and controlled.

'I'd like to thank you Mr Slater for bringing your conversation with Mr Robinson to my attention. I assure you I will be taking this matter up with him in person. About the threats you allege about your Bueno Vista development, I can only repeat that we maintain the highest professional business standards at Mack 'n' Morti's. We are always looking for new opportunities and we'd be happy to explore ways of working with you. But let me reiterate,

Mr Slater, we never apply undue pressure to push our case. As for the nonsense about this Starlight place, you would know that even when you're the innocent party, big companies like ours get blamed. I would appreciate it if you forgot about the whole Robinson discussion.

'As good corporate citizens we have a scheme called Mack 'n' Morti's Family Values. It's a fund to sponsor children's playgrounds with play equipment. I'd like to offer funding for one at Bueno Vista with you as patron. Let's say twenty grand's worth of equipment Mr Slater, as our contribution to supporting kids' health. And of course, it would be a privilege to continue talks about a franchise with you.'

'Actually Chuck, I am about to start designing the Sid Slater Children's Reserve, so play equipment would be a welcome contribution. I'll forget whatever Robinson said, I have no further interest in talking about Starlight Burgers. Sounds like they need to be shut down if they continue to sell cockroach-infested burgers. It's so good talking to you Chuck, I'll be in touch about delivery dates for the equipment.'

Sid hung up the phone, a broad smile across his face.

Great job Sid and what a bonus. I'll have the Sid Slater Reserve sign made huge now I've got decent kids' equipment.

'Mandy!' he yelled. 'Come in here.'

'I was about to go to lunch Sid.'

'Forget that, we've got an urgent media release to get out about the children's reserve at Bueno Vista. I want it to say that I have generously donated twenty thousand pounds' worth of playground equipment for the children of Bueno Vista.'

Mandy stared in disbelief. Sid hated kids and never spent his own money.

'Now get moving. I want this in the paper for tomorrow morning's issue.'

'Sal!' Chuck barked. 'Get Robinson here right now.'

'He's out with clients, I don't expect him back until tomorrow.'

'Damn. Well, who cares? He's fired. Get onto payroll, organise a cheque drawn for whatever he's owed and give it to Crabshaw within the hour. And get Crabshaw back in here.'

The look on Sal's face told Pete Crabshaw to be wary.

'You empty Robinson's personal items from his desk and put them in a box. Then go around to his house and deliver him a severance cheque. In return for his cheque, get the keys to the car and office and any files he has on clients. Remind him he is under a Non-Disclosure Agreement. We'll sue his arse if he gives out any information about the company. He is not to return to these premises under any circumstances and if anyone asks, he left for health reasons, got it? Do you think you can handle it Crabshaw?'

'Of course Chuck,' Pete said without hesitation.

Pete Crabshaw was a close friend of Craig Robinson's and godfather to his children. *Poor Craig, this is going to kill him. Sad, but if I handle this well there could be a promotion on the horizon.*

Pete went into Craig's office and started filling the box with his friend's possessions.

CHAPTER 40
A CAR RIDE

'Bye darling, I'll be home at six.'

Winston Fagg pulled the front door closed and walked towards the bus stop. A black car with tinted windows drew into the kerb. The rear door opened.

'What are you doing? HELP, HELP!'

He cried out in pain as his arm twisted up behind his back reaching his shoulder blade. A hand on his head pushed him through the open door of the car. He lay face down on the back seat. The smell of hessian filled his nostrils as a coarse bag was pulled over his head. The seat sank lower followed by a clunk as the door closed. Hands dragged him into an upright position. He heard gaffer tape being pulled from a reel. The pain from a sudden blow to his stomach stopped him reaching for the door handle. The gaffer tape tightened around his wrists, cutting into his skin, as it trapped his hands onto his knees. A short squeal of tyres signalled the car taking off.

'What do you want, I'm just a council worker?' Winston gasped for air. It was hard to breathe through the hessian.

'My boss wants to have a chat about cockroaches Winston.'

'How do you know my name?'

Julian Witherspoon had been surprised when he received a phone call from Winston Fagg, the health inspector. He usually dealt with his acting agency for all his roles. Though Winston wouldn't tell him how he got his number, Julian took the job. Money was short; he'd received three rejections in a fortnight, despite knowing his auditions were perfect.

Julian was a man fond of routine. He regularly ate lunch in the lounge of the Royal Hotel. Today he ordered a large veal parmigiana with a gin and tonic. A far cry from his usual lunchtime cheese sandwich accompanied by a shandy.

'Won a part in the next Tom Cruise movie, hey Julian?' Mickey the barman joked. 'Looks like you're splashing out.'

'No Mickey. For your information, I have completed a phenomenally successful professional engagement.'

Julian hated Mickey and his smartarse remarks. The barman was too stupid to appreciate the struggle of true artists. Julian was about to get long service leave from his job at the Water Board. He was sure he would crack the big time soon.

The last twelve months had been a roller coaster of highs and lows. There was no arguing Julian's best moment. He recalled surging forward in the crowd of extras in a busy street scene advertising "Mighty Mints, the Macho Mint for Men". He loved the tingle of excitement when the director called out 'action!'

When the mint advertisement screened, you could see

the top of Julian's head from the nose up amongst the crowd. His mother was proud and shared the YouTube clip on her Facebook feed.

But after that came crushing news. He failed to secure the lead in the annual Water Board's pantomime, *Puss in Boots*. They chose Russell Jones, who had no professional experience. As Julian pointed out to the director and producer, it was clearly because someone at the Water Board was friends with Russell.

Mickey delivered Julian a second gin and tonic as he opened the newspaper and read the cockroach story on Sunday's front page for the tenth time. His performance at Starlight Burgers was BAFTA-worthy. He couldn't understand why Winston Fagg refused to let the paper interview him. He ran the dramatic scene with the journalist over and over in his head. Through tears and the occasional gasp, he planned to tell the journalist about his distress at discovering a live cockroach in his burger. For dramatic effect, he had practised a little dry retch for the moment he described splitting the burger apart.

Mind you, I was close to throwing up when I opened the matchbox and dropped the creature onto the burger. Winston didn't tell me it was still alive.

Julian felt a tap on his shoulder and turned round to see his friend Bernie from the Water Board's payroll department.

'Hello Julian, mind if I join you?'

'Of course.'

Bernie and Julian were close. They shared similar artistic aspirations. Bernie was second trumpet player for the H2Os, the Water Board's brass band.

'Things must be looking up Julian. A G&T at lunchtime, what's the celebration?'

Even though Winston made him promise not to whisper a word, he couldn't have meant real confidants like Bernie. He leaned forward, looking round to make sure no one was in earshot.

'See this,' he said, pointing to the newspaper. 'The mystery cockroach man traumatised and in a state of shock; that's me Bernie. That's a re-enactment of my fingers holding the bun. But I can't tell anyone.'

'You've got to be joking, why do you want to keep it a secret? This could be worth a fortune to you.'

'How?'

'Julian, this would make great publicity for your career. Imagine the headlines. "A talented actor is the mystery man in the cockroach scandal. Says he may never be able to act again due to cockroach trauma". You could sue Starlight for millions.'

'Hey Mickey, what do you think?' Bernie shouted across the bar. 'Guess who found the cockroach in his burger at that new Starlight burger place? It's Julian here and the silly bugger wants to keep it quiet.'

'Shush, I told you, I can't tell anyone.'

Mickey slipped into the office. 'Yep, yep, sure, yep, okay,' and hung up the phone. He poured another two gin and tonics and brought them over to Julian and Bernie.

'These are on the house. Julian, you're a dark horse not telling us your news. You're famous now, why did you want to keep it quiet?'

'Er well, I did feel extremely ill yesterday, like the paper wrote but I didn't want journalists bothering my mother. She's elderly and the shock might have given her a turn.'

'Sounds sensible,' Mickey said. 'Tell you what, take your time. I'll get you some ice cream and another G&T on the house.'

After another gin and tonic, Julian saw things more clearly.

Winston Fagg was being selfish. The interview would be in the public interest. Bernie is right; I'd get a fortune if I sue the burger place.

As Julian finished his ice cream, he heard the scrape of a chair and a large man sat down between him and Bernie.

'Hello Julian, my name's Vincent.'

CHAPTER 41
CONFESSIONS

'Come with me Julian, my editor boss wanna meet you. He's interested in ya story. Ya know, about the cockroach in the burger.' Vincent read slowly from a scrap of paper. 'It must have been a real shock to you.' Vincent squinted harder at the paper. 'He says he wants to highlight the emotional stress you've experienced and how brave you were.'

'Sure, I'm happy to help out the media with a major exposé.'

Bernie could be right about the publicity, he thought.

The feeling of elation changed when he got into the car. The driver sped off as soon as he and Vincent were in the back seat. Vincent jammed a rough hessian bag over his head. When he tried to tear it off, Vincent taped his wrists to his knees. The combination of panic, total darkness, gin and tonic and the motion of the car made Julian feel ill.

'I have to get some air, I'm feeling sick.'

'We're nearly there,' Vincent barked. 'You'll have to hang on.'

Julian didn't make it. He tried hard but with one huge, gut-wrenching convulsion it all came out. Desperate to stem the flow, he tried to move his hands but they were taped to his knees. Hot, foul-smelling vomit flowed from the edge of the bag onto the front of his shirt.

'Get the bag off him Vincent, he's starting to choke, quick!' the driver shouted.

Julian struggled and choked as Vincent pinned him to the back of the seat. He grabbed the string under Julian's neck, fighting to undo the knot. Hot vomit poured over Vincent's hands and wrists. The knot came free, loosening the bag. As the bag came off, Julian started thrashing about in panic. The interior of the car became a steaming mess as Julian's excretions spattered over the seats.

The car screeched through the gates of a disused warehouse complex and skidded to a halt. Vincent dragged the still-heaving Julian out of the car and pushed him into the yard. He lay gasping on the concrete, eyes stinging.

'Hose him down,' snarled Vincent to the driver, 'then scrub the car.'

Vincent washed his hands under a tap and stripped off his clothes. He pulled on overalls from the car boot.

The cold blast of water from the hose shocked Julian but the smell receded. He crouched against the wall of the warehouse, shivering.

Vincent cut the tape around his hands and pulled him upright. He pushed him through a side door of the warehouse to a set of metal stairs that led up to a large open area on the second floor. The area was empty except for a single wooden chair in the middle. Vincent forced Julian onto the chair and placed a blindfold over his eyes.

Jack pulled the phone from his pocket. 'Is that Jack?'

'Yes, Jack here, who's that?'

'It's Vincent. We've got your cockroach man and health inspector. Boss says to come over to Griggs Industrial Estate and look for the Grimshaw's Smallgoods building. It's the empty red-brick warehouse at the back. We'll rough em up a bit before you get here.'

'Please don't do that,' Jack begged. 'I'm on my way.'

He grabbed the van keys and ran out of the cafe. He drove fast, imagining a pile of bloodied fingers and a man with broken kneecaps. He wound his way through the industrial estate until he spotted the faded Grimshaw's Smallgoods sign on a large, imposing brick five-story warehouse. The windows on the lower floors were boarded up with plywood and the main doors locked tight. He walked round the side and spotted a small metal door slightly ajar. It creaked on rusty hinges as he pulled it open and walked into a large empty room in semi darkness.

'Hello, anyone here? It's Jack.'

His eyes adjusted to the light. He passed a set of metal stairs and found a door to his right. Through the door a short flight of stairs led him to a corridor with a series of empty offices.

'It's Jack, anyone here?'

He heard the scrape of a chair coming from the far end of the corridor. His heart pounded as he made his way towards the sound.

Ned sat behind an old desk in an office at the end of the corridor. Apart from the desk and three wooden chairs the office was empty. He was pouring tea from a Thermos into a cup.

'Like some tea Jack?' Ned offered him a plastic cup.

'No thank you Ned. How did you get hold of the two blokes?'

'Don't worry about that Jack. I've told Vincent and the boys to hold off softening them up until you're ready to ask them questions.'

Jack gulped; he felt like he was in a *Luther* episode on TV.

'Can we try another way first?' Jack tried not to sound shocked.

'Tell me what you're thinking.'

Ned sat back in the chair; fingers laced behind his head as Jack laid out his plan.

When Jack finished, Ned leaned across the desk. 'This is the deal. I'll follow your plan up to a point. These characters need to feel threatened, so I'm going to add some pressure. If I think they're wasting my time, I'm going to do it the traditional way with Vincent and the boys, if you get my drift.'

'Ned, I'm curious. Can I ask you a question?'

'Sure,' Ned said. 'Fire away.'

'Why are you helping me?'

'Ha! It sure isn't because I think you're a good bloke! But you gave Harry a job. If he succeeds with you, then Harry is off my hands. The lad's a bit of a liability in my line of business. And Cassie. She loves that place of yours. She's proud to be part of it. I suspect there's something more than burgers going on with the tall bloke, Ben. Harry and Cassie both had a rough time as kids with useless parents and I'm fond of them. They're family. By helping you, I'm helping them.'

Julian clenched his muscles to keep the chair still. He pushed against the ropes trying to scratch his nose. The itch was becoming unbearable. A door creaked and footsteps approached. He'd watched *Reservoir Dogs* and knew what to expect. His legs began to wobble as he fought to keep his feet from drumming on the concrete floor. He expected a cold steel blade to rest on top of his ear at any moment. Terrified, he clenched his jaw so tight that he thought his teeth would shatter. The rope chafing increased with every movement.

'Julian, relax,' a calm, steady voice said near his left ear. 'I want to know about a cockroach that ended up in a burger.'

Julian smelled Brylcreem. He conjured up an image of a middle-aged gangster with a scar down his left cheek and knuckle dusters at the ready to give him a beating.

'You see Julian, the thing is the place you helped shut down is a favourite spot of mine. We know you planted the cockroach under orders from someone else. I said to my associate here: "Julian looks like an honest sort of person. He would only do something like that if he'd been forced to." Isn't that what I said, lads?'

'Yeh boss,' Vincent said.

The voice grew more menacing.

'My associate was all for removing any chance of you becoming a father, if you get my meaning. But I said no, I don't think that's necessary. I'm sure Julian will tell us everything we need to know. Am I right or am I wrong, Julian?'

'It wasn't my idea,' Julian blurted, tears streaming down his cheeks. 'Winston Fagg, he's the one you want, not me. He made me do it. I didn't even know the burger place existed. He sourced the cockroach and made me take it to Starlight Burgers.'

'Tell me Julian, why would Mr Fagg want to harm the Starlight?'

'I don't know, although he did mention something about the cafe upsetting friends of his. He said he was protecting their interests. That's all I know.'

The room went quiet except for the sound of receding footsteps followed by the sound of a heavy metal door sliding open. Suddenly, he was lifted still tied to the chair.

'We're going for a little walk,' Vincent said. 'Nothing to worry your little noggin about.'

Julian felt a waft of cool air as he was carried to another room and plonked down.

He caught the familiar whiff of Brylcreem. 'Julian, I'm thinking you might know the gentleman you're about to meet. And don't talk until I ask you to.'

Julian heard someone being dragged into the room.

'Ouch,' Winston cried as gaffer tape was ripped from his hands. He was roughly pushed onto a chair. Heavy footsteps echoed around him.

Sweat trickled down Winston's face in the confines of the hessian bag. Vincent removed the bag, replacing it quickly with a blindfold.

The menacing voice spoke again.

'Why did you stitch up our friends with that cock-and-bull story about the cockroach?' Winston felt someone grip the back of the chair.

'I had no choice. I issued the closure notice after a customer came to see me with the burger and cockroach. My job is to keep the public safe, so I determined the cafe should close pending further investigation. You must understand my position; it was the second major offence, so I had no choice.'

The grip on the chair turned to a light tap. 'Tell me about the man who made the complaint. Have you met him before?'

Winston kept up his story. 'I've never seen him before. He came to the office to make the complaint and gave a false address. I've no idea where he is. I'd like to help but I can't tell you any more than that.'

'Julian,' the voice said. 'I'd like you to go over what you told us about Mr Fagg. You mentioned he gave you a cockroach?'

'I'm sorry Winston,' he sobbed. 'They made me tell them what happened. I thought they'd kill me if I didn't confess.'

You stupid idiot. Winston's head was racing.

'I've never seen this man before. He's making it up, I swear,' Winston said with a trembling voice.

'We know that's not true, Winston. Don't waste our time. Now, why don't we see if we can sort this out? We have two options. First, we can make your slimy scheme public by leaking the facts to the media. I guess you would be fired after that. And you Julian, would be completely humiliated in front of your family and friends. Second option is that you Winston, publish a full apology to the Starlight. The apology will say that, after further investigation you discovered the cockroach had been deliberately placed in the burger. Plus, you tell me who you are working for. As for you, Julian, all you have to do is keep quiet.'

The room fell silent, except for an occasional sob from Julian. After a long pause, Winston spoke.

'I can arrange an apology but I can't tell you who I'm working for. They'll kill me.'

'No deal, we're not planning to involve you any further than the apology. We want a name and that's the last you'll hear from us.'

Winston stayed silent.

'Come on Winston. The name, then you and Julian can go home. If not, I'm going to leave you with Vincent and some of his friends. My colleagues have painful ways of getting people to talk, even if it takes a week or so.'

Julian heard the flick of a long-bladed knife. He broke down, sobbing uncontrollably.

'Winston, for god's sake, tell them what they want to know. Wasn't it someone from Mack 'n' Morti's?'

'Mack 'n' Morti's,' the voice said in surprise. 'What the hell have they got to do with this?'

Winston sighed. *I shouldn't have told Julian anything. I thought if I took him into my confidence, he'd keep quiet. He's really dropped me in it.*

'Okay, I'll give you a name. Then I'll release an apology to the media but I'll deny everything if you try and pin stuff on me. The apology will state that I was doing my job and keeping the public safe. I'm not responsible if a crackpot like Julian fabricates a stupid story.'

'I'm not a crackpot, this was all your idea.'

'Winston, we will keep you out of this but give us the name.'

'Frank Wilson. He's an executive at Mack 'n' Morti's who keeps a watch on potential competitors. Starlight got singled out because they were close to one of Mack 'n' Morti's franchise operators. They make healthy burgers and people were pouring through the door. Wilson was worried a journalist might start doing health comparisons with the local Mack 'n' Morti's franchise.'

Ned was confused. 'I can't believe they did all that because a small joint like Starlight cooks decent burgers.'

'Mack 'n' Morti's is ruthless about potential competitors. That's why they're so successful. They're control freaks.'

'Vincent, drop Julian off and go with Mr Fagg to meet his press contact. Make sure the apology is headline stuff. Not some column under the crossword or obituaries where it's hard to find. Do you understand, Winston?'

'I get the picture.'

CHAPTER 42
AN APOLOGY

The Mini driver had his hand on the horn, mouthing, 'Fucking idiot!' Jack held his hand up in apology for cutting him off.

He turned onto the A12 and phoned Ben. 'Ben, you won't believe this! Ned's sorted out Winston Fagg. He called me to meet him at an abandoned factory on the Griggs industrial estate. He had the health inspector and the man with the cockroach tied up. It was incredible, just like the movies.

'Cockroach man confessed and Ned forced the health inspector to issue an apology in the media. It means we can open the Starlight tomorrow! And I have more news.'

'How did they get them to confess?'

'I'll tell you more about it tomorrow but there's another problem.'

'What do you mean?' Ben said, alarmed. 'They didn't kill cockroach man, did they? I don't want to be an accessory to murder. Why did they kill him for Christ's sake?'

'Ben, calm down, I'll see you tomorrow.'

Jack turned up the radio and tapped the steering wheel to the rhythm of 'Uptown Funk'.

Vincent was also on the road. He drove Winston to the offices of *The Hackney Gazette*.

The doors opened on the seventh floor. 'I need to see Jim Croker, it's urgent.'

'I'll see if Mr Croker is in.'

The sight of the gorilla-like man with a cauliflower ear towering over the dishevelled health inspector made the receptionist nervous. She dialled quickly.

'Jim, the council health inspector is here to see you, says it's urgent.'

The receptionist nodded and hung up the phone. 'Jim's in his office, you can go through.'

Jim stood up from his desk, surprised at Winston's appearance.

'What's happened to you Winston?'

'Nothing, been a busy day.'

Jim shook Winston's hand and looked up at Vincent.

'Oh, this is Vincent, a colleague of mine. He's helping with the burger case.'

Vincent left Jim's offer of a handshake in mid-air.

'Jim, I need you to publish a story for tomorrow morning.'

'Front page, lead story, don't forget Winston?' Vincent squeezed his shoulder.

Jim gave Vincent a curious glance. 'You're pushing the friendship Winston; we've finished the copy for tomorrow.'

'I'll owe you a big one Jim.'

Winston's voice trembled and Jim saw the panic in his red, watery eyes.

'The council wants to publish an apology to the Starlight:

We want to assure the public that Starlight Burgers was

in no way responsible for the cockroach in the burger. A mentally unwell member of the public planted it in the burger and an arrest has been made.

'Jim, you can add something about me. You can say I became suspicious and investigated the case. That I single-handedly uncovered the deception. You can end with me exonerating Starlight Burgers from any suggestion of poor health practices. You know the sort of thing.'

Jim Croker scratched his head.

'That's what I like about you Winston, you never let an opportunity slip by. You owe me for this one. I'll get the story out as soon as I've written it.'

Jim cursed Winston for making him re-arrange the lead story. But Fagg's money on the side was handy for a poorly paid journalist. He could cut back the Sid Slater Children's Reserve announcement and put the boat people story at the back of the paper. Local stories mattered.

Outside, Vincent patted Winston on the back.

'Good job Winny. If this gets done proper, you won't see us again. Don't stuff it up or else.'

Vincent drove away, leaving Winston feeling sick.

I can't tell Frank Wilson I've ratted on him. I'll have to act shocked and surprised when he rings after he reads the news. Who am I kidding? He's going to know it was me. I'm in the shit if he wants the money back. The builders have already started on the patio extension. What am I going to do?

CHAPTER 43
THE AGREEMENT

'I can't believe Mack 'n' Morti's thought the Starlight was a threat to them,' Jack said. 'It doesn't make sense. I'm sure customers will come back once they see the headlines.'

Julie looked across at Jack, a tinge of sadness in her voice. They were in the car on their way to the cafe.

'Don't forget Stan still wants it back as a sandwich bar.'

'I know, I've told him I'm not interested unless we sign an agreement for the sale of the Starlight. We have to sit down with him today and decide what to do.'

They arrived at the cafe in silence and found Stan waiting outside. 'How's life, Stan?' Jack said, trying to sound cheerful. 'How's the cat?'

'Bloody neighbour complained about me harassing his cat.'

'Well, you did Stan.'

'Beside the point. It shouldn't have been stalking birds. Some idiot arrived at my door from the council and I told him to get stuffed and get a proper job.'

Stan surveyed the inside of the cafe while Jack turned on the espresso machine to make coffee.

Julie turned to Stan. 'Let's sit down.'

Stan chose a table at the back of the cafe.

'It's a bit of a shock I suppose Stan.'

'You're not wrong love, I don't recognise the Starlight anymore. As I said to Jack, the funny thing is that if Ruby were alive, she would think this update looked great. She always wanted to specialise in one food like a burger. Ruby was ahead of her time but I could never see it. I realise now I wasn't fair to her.'

Jack brought the coffees over and sat next to Julie.

'Stan, good news about the health inspector. Vincent picked up Winston Fagg on his way to work and started questioning him about the cockroach.'

'Who's Vincent?' Stan asked.

'He's an ex-heavyweight boxer. A kind of minder for Ned.'

'I'm confused, who the hell is Ned?'

'Sorry Stan, it's a long story. Ned is Ned Cleghorn, head of the Cleghorn family. He's been helping us sort out the cockroach problem.'

'The Cleghorns are criminals,' Julie added.

'And we've found them to be extremely useful criminals,' Jack said. 'Cassie says Ned is more of an Arthur Daley than a serious criminal. And before you ask, Cassie is Ned's niece. She came up with the Starlight design and did the painting. Anyway, Ned got a tip-off about the cockroach.'

Stan stared at Jack in disbelief.

'You're winding me up Jack.'

'No Stan. It's all true, isn't it Julie.'

Julie nodded and Stan leaned forward.

'Go on Jack, what happened next?'

'Cockroach man, his name's Julian, was in a pub having lunch. He's the one who ran out of the Starlight saying there was a cockroach on his burger. Vincent picked him up and took him to the warehouse.'

'What warehouse?'

'I don't know Stan. An old brick warehouse on the Griggs Industrial estate. I think Ned might own or rent it. He stores some of his imported goods there.

'Ned told me they'd found Julian and Winston Fagg, so I went over to the warehouse. They got Julian to confess.'

'Did they kneecap him?' Stan said excitedly.

'No Stan, they agreed to try a less-drastic plan first.'

Stan's disappointment showed on his face.

'But I don't understand. Why is Mack 'n' Morti's interested in the Starlight?'

'Fagg said a man called Frank Wilson from Mack 'n' Morti's said our burgers are a threat because they're healthy and we're getting too popular. We're close to one of their franchises and they don't want to risk a direct comparison in case it harms their business. It seems extreme to me but I can't think of any other reason. I wanted to speak to you about our next move.

'As it stands, we can start up again tomorrow, with the apology published in *The Hackney Gazette*. We shouldn't suffer any backlash from customers. But from what Fagg said, Mack 'n' Morti's are a ruthless pack of bastards and they will try and find another way of closing us down. I'm ready for a fight, I don't care how big they are. Ned said he'd lean on this Frank Wilson to find out more but it depends on what you plan to do.'

'Mack 'n' Morti's is only after us because we sell burgers.' Stan sipped his coffee, leaned back in his chair and scratched his head.

Jack continued. 'I didn't know what to expect when you offered to sell the Starlight. Since we made the changes, I've come to love this business and our customers. Even though I've only been at it a short time.'

Jack's voice grew more serious. 'I want to buy the Starlight and keep it as a burger bar for our future and, with your help, take on Mack 'n' Morti's.'

Stan drained his coffee cup and let out a small belch. He thumped the table, nearly landing his empty cup on the floor.

'If you think I'm going to let those corporate creeps off the hook, then you have another thing coming. How dare they try to wipe out Starlight after thirty years of hard work. It makes my blood boil.'

'But Stan, you told me the other night you don't want to sell the Starlight? If you turn it back to a sandwich bar, they won't bother you.'

'I know I'm old but I'm not stupid. If Mack 'n' Morti's are doing this to keep Starlight burgers off the streets, then you must be making bloody good burgers. I've seen the figures. You're more profitable than I ever was. Besides, if Ruby were alive, she would be proud of what her nephew's done.'

Since his last visit to the Starlight Stan's conscience had plagued him. Recurring dreams of Ruby became a source of both comfort and sadness. Ruby had made him realise his attachment to the cafe was about friendship and belonging rather than owning. He understood now that Jack was earnest in making a long-term commitment to the Starlight recognising the same ambition he once had.

'I've been thinking about our talk the other day Jack.

I'm sorry I've been so indecisive but I've made up my mind. I want you to own the Starlight; Ruby would want it. Julie, draw up a formal contract for the sale of the Starlight Cafe and I'll sign it.'

'Oh Stan, that's fantastic. I promise to look after it and you are welcome here anytime. Your burgers are always on the house.'

'You can reserve me the same table by the window you had as a boy. I'm a customer now.

'But on one condition. I want to be in on this fight. I've got a score to settle with Winston Fagg and Mack 'n' Morti's. That weasel has tried to close this cafe down twice now.'

'If we nail Mack 'n' Morti's, then Winston Fagg goes down as well Stan. Julie's planning to get more information about their whole operation.'

Julie turned to Stan. 'I'll find out when they were incorporated, their parent company details, the registered company officers and any litigation disputes they're party to.'

On the way out of the Starlight, Stan ripped the Health notice off the window, screwed it into a ball and threw it in the bin.

'Stan, are you sure about this fight? It could get rough.'

'You've got to be joking. I wouldn't miss this fight for quids; it's a lot more exciting than fishing.'

Stan skipped across the footpath to his car.

'Fiery old bugger your Uncle Stan,' Julie said.

Jack laughed. 'At least the cat will get a break.'

CHAPTER 44
FRANK GOES JOGGING

The alarm went at 5.30am in Frank Wilson's apartment. He turned it off and lay on his back checking his Facebook feed. He scrolled quickly through the new posts, finding nothing of interest. He sat up, stretching his arms in the air. *The Magic of Thinking Big* sat on his bedside table.

He pulled a tracksuit on and went into the kitchen. Jogging on the spot, he grabbed a carton of almond milk from the fridge and turned on the coffee machine. Frank added a sliced apple to his bowl of muesli and poured on the milk. He crunched through the muesli, impatient to get on with his run.

He finished the last of his coffee while reading his emails. He was happy to read that Craig Robinson had left Mack 'n' Morti's for health reasons. Whenever a staff departure stated health reasons you knew Chuck had fired them. Craig had been helpful to Frank when he started but he'd got cocky and became a liability. Frank could get more responsibility with Craig leaving. He made a mental note to find an excuse to see Chuck. He would wear his new suit and give Chuck the good news about Starlight Burger's closure.

Chuck continually lectured his employees that a healthy body was essential for a healthy mind. He planned to introduce extra jogging sessions for the management team next month, so Frank wanted to make sure he was the fittest. He used his treadmill in bad weather and ran around Walthamstow Marshes at other times.

Outside Frank's apartment Vincent yawned and offered another strip of chewing gum to his driver and accomplice. He'd been outside Frank Wilson's apartment since 5 a.m., watching the building's car park barrier for Frank to appear. With the telephone details extracted from Winston Fagg, it was easy to find Frank's address. He also had a physical description and photo of Frank's face obtained by Ned.

The main door of the apartment block opened. Frank jogged out and stopped at the entrance. He went through a series of stretches, hanging onto the apartment door handle. He jogged down the apartment steps.

'Easier than I thought,' Vincent nodded to his accomplices.

Frank didn't notice the large black car following him as he approached the Marshes. Vincent jumped out of the car and sprinted towards Frank. The gap narrowed near the entrance to the Marshes but Frank increased his pace as he reached the old railway arch. Vincent pumped his arms to increase his speed but he wasn't gaining. A train rattled over the bridge, muffling his heavy breathing. When Frank reached the football field, he increased his pace.

Vincent's tight suit trousers started to chafe against his sweating thighs and his breath began to labour. He collapsed on a bench trying to catch his breath, Frank disappeared. Vincent returned to the bridge and hid. Thirty minutes later he heard someone jogging towards him. He peered around the corner to see a hot and perspiring Frank approaching. Vincent stuck out his foot and Frank sprawled across the footpath.

'What are you playing at you idiot?' Frank picked himself up from the ground.

'Sorry, Franky, let me give you a hand.'

Before Frank could get his breath, Vincent punched him in the ribs. Frank fought for breath as Vincent half-carried him towards the road. Vincent pushed him face first onto the rear red vinyl seat of the waiting car. Frank kicked out as he felt a thick hessian bag drawn tightly under his chin plunging him into darkness. A rough pair of hands dragged him upright in the seat. He flailed out with his fists until a sledgehammer blow to the side of his head made him stop. Frank heard gaffer tape being pulled from a reel. His hands were pushed onto his knees and the tape wound around his wrists and legs.

'I don't know what your game is. I work for a large corporation and you are going to be in big trouble!' Frank screamed through the bag.

'I wouldn't waste your breath making that racket,' Vincent replied.

Frank struggled to get his hands free but they stayed

firmly taped to his knees. He threw himself sideways to escape but the door had been closed. 'Ow!' he yelled as his head banged into the window. The temperature inside the bag was rising rapidly with the exertion. Sweat poured down his face creating a small sauna. The gel from his hair softened to a liquid and trickled down his face, stinging his eyes.

A large hand gripped him around the throat. He tried to speak.

'Ltmgo cbrth.'

'Can't hear you Franky, you gonna be a good boy now?'

Frank nodded and the hand eased the pressure. He felt a large body sit down next to him as the car engine started.

He tried to remember the mindfulness podcast he listened to: 'I am breathing in, I am breathing out, I am breathing in, I am breathing out, I am bre—'

'Shut the fuck up or I'll break your neck.'

The car wound its way through the Griggs industrial estate and stopped at the side entrance to the factory. Frank's feet dragged on the pavement as Vincent pulled him from the car and into the factory. He was half-pulled, half-walked up a set of stairs to a closed metal door. Vincent cursed; the door was jammed.

'Hang onto this railing while I get this open.'

Frank clutched the railing. He felt lightheaded from the hot wet heat inside the bag. His hair gel stung his eyes and ran into his mouth. Suddenly, he felt sick with vertigo and toppled backwards down the stairs.

Vincent heard a thump as Frank landed.

'Fuck.'

He bounded down the stairs and ripped the bag off

Frank's head but Frank's red puffy face slumped to one side.

'Frank, Frank, wake up.'

Frank didn't move. Vincent ran outside to get his accomplices. Three men stood peering down at Frank.

'Reckon he's dead Vincent' the driver asked.

'Dunno, how do you tell?'

'Ned won't be happy.'

Vincent bent down, raising his hand. 'I'll give him a slap.'

'Wait,' the accomplice said. 'His foot moved.'

They saw Frank's chest rise and fall in short breaths.

Vincent wiped his forehead. 'Thank Christ for that.'

Vincent hoisted Frank over his shoulder and carried him back up the stairs.

CHAPTER 45
WHERE'S FRANK?

'What the hell is going on?' Chuck Adams, the CEO of Mack 'n' Morti's, exploded.

He read the front-page story of *The Hackney Gazette* again, then picked up the phone.

'Get in here Crabshaw. Now!'

'Have you read this?' Chuck tossed the paper at Pete Crabshaw.

Pete had read the article at home. This was dangerous territory and he wanted to keep his head down. Although it was Frank's problem, Chuck was unpredictable and could lash out at anyone. Pete pretended he was reading the article for the first time.

'Starlight Burgers health scare set up by deranged diner. Cafe innocent of all charges.'

'Wilson was supposed to close them down. Not give them free fucking advertising and endorsements. What the hell's going on Crabshaw? Do you know anything about this?' Chuck demanded.

'Of course not Chuck, the inspector is Frank's contact. I don't know what's going on.'

'I mean, I knew he was working with the inspector to get the cafe shut down but I didn't know the details.'

'Go and find out what's going on Crabshaw. I won't tolerate these cock-ups.'

'Looks like you've seen a ghost,' Sal said, as Pete steadied himself on the edge of her desk.

Sal Baker had been Chuck's PA for six months. At thirty-two she had married a merchant banker and lived in an upmarket house near the office. Sal enjoyed a bit of easy work and, when the position at Mack 'n' Morti's came up, she applied. Chuck thought Sal was perfect, smart and most importantly, attractive.

Her phone rang.

'Sal!' Chuck yelled down the phone. 'Get Wilson in here now.'

'Sorry Chuck, he hasn't come in yet. Should have been here at 8.30 for a meeting but no one's seen him.'

'When he gets in, tell him to get his arse here straightaway.'

Pete winced at Sal and waved a silent goodbye. Sal sighed. *Looks like another call to HR coming up.*

CHAPTER 46
A NIGHT AT THE FLICKS

Ben browsed the shelves of the Fonlin Book shop in Hackney. He flicked through books specifically with graffiti in their title.

'Do you need some help?' A tall woman with short cropped white hair and red glasses smiled at Ben.

'I want to buy a book on graffiti art for my girlfriend.'

It felt strange but exciting calling Cassie his girlfriend.

'What style is she interested in?'

Ben looked confused.

'We've got books on Throw-up, Tag, Blockbuster, Heaven, Wildstyle, Stencil, Poster, Sticker and Piece. What type of graffiti are you looking for?'

'Er, um.'

'Let me show you.'

The woman flicked through examples of graffiti styles in several books.

Ben pointed to a book filled with colourful images on shiny gloss paper. 'This one looks good.'

'Ah yes, this is the book I'd recommend too. It has great examples of the Piece style, I'm sure your girlfriend will love it. Let me gift wrap it.'

Ben spent the rest of the afternoon cleaning and re-tidying his flat. He lay his brown moleskin jeans and dark-green shirt over the warm radiator and smoothed out the wrinkles with his hand. *Must buy an iron one day.*

His alarm sounded "Kitchen Mix" at 6.30. Ben checked his hair in the mirror, picked up Cassie's gift and walked to the bus stop. *Wish Dodger had the Golf ready.* Ben had sold the motorbike in part-exchange for a ten-year-old Golf. He wanted to surprise Cassie but the Golf failed its MOT test.

The bus pulled up within a short walk to Cassie's shared house.

Colin barked as Ben rang the bell. He could hear him snuffling on the other side of the door.

'Come in Ben.'

Cassie held Colin's collar as Ben entered the hallway. She led him into a small sitting room where he met her housemates, Sylvie and Lucy. Two pairs of critical eyes examined him as he spoke.

'Hi, it's nice to meet you both.'

Silence. Colin sniffed his shoes.

Cassie took his hand. 'See you later girls,' and led Ben to her bedroom.

'Sorry about them, they can be real bitches. But the rent's cheap.'

'It's okay. I wanted to give you this.' Ben handed her the present.

Cassie looked surprised. She carefully unwrapped the paper and stared at the book cover: *Trespass: A History of Uncommissioned Urban Art.*

'This is fantastic Ben, I love Carlo McCormicks's work.'

She turned the first few pages and then closed the book.

'Thank you so much Ben, I don't know what to say.'

'I'm glad you like it. The woman at the book shop was extremely helpful. I had no idea there were so many different styles of graffiti. So clever and colourful. We'd better get going or we'll miss the movie.'

The opening credits of *The World's Fastest Indian* were rolling as they took their seats. Burt Munro commenced his journey from New Zealand to the Bonneville Salt Flats in Utah. In the warmth of the darkened cinema, Cassie nestled into Ben's shoulder as he gently held her hand. Cassie swore at the screen when the officials tried to stop Burt racing. She clutched Ben's arm tightly as Burt flew across the salt flats at over two hundred miles per hour.

'Great movie Ben, what a legend Burt Munroe is.'

Ben spied a mobile chip van. 'How about we get some chips?'

'Nice chips,' Cassie said as they ambled down Holloway road.

Ben desperately wanted to ask Cassie something but his confidence was fading. He lapsed into an uncomfortable silence.

'What is it Ben?'

Cassie couldn't see him blushing in the dark.

'Well, I was wondering...'

'Yes Ben?'

'I was wondering if you would like to stay at my place tonight?'

Cassie stopped walking.

'Are you sure Ben?'

'I've never been so sure in my entire life. I love you Cassie.'

CHAPTER 47
OPEN FOR BUSINESS

The alarm woke Ben at 6.30am.

Cassie's arm lay across his chest. He gently kissed her on the lips as she opened her eyes.

'Have to go to work, want some breakfast?'

Cassie wrapped herself in a sheet and sat on the couch watching Ben pour the tea. They sat close to each other, eating toast.

'Do you have to go Ben?'

'I have to, it's only me and Jack this morning.

'We're re-opening the Starlight at lunchtime. Jack's worried we might not get any customers back after the cockroach scare.'

Jack and Ben were sticking a sign in the cafe window:

Celebration!
Re-opening this lunchtime.
All burgers 20% off

They heard the rattle from a familiar old car making its

way towards the cafe. The driver's door opened with a high-pitched squeak and Stan appeared.

'I'm on my way to the shops and thought I'd see how the re-opening's going.'

Stan spotted the sign in the window. 'Hmm, a lot better than the last one I saw.'

The tobacconist came out of his shop next door when he saw Stan's car.

'How are you my old friend?'

They shook hands.

'Saw the paper this morning. Congratulations on your win with the council. I've been missing our chats. How are the cat wars going?'

'Oh, you know. Bloody thing's still on the loose and causing havoc.'

'I remember you once had a run-in with the council before Stan. But they didn't close you down as fast as they did with your nephew here. Great photo of the cafe in the paper by the way,' the tobacconist said as he returned to his shop.

Jack showed Stan the headlines from the Hackney Gazette.

Stan threw the paper on the counter. 'You can't buy this sort of advertising Jack.'

Jack's phone rang.

'Hello Vincent. What's that? Frank who?' Jack strained to hear. 'You've found him? That's great. OK. See you soon.'

'That was Vincent, they've found Frank, the hot shot from Mack 'n' Morti's. I'm going to the warehouse to find out what's going on.'

'Not without me you aren't,' piped up Stan.

'You don't need to get involved with this Stan. Neds on top of it. Why don't you give Ben a hand while I'm away?'

'Not a chance. I'm not missing this for anything.' He trotted over to his car and flung open the passenger door. 'Come on Jack, get in.'

Stubborn old bugger.

'Hey Ben, get onto Cassie and see if she can come in to give you a hand while I'm away.'

Jack's phone rang as they turned into the Griggs Industrial estate.

'Hi Julie. I'm on my way with Stan to see Ned. We're going to meet Frank Wilson, the bloke from Mack 'n' Morti's.'

'Okay Jack, just to let you know I've found some information on Mack 'n' Morti's. They are a subsidiary of The Vine Tobacco company based in Virginia, USA. The records show many other companies owned by Vine. They include a pancake chain, waffle chain and a barbecued chicken group. All the affiliates are major franchised fast-food outlets in the USA. Only Mack 'n' Morti's operates in the UK. There's an odd connection between Vine Tobacco and a bakery in Hackney but that's all. Looks like everything is legal and above board.'

'Guess the bakery makes their buns,' Jack said. 'Anyway, thanks for the info, I'll speak to you later.'

'Hang on, what do you mean Stan's with you?'

'Couldn't stop him, Stan's spoiling for a fight.'

CHAPTER 48
FRANK GETS FRESH AIR

Frank woke to find himself tied to a chair in a small, windowless room. A single lightbulb hung from the ceiling. Cream-painted plaster stained with faded brown marks covered the walls. What Frank thought to be meat hooks jutted from one wall. The room, enclosed by thick brick walls, had a single metal door for entry. A shallow gutter ran down the centre of the concrete floor. A long metal rod ran the length at head height.

Frank sniffed. He smelt a sweet fatty odour. *Must be a meat storage room.* He strained his eyes and deciphered the words Cosa Nostra in faded letters on the opposite wall. He swallowed hard as he saw smeared blood-red hand-prints below the words. *What do they want with me? I can't understand why I've been kidnapped. Maybe it's connected to the Starlight, I'll deny everything.* A door slammed in the distance. A terrifying sense of foreboding took hold.

Ned looked annoyed when Jack arrived. 'What's that old

geezer doing here? I don't want any complications; the less people the better.'

'Sorry Ned, he's my Uncle Stan. He used to run the Starlight. He's had run-ins with Fagg before and wants to get stuck into the Mack 'n' Morti's bloke. I've told him it's under control but he still wanted to come.'

Ned looked across at Stan. 'Well, if he's family I can understand why he wants to help you. You've gotta respect that.'

Ned spoke to one of Vincent's offsiders, who led Stan away to Ned's office.

'Come on Jack, we've got Frank upstairs.'

'I don't know anything about a Winston Fagg or the incident at Starlight,' Frank pleaded as Jack and Ned entered the room. 'You've got the wrong man, I promise. The person you want is Craig Robinson. They sacked him. He's involved in this and that's why he got sacked from Mack 'n' Morti's.'

Ned cracked his knuckles with a loud crunch. 'I don't recall mentioning Winston Fagg or Starlight Burgers. I'm disappointed in you Frank. I hoped you would cooperate but I can see my colleague was right. We're wasting our time. You know what to do Vincent.'

Frank felt the hairs rise on the back of his neck. He squeezed his eyes shut and tensed his body, waiting for the blows to start.

The breeze felt cool on Frank's face as he hung by his ankles from a rope. He swung gently from the rusting gantry of the warehouse, sixty feet in the air. His terrified mind raced over the situation. *They must have found proof I got the cafe closed. Oh God, get me out of here. I don't want to end up in a concrete flyover.* Frank started shaking. The rope tightened around his ankles. He tensed his body to keep still. *Winston Fagg's told them everything. Maybe I can negotiate a deal, get immunity somehow. Think Frank, think.*

Vincent leaned out of the warehouse window near the gantry.

'Enjoying yourself Franky, how good are you at flying?'

Vincent nodded towards the ground.

'Your mate Winston didn't seem to get the hang of it.'

Frank craned his neck and looked down. He caught the sound of whistling as an old man hosed a pool of blood off the concrete into a gutter that ran towards a drain. A red trail trickled towards an opening in the warehouse.

Tears streamed into Frank's hair and his bladder released a stream of urine.

'OK, I'll tell you everything. Please get me down, I don't want to die,' Frank cried.

Ned appeared at the window. 'Well Franky, glad to see you want to cooperate. Before we let you down tell me why Mack 'n' Morti's tried to close the Starlight. I use the word "tried" Franky because it's open again.'

Jack hung a copy of *The Hackney Gazette* upside down so Frank could read the headline.

'So you see Franky, the good guys always win. Don't give us any shit. We will find you no matter where you go.'

Vincent swung the gantry back to the window and hauled a sodden, trembling Frank inside.

Jack helped Frank onto a chair. 'Start talking Frank.'

'Well,' stammered Frank, 'my job is to check out the competition. I mentioned Starlight Burgers because we analyse competitor's burgers. Starlight's are more nutritious, taste better and are much lower in saturated fats and sodium. The boss wanted Starlight shut down because they're too close to one of our top franchise operators. Especially as that franchise is trialling our new toddler burger. We couldn't risk any detailed food analysis by nosey journalists.'

Jack was curious. 'Why would you worry about an analysis comparison? Most people know there are likely to be additives in food these days.'

'That depends on the additive,' Frank half whispered.

Ned towered over Frank. 'What do you mean Franky? Is there something a little extra in Mack 'n' Morti's burgers?'

'They have an extra ingredient.'

Frank bit his tongue, he felt cold and clammy. He couldn't stop his left eye twitching. *Please don't ask*, he prayed.

'Tell us about the extra ingredient Frank.'

He looked at Ned then back at the gantry, his shoulders slumped in defeat.

'The toddler burger contains low levels of nicotine. It's part of the Hook 'Em Early campaign. Our parent tobacco company is using its fast-food chains, like Mack 'n' Morti's, to addict toddlers.'

Jack shook his head. 'Wow! that's shocking.'

'They bought a bakery in Hackney as a secure in-house

supplier for the toddler burger buns,' Frank continued. 'That's the place where they add the nicotine.'

Ned drew up a chair opposite Frank. 'I'm confused, I thought tobacco companies only sold cigarettes. Why are they developing products for two and three-year-olds?'

Frank explained, looking across at Ned. 'Tobacco companies sell cigarettes using their prime product, nicotine. Without nicotine, you wouldn't smoke cigarettes.'

'It doesn't make sense,' Jack said, 'you can buy low-nicotine cigarettes so it can't be that important.'

Frank shook his head. 'You have to be joking. Nicotine is essential. The nature of nicotine is that you need a hit about every forty minutes. It's why they put twenty-five cigarettes in a packet, which lasts around a day.'

'But what's that got to do with putting nicotine in toddler's burgers?' Ned asked again.

'It's our cradle-to-grave strategy. Creates brand loyalty by hooking them as young as possible with nicotine. They'll take to cigarettes at a much earlier age. If you start toddlers on our burgers at pre-school age, they become addicts earlier. The transition to cigarettes becomes a natural progression as they grow older.'

A look of disgust crept over Jack's face. 'So the only reason you want to sell toddler burgers, is to get two-year-old kids hooked on drugs.'

'Pretty much and our secondary strategy is to give away free toys to encourage kiddy sales.'

'We've heard enough.' Ned signalled to Vincent. 'Take Franky back to the meat storage room, give him a drink and we'll work out what to do with him later.'

CHAPTER 49
MEET THE PRESS

Ben watched Cassie hop off the 292 and walk across the road to the Starlight. He ran out the door, impatient to see her and lifted her up in a bear hug. They kissed each other slowly as they entered the Starlight.

'Oi you two, how about some service?' a burly workman in hi-visibility vest yelled.

'Righto,' Ben danced happily behind the grill.

Cassie took over the till and espresso machine.

'One Cocky burger and chips please.' Lizzy was a Starlight regular.

'How are you, Lizzy?' Ben shouted.

'Great thank you Ben, glad to see you open again.'

'Do you want the Cocky dead or alive Lizzy?'

'Alive of course Ben!' she laughed.

Ben had cooked fifteen Cocky burgers. It became a standing joke with customers. He'd written it on the board as a lunchtime special. It consisted of a burger with sun-dried tomatoes, baby spinach and halloumi cheese.

Cassie looked across at Ben. She loved his tall, lean figure and the look of concentration as he prepared the burgers. His initial shyness had disappeared as they grew closer. Cassie felt a new sense of happiness.

A steady stream of customers continued throughout

the morning; Ben felt calm as he looked across at smiling happy customers munching his burgers. *I think we are going to be all right.*

Jim Croker, the journalist from *The Hackney Gazette* arrived. He ordered a Bombay burger and introduced himself to Ben and Cassie.

'We've had a lot of calls about your story and the mystery cockroach man. We'd like to do a short follow-up. You know, how you got started, how you felt when the incident occurred, that sort of thing. I've been told you sell reusable containers and that you have a weird machine to clean them.'

Ben pointed towards the machine. 'You mean the world-famous bin burger containers and the Bin-O-Matic. We can give you a demo when the queues are smaller.'

Jim sat at a table with his Bombay burger, writing notes. As the lunchtime crowd faded, Ben and Cassie joined him at the table.

'Stan Morrison owned the cafe for thirty years,' began Ben. 'It was a typical cafe of its time. He sold sandwiches and drinks plus a few hamburgers. The cafe came under pressure from the new deli-style cafes and Stan retired, selling the business to his nephew. Jack turned it into the place you see today. Cassie did all the amazing artwork.'

'We were gutted when the cockroach turned up in the burger,' Ben continued. 'We tore the place apart but didn't find a trace of an insect. The inspector turned up a short time later, out of the blue.'

Jim looked puzzled. 'Did the health inspector mention who complained?'

'No, he just said he received a complaint.'

'Did he show any evidence?'

'No, he only gave us the notice to close.'

Jim frowned. 'Strange how the story was retracted so quickly. I wonder what happened.'

Cassie looked at Ben. 'Yeah, strange that,' Ben said, keeping a straight face.

'Thank you for the burger and information. I'll send you a copy of the finished article.'

Jim had parked on the opposite side of the road. He sat in his car looking through his notes. Tap, tap, tap, his pen beat a steady rhythm on his notebook. *Winston, you shifty bugger, what are you mixed up in?*

CHAPTER 50
WEIGHING UP THE OPTIONS

'Come on Franky, less of that unless you want another slap.'

Frank gave up the struggle as Vincent's boa constrictor grip tightened around his chest. In a last hopeless effort, he jammed his leg against the architrave of the cold room door.

'Please, please don't lock me in there. I've told you everything. For god's sake let me go. I won't tell anyone.'

His leg spasmed in pain as Vincent stamped on his foot and he fell to the floor. He heard the door close and a click as the lock turned.

Vincent joined Ned, Stan and Jack, sitting on wooden crates near the front of the room.

'Ned, we should get hold of Chuck Adams and beat the shit out of him. That'd teach him a lesson.'

'Worked in the old days,' Ned said. 'I don't think they would dare bother you again Jack.'

Stan stared at Ned and Vincent in awe. *This is great, I can't believe I'm in a gang.* Not to be outdone he said, 'I think we should dip Chuck in acid, burn the bakery down and drown that bastard Winston Fagg in concrete.'

'Like the way you think Stan,' Vincent agreed. 'I'm with you.'

Frank strained to hear the conversation, ear flat against the cold room door. *Thank God they didn't turn the cooling on. I'd be an ice block already.*

The thickness of the door made it hard for Frank to hear. He made out a few words. *Christ, I knew it. They're going to throw me in an acid bath or bury me in concrete. I'll end up as part of the new flyover. I've got to get out of here.*

The cold room was completely sealed, apart from a box containing a fan near the ceiling. Frank remembered a scene from *Mission Impossible*. Ethan Hunt leaped up to a similar unit and managed to crawl through ducts and make his escape. Frank steadied himself, then ran leaping in the air to grasp the box. Missing the bottom of the box by six inches, he fell on the floor. 'Sod it!' he yelled. 'Tom Cruise is a short runt; I can do this.'

There were shelves along one side of the room. Frank dragged them nearer the unit. Scaling the shelves, he reached the box. Six screws held the outer casing firmly to the wall. Frank wrapped his arms around the box and tried pulling it off. He left the security of the shelves and his legs thrashed wildly mid-air. The casing refused to budge. Frank threw his weight back and forth. He threw his legs violently to the right, hitting the shelving. His hands slipped off the casing and he crashed to the floor, bringing the shelving down on top of him.

Jack looked up. 'Did you hear something?'

They shook their heads.

'We don't need to resort to violence to get what we want,' Jack argued. 'How about we just try and put Mack 'n' Morti's out of business? Let's prove they're putting nicotine into toddler burgers. The press would have a field day.'

'Seems a bit airy-fairy to me.' Vincent preferred a good physical solution.

Ned compromised. 'Tell you what Jack, let's try your idea. If nothing turns up, we do it our way.'

Vincent and Stan looked disappointed.

Stan drove Jack back to Starlight. His uncle's weaving in and out of the traffic reminded Jack of a dodgem car. He closed his eyes and sank lower in the seat.

They arrived at the cafe and found Cassie sitting on Ben's knee, deep in conversation.

Ben looked up. 'We've just finished cleaning up, first chance to sit down.'

Stan put his coat on the back of a chair and sat down. 'Could murder a coffee Ben.

'How was business' Jack asked.

'Flat-out over lunch. The Cocky burger is a real hit, we should add it to the menu. Cassie saved our bacon again and I reckon she makes a better latte than you now Jack. What did you find out?'

Jack turned to Cassie. 'He might be your kind Uncle Ned Cassie but you wouldn't want to get on the wrong side of him. Frightened the life out of me.'

'What do you mean?' Ben asked.

'They tied the Mack 'n' Morti bloke up by his ankles

and dangled him out a window six floors up. Just like the gangster movies. I thought they were going to kill him.

'They let him hang in the breeze until he told us what we needed to know.'

'No way.' Ben clenched his fists after Jack finished telling them about Mack 'n' Morti's plot. 'They can't do that to little kids; get them hooked on nicotine.'

Jack slumped onto a chair next to Stan. 'They're doing it right now, which is why we need to expose the bastards.'

Ben handed Stan his coffee. 'Jim Croker, that journalist from *The Hackney Gazette* was in earlier, let's talk to him.'

'I reckon he's in with Winston Fagg,' Jack said.

Stan stirred three teaspoons of sugar into his coffee. 'He's probably got some dodgy deal going Jack but I don't think Winston or Jim have a clue what Mack 'n' Morti's is really up to. It's a journalist's dream to crack a story like this.'

'Are you okay to lock up tonight Ben? I'm picking Julie up from work. We're thinking of getting a rescue dog from Battersea Dog's Home.'

'Oh good,' Stan said. 'It can come over and scare off the cat.'

Ben and Cassie watched Jack give Stan a hug on the pavement as they walked to Stan's car.

'I've got a couple of things to do before we lock up Cassie. How about we go for a walk along Regent's Canal and have a pint?'

'Great, I asked mum to look after Colin while I was at the Starlight. I promised I'd pick him up after I finished work.'

'No problem, he can come with us. Does she mind looking after Colin?'

'Depends on her mood. You never know until you get there but she was okay today. I don't want to push my luck with her.'

'Has she always been like that?'

'She got worse after Dad left. She didn't let me have friends around, so I spent a lot of time on my own. I loved drawing so that kept me busy. Ned was great. He'd drop by and make sure we were okay. He took me and Harry to Whipsnade Zoo for a day after Harry escaped the cult. I'll always remember that day. First time Harry and I had seen an elephant, couldn't believe it.'

Cassie looked up at the clock. 'I'll help you finish up so we can get Colin.'

'What do you think?'

Ben stood on the pavement with Cassie, admiring his newly purchased Volkswagen Golf.

Cassie clapped her hands in excitement. 'It's so cute, it even has room for Colin. Can we go down Dalston Lane on the way?'

'Sure.'

Cassie continued. 'I had this strange call from a girl called Sarah. She owns the Beans A Go-Go coffee shop next to Marks & Spencer. She saw the photo of the Starlight in the paper. She wanted to send me some information via email. It's all very mysterious and I don't know how she got my number. I'd like to check the place out.'

Ben double-parked opposite the Beans A Go-Go coffee shop. 'It's still open, you go in and I'll park. Let's see what it's like.'

The cafe was in a row of solid three-storey pre-war shops. On either side stood a noodle shop and a boutique selling cheap jewellery and clothes. Opposite was a badly maintained 1960s cream brick six storey block of flats with shops on the ground floor. The more fortunate tenants had narrow balconies. Cassie could see a neatly pegged row of men's underpants and socks drying on a line on the fourth floor. While she waited for Ben, she studied each shop in the row. A Caribbean cafe, vaping shop, social care, barber, launderette, betting shop and supermarket.

She saw Ben run across the road to join her.

Ben checked out the cake cabinet. 'What would you like, love?'

The cake cabinet was empty, apart from a plate of donuts and half a dried carrot cake. 'Two flat whites and two donuts please.'

A row of empty tables ran neatly down each side of the cafe. The interior was decked out in dark wood panelling.

The coffee arrived in soup-sized cups.

'It's a bit dingy,' Cassie whispered. 'And the coffee is terrible; it tastes like hot milk.'

Ben held Cassie's hand. 'I wonder what they want to talk to you about?'

Cassie shrugged.

They left the cafe leaving the coffee undrunk and drove to Cassie's mother's house.

Colin came puffing out to see Cassie and eyed the bright-red Golf with suspicion. Cassie opened the rear door and with a gentle push Colin jumped onto the back seat and lay down.

'See Colin, not so bad, is it?'

Ben parked in Regents Row. It was late afternoon and a cool breeze blew along the canal. They walked to the pub with Colin exploring with his nose behind them. Canal boats full of smiling passengers chugged past.

'Would be great to live on a boat, don't you think, Ben?'

'Yeah, imagine it. Pulling up anchor and going wherever the canal took you.'

They reached the Narrowboat pub.

'Do you have a booking?'

'Yes, a table for two on the balcony in the name of Ben.'

The manager scanned a page of names on a clipboard and summoned a waiter over.

'Charlie, table three.'

Charlie led them onto the balcony overlooking the canal.

'Would you like to order some drinks?'

Cassie looked up at the blackboard.

'I'll have pint of London Original please.'

'And I'd like a pint of London Special,' Ben said.

Colin lay at Cassie's feet under the table.

'This is lovely Ben, when did you arrange this?'

'Yesterday but I wasn't sure you'd be free with such short notice.'

'Harry and I hang out sometimes but I usually work on my artwork at home with Colin.'

'I imagined you'd have lots of friends,' Ben said in surprise.

'Not really. I've got a couple of friends at college but we're not close. It's funny Ben, the Starlight's been the best experience I've had in a long time. I wasn't sure when I met you at the railyard but you and Jack have been great. Jack had enough faith in me to re-imagine the Starlight, Julie's so smart and kind, she's become like a big sister. Stan is a funny old codger and makes me laugh. I feel I can trust them, like I'm part of a family.'

Ben smiled, pointing his finger at his chest.

'Oh, and you're not so bad either,' Cassie laughed.

The sun glinted on the canal as Colin snored happily at their feet. Cassie stared down at the water. She couldn't remember a time she had felt this content.

They walked back along the canal, hand in hand, as the sun went down, Colin staying close on Cassie's heels.

CHAPTER 51
CALLING IN SICK

Frank looked up from where he lay on the floor; he heard a lock was being turned. A draught passed across his face as the cold room door swung open. Frank clutched the leg of a shelf.

'I don't want to go, leave me alone. Please don't kill me,' Frank sobbed.

Vincent pulled him from the cold room by the ankles. He tried to hold onto the shelf but it slipped from his grasp.

'How are you doing, Franky?' Vincent pulled Frank roughly up onto his feet. 'Come with me.'

So, this is it. They're going to use my body for a bit of ballast in a multi-storey car park. Acid bath, bullet in the back of the head, couple of yards of concrete.

Vincent turned his head to one side. 'You stink.' Frank's tracksuit was still damp from when he wet himself.

Vincent looked around at the broken shelving. 'Been busy have you?'

'Come on Franky, get moving, haven't got all day,' Vincent pointed to the doorway. Frank stumbled through and descended the stairs. Vincent pushed him into a grimy locker room.

'There's a shower and toilet. Clean yourself up and put this tracksuit on. Vincent pointed to a chair.

The shower helped calm Frank's nerves and he felt a glimmer of hope as he put on fresh clothes. Vincent was waiting by the locker room door and motioned Frank into a small office with three chairs, a table and an old phone.

'First Franky, you ring Mack 'n' Morti's and tell them you're ill. You've got food poisoning and won't be back for a couple of days. Remember, any funny stuff and you're dead. Here's the number.'

Vincent handed Frank a scrap of paper and Frank picked up the phone. Sal answered.

'Hi Sal, it's Frank. Sorry I didn't call earlier but I've been throwing up—food poisoning. I'm not going to be in for a couple of days.'

'Frank, Chuck is exploding. Have you seen today's headlines? To quote him: "Unless he gets his arse into gear and fixes this mess, he can join Robinson on the dole queue." He's serious Frank. You'd better get in here tomorrow and sort it out.'

'I can't get in tomorrow Sal, I'm too sick. Can't you calm him down for me?'

'It's your funeral Frank, don't say I didn't warn you.' Sal hung up.

Frank felt sick. Vincent towered over him, unsmiling. Staying alive was his number one priority. Making a run for it out of this Mafia-style stronghold would be impossible. His career at Mack 'n' Morti's was over no matter what happened.

Vincent led Frank to an old first aid room. Graffiti covered the cream walls. Remnants of safety-first posters lay amongst the empty cans and discarded wrappers scattered on the concrete floor.

A camp bed was set against the wall with a blanket folded on top. Vincent brought in a box of pizza and a black bucket.

'Why can't I go home now?' Frank begged. 'I've told you everything I know.'

'We've got a job for you in the morning. Do as you're told, then we'll let you go home with all your fingers.'

The bed creaked as Frank sat down. He placed the pizza box on the bed and looked in the bucket. Inside was a plastic bottle of water.

'Get some sleep, I need you up bright and early in the morning.'

Vincent locked the door, leaving Frank in pitch darkness.

Despite his terrifying ordeal, Frank was hungry. He put the pizza box on his lap and opened the lid. At the first bite, he realised the pizza was cold. 'It's still half frozen.' He spat the second bite back in the box.

'Anchovies, bloody anchovies. I hate anchovies.'

CHAPTER 52
GIVING A HAND

Stan looked at the clock on his mantelpiece. It ticked 6.56 p.m. After the excitement at the warehouse, he needed a quiet evening at home. But he couldn't settle. He turned on the TV, flicking through the channels.

'Nothing but stupid reality shows,' he muttered.

He switched off the TV and went into the kitchen. He peered out the window, hoping to catch the cat but nothing stirred.

Guess I could try a burger instead of eating at home. Pop into the Starlight for a few minutes. I wouldn't interfere; I'd be like a regular customer as we agreed. Stay half an hour at most.

Finding somewhere to park near the cafe was difficult. He managed to squeeze into a spot after aggressive touch parking. It was funny seeing the premises at night, packed with people. He had to admit the old place was buzzing. It gave him a warm feeling to see the Starlight busy as it once was in its heyday. Jack spotted him as he joined the queue.

'Hey Stan, thought you were going to have an early night?'

'Got bored Jack, thought I'd get something quick to eat.'

'Well don't queue Stan, go and grab something from Ben.'

Jack could tell Stan felt awkward; trying not to interfere but itching to help.

'We're busy tonight, don't suppose you've got half an hour to give Ben a hand?'

'Yes of course, I'd be happy to help,' Stan replied with a sense of excitement.

Jack had an impulse.

'Before you see Ben, I want to say something.' He clapped his hands together to get people's attention and then put his arm around Stan's shoulder.

'I want to introduce you, our customers, to my Uncle Stan. Stan created the original Starlight over thirty years ago. Like me, some of you will remember coming here for a sandwich and milkshake. I want to take this opportunity to thank my uncle for entrusting me with the cafe's future. Please put your hands together for Uncle Stan.'

The customers clapped and whistled. Stan hugged Jack and tears ran down his cheeks. He dabbed his face with a napkin. Several people came up to him, patting him on the back and reminiscing about the days he ran the cafe.

Stan beamed as he stood behind the counter again; Ben asked him to look after the buns and fillings. He assembled the burgers and put them in wrappers. *This is so much easier than sandwiches; no messy mayonnaise or filling combinations to worry about.*

'We're killing it Stan, great teamwork.'

Stan peered into the chip fryer. 'That chip oil looks strange, I can see to the bottom of the pan. What happened to the stuff I used?'

Ben smiled.

'Reckon you bought ex-army tank oil Stan; it was so thick.'

Jack said goodnight to the remaining customers and closed the Starlight. Stan stretched to ease the ache in his back and leaned against the counter next to Jack.

'You okay Stan.'

'Never better Jack, I don't know where the time went.'

'I would love you to help us from time-to-time Stan. You know, keep it flexible so you can still do a bit of fishing. That way, we all benefit. After all those years of opening the cafe at 7 a.m., you might enjoy the extra sleep in the morning.'

'It was just like the old days Jack,' Stan beamed. 'So full of life and warmth. I don't know why I was so hung up on selling sandwiches. The Starlight's what matters. It's a place where people meet, share something good to eat and catch up on news. You've opened my eyes Jack. I'd love to help out when you need me.'

Stan felt alive. Finally, he was able to relegate the yellowing walls and rows of sandwiches to history.

'How did Ned go with the Mack 'n' Morti creep? Didn't kill him did they Jack?' Ben asked.

'No, frightened the life out of him though. By the way, big day tomorrow. Frank Wilson has been, um encouraged to talk to Jim Croker. Jim's meeting us at a cafe near the warehouse. It belongs to a friend of Ned's; he's organised a private room for the interview.'

Stan drove home tired but happy. He made himself a cocoa and fished through his sideboard for a photo album. At the start of the album were photos of the Starlight when it first opened. One photo showed Ruby standing behind the counter with a broad smile, making a milkshake. Later in the album he found a photo of a little boy—Jack—with an empty plate in front of him, the biggest smile and cream around his lips.

'Well Ruby, the old place is in good hands now.'

CHAPTER 53
A DARK SECRET

'Sure you're not hungry Franky?' Vincent's knife and fork resembled child's cutlery in his huge sausage like fingers. He devoured an overloaded plate of eggs, bacon, sausages and baked beans. 'Breakfast is the most important meal of the day. I get hangry if I don't get a decent breakfast.'

Frank looked away. He couldn't bear to watch the egg yolk dribbling down Vincent's gnarled chin.

It had been over an hour since Vincent unlocked Frank's room and pushed him into the back of the car. They drove to the Golden Gates cafe on the industrial estate and sat in a small, grubby room that stank of old cooking oil and perspiration. Vincent mopped up the grease and egg yolk with the last of the bread and pushed his plate aside. After gulping down the rest of his tea, he leaned towards Frank and gave him his instructions.

'My boss and the Starlight bloke have just arrived. Remember, cooperate and you'll live. Fuck it up and you're part of the new flyover. It's your call. In a few minutes, the journalist from *The Hackney Gazette* will be here as well. Tell him all the stuff you told us. If it stacks up, you'll be OK.'

❖

Jim Croker drove through the neglected industrial suburbs on the west side of town. Successive government deregulation and importation of manufactured goods from overseas had taken a massive toll on the once-thriving blue-collar heartland. Jim passed empty warehouses and factories and nature strips strewn with rubbish. Locked gates and weather-beaten signs were everywhere:

"For Lease—Excellent Opportunity".

The whole area depressed him.

He was curious why Jack wanted to meet him in this part of town. The Golden Gates neon sign flickered intermittently above the entrance. A stack of empty crates leaned against the wall. The greasy windows emitted a yellow glow. Jack was waiting for him at the entrance. Jim's curiosity increased when he saw Ned Cleghorn standing next to Jack.

What's Ned Cleghorn got to do with all this? Ned's reputation was well known at *The Hackney Gazette*. The Cleghorn clan made careers of crime; it was almost a calling and Ned was the head priest. They had a reputation for illegal betting, handling stolen goods and protection services. Every journalist at the paper had heard of the Cleghorns.

'Hello Jim, meet Ned Cleghorn, a friend of mine.'

Ned glared at Jim.

'We're giving you this story on the understanding that you don't mention our involvement, understand?' Ned poked his finger hard into Jim's chest.

'Of course.' Jim started to feel his knees tremble. 'Not a word.'

'The man we have inside is a big-wig with Mack 'n' Morti's. He's told us about trying to shut down Starlight Burgers and now he's going to tell you the full story. If he asks about your mate Winston Fagg, you say you haven't seen him for a few days. I know you're on the take from Fagg. Now, let's go.'

Jim followed Ned and Jack to the back of the cafe into the small room where Vincent and Frank sat. Jim's eyes widened. Vincent was talking to a pasty-looking man with dark blue circles under his eyes.

Shit a brick, that's Vincent Stubbs. I saw him with Winston at my office.

Jim knew about Vincent from his younger days when Stubbs was a professional heavyweight boxer. He had heard Vincent was a standover man for Ned Cleghorn.

Ned signalled Vincent to stand up and let Jim have his chair opposite Frank. 'Franky, this is Jim Croker, the journalist we mentioned. All you have to do is tell Jim what you told us.'

Frank looked pleadingly at Jim as he sat down. 'I'm in charge of competitor intelligence at Mack 'n' Morti's,' he began. 'I heard about the Starlight cafe changing its operation from selling sandwiches to burgers. It's close to one of our franchise operations, so the competitor intelligence analysis showed we needed to keep a watching brief.'

'There's a big difference between keeping an eye on us and shutting us down,' Jack said.

'I know but our CEO wasn't happy because we were running a secret trial at our franchise nearby. He wanted the Starlight shut down and it was my job to do it. I contacted Winston Fagg, the health inspector. I've used him for a few jobs. He likes a bit of money on the side. If we get complaints about food poisoning, we get Winston to sign an all-clear notification.'

'You're saying Winston's on Mack 'n' Morti's payroll? Anyone else?' Jim asked.

'I don't know, my arrangement is with Winston.'

Frank continued.

'I came up with the idea of the cockroach and Winston hired an amateur actor, Julian Witherspoon. Winston gave Julian the cockroach and told him to order a burger and slip it on top of the meat. Julian was to make a song and dance about it in the cafe. He had to show it to other customers and make out he felt sick. Once the chaos started, he had to disappear and report to Winston.

'Winston waited a day, then went to the cafe and closed it down with a health notice. Our next step was for Winston to convince you Jim, to report the cockroach incident in *The Hackney Gazette*. I figured that would close Starlight down for good.'

Jim looked confused. 'Why go to all this trouble to shut a pissy little place like Starlight? It doesn't make sense.'

'Well, it does if you've got something to hide and don't call the Starlight a pissy little place,' Jack said, feeling offended.

'Hey Franky,' Ned interrupted, 'tell Jim about the toddler burger and the nicotine.'

Jim stared open-mouthed as Frank explained Mack 'n'

Morti's strategy to feed nicotine-laced burgers to small children.

'But surely the health authorities would detect nicotine. I can't believe Mack 'n' Morti's would take the risk. I know tobacco companies don't have scruples and use dishonest marketing to sell nicotine but getting caught poisoning toddlers, that's dynamite.'

'It's not difficult, cigarettes contain hundreds of additives to disguise the taste of nicotine. Our company has developed a masking agent that makes the substance undetectable in small doses. The toddler buns contain a miniscule amount. It's enough to make toddlers get their system used to nicotine and then want more. That way, they want to start smoking at a much earlier age and will prefer Vine's stylised form of nicotine.'

'So, you're saying that if I took a toddler burger to be analysed, the tests wouldn't detect nicotine?' Jim asked.

'You have to remember that the chemical labs at Vine are more sophisticated than those at our government testing labs. Vine Tobacco spend millions on research and governments don't have a hope in hell of matching that.'

Jack drummed his fingers on the table. 'What about the bakery outlet? Wouldn't we find evidence there?'

'It's a secure site, you can't wander in and have a look around. They keep the concentrated chemicals there. It's the only place you can detect the nicotine but you'd have to find a way of getting your hands on the stuff.'

'Is there anything else you need to tell the journalist,' Ned looked across at Frank.

'No, that's all of it.'

'I'm shocked,' Jim laid down his notepad. 'This is an

assault on vulnerable young children. I'll make sure this investigation gets the priority it deserves in *The Hackney Gazette.*'

'If there's nothing else, you can get on your way,' Ned motioned Jim to the door.

Jim Croker was glad to head back to his office. He offered to give Jack a lift back to the Starlight.

Jim kept asking Jack questions as they drove through the traffic.

'Why did Ned want me to keep quiet about Winston?'

'Right now, it's helpful for Frank to think Ned killed Winston. Keeps Frank on the edge of his seat, so to speak.'

Winston's in a lot of trouble, thought Jim.

CHAPTER 54
REDUNDANCY

Through the greasy window of the cafe, they watched Jim Croker and Jack drive away. Ned grabbed Frank's arm. 'We're going to visit your flat to check for extra evidence Franky. You'll be our guest for another couple of days. You did well today but there are a couple of loose ends to tie up before we release you.'

Frank turned to Ned. 'I want to come along to get some of my own clothes.'

He guessed they would hang on to him until Jim checked his facts. Vincent drove to the apartment with Frank and a second minder sitting in the back. When they arrived on Frank's floor, a cardboard box sat outside his door. Frank picked it up and took it inside to open.

'The bastards.' He passed Vincent the letter that had been taped to the box.

Dear Mr Wilson,

Due to a restructure at Mack 'n' Morti's, your position with the company is now redundant. A cheque covering your statutory entitlement will be available on return of your office fob and laptop. We wish to remind you that you signed a binding non-disclosure agreement. You must keep all company information confidential. Please contact our office to arrange a time to return all company property. We wish you well in the future.

Sal Baker, on behalf of Chuck Adams.

The box contained Frank's framed photograph of a Ferrari, his lucky penguin, his *Little Book of Calm and* an opened packet of jellybeans.

'Guess you won't be getting a farewell present then.'

'It's not funny Vincent. My whole careers down the toilet. Look what I've got to show for it. I'll show them what happens when they screw with Frank bloody Wilson.'

'I'm watching you.' Vincent shadowed Frank around the apartment. 'No tricky stuff or else.'

Frank sat at his desk and fired up his laptop. He clicked the smiling icon of Mack 'n' Morti, then entered his user ID and password for the company's intranet site. Invalid UserID/Password flashed up on the screen.

'You must have typed it wrong,' Vincent peered over his shoulder.

'No, they've cancelled my access. I'll try something else.' Frank entered pcrabshaw and password bigboy. An email menu appeared on the screen and Frank laughed.

'Pete, you're a slack bastard. He's hopeless with computers; always gets me to help him change his settings and password. I told him to change his password to something else but I knew he wouldn't get around to it. Company policy is to double-delete all sensitive emails. With Pete, no matter how many times I remind him, he forgets.'

Frank clicked on the list of folders and selected

"Deleted". It contained pages of deleted emails. Frank scrolled down and found what he was looking for.

'Bingo! I'll forward it to Jim.'

The email's subject line said, "TOP SECRET—DELETE—Toddler burgers".

Frank rang Jim at *The Hackney Gazette.*

'Put the phone on loudspeaker,' Vincent demanded.

'Read the email I forwarded you Jim. It's from Mack 'n' Morti's. Ring me back before you do anything with the bakery. I can help you nail this story.'

Frank closed the laptop and sat back in his chair. 'Teach you to sack me Chuck Adams, you mongrel.'

Martin Bates, editor of *The Hackney Gazette*, let out a slow whistle as he read the email.

'This is incredible Jim. We must be careful. Tobacco companies have bottomless pockets when it comes to self-protection. You need to gather as much evidence as you can before we print a word. This could be the biggest story we've had in years. Drop everything else. I want you on this full time. Let me know if you need help.'

Jim smelled promotion. Perhaps an offer from one of the national dailies or Channel 4 TV.

CHAPTER 55
MOBILE BURGERS RETURN

Jack and Stan were cleaning out the espresso machine when Magpie walked in.

'Hello Magpie, how did you go with the van?' Jack said.

'It's ready to go again, didn't take long to put all the original stuff back.'

'Sorry Magpie, I could have driven it to your place to work on instead of you dragging your tools over here.'

'Then I'd have to lend you my van to get back here. It hasn't been the same since you borrowed it. It's a delicate piece of machinery and it doesn't like strangers.'

'It's a death trap.'

Magpie looked hurt. 'You don't know how to handle her. That's the trouble with you youngsters.'

'You tell him,' Stan shook hands with Magpie. 'They don't teach them how to drive these days. Need everything done for them; auto this and power-assisted that.'

'Best news is,' Magpie continued, 'that I've managed to find a new counting display. It's not quite as flash as the last one but it does the job. Came out of a supermarket. It was used to show the next customer number in the deli section.'

'You sure it doesn't show other messages?' Jack asked. 'Like sausages fifty per cent off?'

'Very funny, I've tested it several times and it only displays numbers. Now, give me one of your Stan burgers and some chips, or I'll make it display something rude.'

Fascinated by the burger van, Stan peered inside.

'What are all those buttons for Magpie?'

Magpie offered Stan a chip. 'Hop in and I'll show you.'

Stan climbed in and poked his head out of the serving hatch.

'These switches control the heated trays for the burgers.' Magpie licked salt from his fingers. 'This one lights up the Starlight sign on the roof. This big red button counts the burgers you've got left.'

Stan chuckled as Magpie hit the counting button.

'Magpie, you're a genius. If this takes off, they could have half a dozen vans travelling around town. Maybe even a franchise.'

'See you later!' Stan shouted. Magpie's van spluttered up the alleyway leaving a fog of blue smoke, making Stan's eyes water. He went back inside the cafe and met Ben, who had arrived for his shift.

'What's up Stan? you look like you've been crying.'

'Magpie's van, it burns a bit of oil.'

'Big mistake standing anywhere near it, should be in a scrapyard.'

'Jack,' Stan said, 'I'd like to have a go in the van tonight.'

'Sure, why don't you come back about nine? I want to give it a run myself. I'm going to catch the greyhound crowd as they leave.'

Stan was impatient to try out the van and arrived at the

Starlight early. He helped Jack pack the burgers into the van. 'Let's go Stan!' Jack yelled. He started the van while Stan stood back, checking the signage on the roof.

'I can't stop looking at the burger sign Jack. That Cassie is a talented girl. She's got a real eye for colour.'

They arrived at the greyhound track, positioning the van between the exit gate and car park. The last race announcement came over the loudspeaker. Stan sat on a stool, staring out of the serving hatch. The waft of warm burgers floated around him and he dozed off into a peaceful sleep.

'Stan, Stan! Wake up, they're coming. Stan yawned, opened his eyes and panicked. A wall of people was heading straight for the van.

'What do I do, where's the cash tin? What if we don't have enough burgers, where are the drink straws?'

Jack began laying out the burgers. 'Stay calm Stan.'

The wall of people slowed and a queue formed in front of the serving hatch.

'Want a cola with your burger Naz?' Dean reached for his wallet.

Stan passed Dean his order and pressed the counting button twice with his foot.

Jack peered out the hatch. Dean pushed up his Oakleys, looking intently at Jack's face.

'Well, if it isn't Sid Slater? Remember us? You tried to sell us Bueno Vista. Well look at you now! Selling burgers out of an old van. Why aren't I surprised?'

'Arghhh, Deano. Someone's sniffing my bum!' Naz shrieked.

Dean swung round, fists at the ready.

'Rocket, Bobby Dazzler, come away. Sorry mate, they're only being friendly.'

Dean stared down at two large, muscular black greyhounds held by their trainer.

Stan reached out of the hatch and scratched Rocket's ears. 'Beautiful dogs these.' Rocket nudged Stan to keep scratching.

'Here you are Dean.' Jack handed him the burgers.'

'Thanks Sid, hope things pick up for you.'

'Who's that?' Stan watched the couple wander away.

'Long story Stan. Not worth telling. But the good story is we've sold our last four burgers so you can turn off the heaters. I'll close the hatch and then we're on our way.'

'I had a great time tonight Jack; don't think I'm cut out for retirement yet.'

CHAPTER 56
THE SAMPLE

Winston Fagg felt nervous about his meeting with Jim Croker. When Jim called, the journalist wouldn't tell him any details; only that it was about Starlight Burgers. Winston's mind raced out of control. *What if I've been exposed after all? What if those crooks changed their minds and told Jim the whole story?*

He could see the headlines. His wife, Clementine would leave him straight away; she wouldn't be able to bear the shame. He pictured himself a broken man, jobless, the neighbours avoiding him. His pots and pans would remain unwashed in the sink and he would become an alcoholic. Thrown out for not keeping up with the mortgage repayments, he would have to sleep in the car. Within a month he'd be lining up at a homeless shelter. His head drooped as he waited for Jim to arrive at the pub.

A tap on the shoulder made him jump, bringing him back to the present.

'Hello Winston, glad you could make it, let me buy you a beer.'

The vision of an alcoholic tramp on the streets persisted and kept flashing across Winston's mind.

'An orange juice, thanks Jim.'

The two men settled into a quiet corner of the pub. Jim

recounted his discussion with Frank Wilson at the Golden Gates cafe. Jim was careful not to accuse Winston of working for Mack 'n' Morti's. He referred only to someone at the council. Winston read the email Frank sent to Jim.

'This has to be a hoax Jim. A company the size of Mack 'n' Morti's would never get involved in this.'

'Why not Winston? If they lace toddler burgers, they have a whole new generation of customers coming through. Winston, I need you to do a surprise raid on the bakery to find the nicotine concentrate. It's the only way we can prove our case.'

Winston began to feel queasy, his stomach churned and he felt a sudden wave of nausea. He was wary of telling anyone about his recent ordeal.

'You OK Winston, look like you've seen a ghost.'

'I'm a bit under the weather, I'll be OK in a day or two. But I can't raid a place without a legitimate reason Jim. This isn't the Wild West; we have rules and regulations to follow.'

'You didn't have much trouble with regulations when you closed Starlight Burgers,' Jim said, with a smile.

'Well, I had hard evidence from a member of the public. There was a live insect in the burger.'

Jim persisted. 'What if I get hold of a sample of the toddler bun chemical for you? You can check it out, see if your experts detect nicotine. Then if the result is nicotine, you have a legitimate reason to organise a raid.'

Winston considered his options. *If the gang of killers find out I'm protecting Mack 'n' Morti's, they will likely torture me again. Probably lose some vital organs. If I organise a raid on Mack 'n' Morti's they will cut off my bonuses and might expose the favours I've done for them. I'm done for either way.* A terrifying vision of Vincent holding a meat cleaver made up his mind.

'I suppose we could raid the place if we have more proof. Tell them we have reliable information that some of their ingredients are illegal. But I'd want to make sure. We'd look pretty stupid after the cockroach affair.'

'Think of it Winston, the raid would be a coup for whoever conducted it. I can see the headlines now: "Brave Health Official Smashes Drugs Racket. Saves Children."'

'Guess it's a coup for the journalist who breaks the story as well.' Winston winked at Jim.

Winston looked at Jim slyly. 'No need to repeat the early stuff though, is there? You know, the stuff about shutting Starlight Burgers down?'

'No, no, no,' Jim assured Winston. 'It's best to leave those things in the past, other than the stuff we've already printed. After all, you were only doing your job and protecting the public from an insect infestation.'

'Do you think there's a chance of trouble at the bakery Jim if we proceed with a raid?' Winston asked with a nervous laugh.

'Let's get the police involved,' Jim suggested. 'It adds weight to the story and our photographer will get more dramatic shots.'

Jim stirred his coffee slowly. 'So how about it Winston? When do you want your sample?'

Winston's mind wandered. Perhaps this solved a sticky situation. He imagined the 'Citizen of the Year' medallion hanging around his neck; Clementine beaming at his side at the civic reception. Her father would rush up to him after the reception and apologise for calling him a 'snivelling little turd'. He'd never forgiven him since the incident when the fire alarm malfunctioned and Winston trampled over Clementine at the cinema in a panic to escape.

'OK, find me a sample and I'll have it analysed.'

CHAPTER 57
SECRET MISSION

Vincent and Frank had returned to the warehouse. Vincent tapped on the glass door of Ned's office. He signalled them to come in while he finished a phone call.

'What does he expect for three pounds a bottle? Grange Hermitage? My suppliers make a very exclusive drop. Tell him I've got other people lining up so he'll have to be quick, or I'll sell it elsewhere. Goodbye.'

Ned put down his phone and turned to Vincent and Frank.

'I've had a call from that journalist at *The Hackney Gazette*. We need to get hold of the chemical concentrate at the bakery so he can check its nicotine content. I've already had someone check out the bakery's security; one guard at the entrance. The health inspector won't sanction an official raid unless we can prove the chemical exists. How do we get the sample Frank?'

'If the guard hits the alarm all the doors lock and you can't get out. The chemical concentrate is in the safe. Staff don't know anything about the chemicals. They're only told it's a trade secret and has to be kept under lock and key.'

Vincent clicked his fingers. 'Piece of cake. We break in,

knock out the guard, blow the safe and pinch the chemicals. Bread and butter operation.'

'Won't work Vincent,' Frank explained. 'Mack 'n' Morti's is paranoid about this stuff. As soon as they realise the safe's opened, they'll close the bakery. They'll destroy any trace of documentation or evidence. It's got to be legal. This type of corporation has the best barristers coming out its ears, so if you do anything illegal the charges won't stick. If you only need a sample, we can get a swab from one of the used cans in the disposal security bin. They won't even know it's gone. The bin has a big padlock and it's cleared once a week by a security company. The bin is supposed to be kept inside but staff hate the stink. They store it outside under a carport in a secure area. It's the weak link in the whole system. If you've got someone who can scale a high wall covered in glass shards at the top and open the secure padlock, you can grab the sample.'

Ned smiled. 'Vincent, give my nephew Sammy a call. He owes us a favour. And grab anyone else you think can help.'

'Ned, how about me? I know the layout of the place and can make sure you get the right stuff. I've got a score to settle with Chuck Adams.'

'Congratulations Frank, I'm pleased you've decided to join us.'

CHAPTER 58
FINDING A SAMPLE

'Arrgh.'

Vincent wound down the van window for fresh air.

'Blimey, pack it in Frank.'

'Sorry, it's that pizza you gave me. I hate anchovies, they give me terrible wind.'

Vincent wound up the window again, leaving a small gap. The only light inside the van came from Vincent's phone. Apart from the occasional set of headlights, the road to the bakery was deserted.

'We'll pick up the others on the way. We're not far now.'

Vincent reached into the back of the van and pulled out a handful of clothes from a cardboard box.

'Here, put these on.'

Frank pulled a black pair of overalls over his clothes and placed a balaclava over his head. Looking in the rear-view mirror, he felt a thrill of excitement. He was working with real criminals. It was like starring in a James Bond movie.

Vincent slowed to a stop. There was the bang of a fist on the rear doors and Vincent let two men into the van.

'Frank, these are friends of mine. Lewis provides muscle and this is Sammy our lock specialist.'

Lewis towered over Frank, muscles bulging out of his overalls. Sammy was wirier, with darting eyes and a nervous laugh.

Vincent turned around to Sammy. 'I hear Ned gave you a bollocking Sammy.'

'Yeah, I never thought Harry would be so stupid to park in Smith's car park with the bloody sign lit up for all to see.'

'That's Harry for you,' Vincent said.

Vincent started the van and drove on to the bakery.

'Down here,' Frank pointed to a narrow lane. 'Go left at the bottom and pull up in the alleyway beside the wall.'

Vincent switched off the headlights and followed Frank's instructions. The alleyway was in darkness. He parked close to the wall and cut the engine. The brick wall looked over twelve feet high and they could make out solid metal gates shining in the moonlight.

Frank pointed to the gates. 'Those gates have alarms and security bars on the inside. The only way in is over the wall.'

Vincent looked at Lewis.

'Go back to the main entrance, ring the bell and keep the guard talking.'

Lewis ambled out of the van and walked back to the front of the bakery.

They waited until Lewis was out of site. Climbing on top of the van they surveyed the wall. Cemented into the top were shards of glass. Vincent laid several sacks over the shards before throwing a rope ladder over.

'Off you go Sammy.'

Sammy's speed up the ladder and over the wall took Frank by surprise.

Frank followed cautiously. He climbed the rungs to the top and eased himself over the sacks. The climb down was more difficult. The ladder swayed and he scraped his knuckles against the wall as he descended into the bakery yard.

Using Sammy's torch, they found the carport and located the security bin. Sammy unfolded a slim wallet and selected what looked like a dentist's instrument. He held the torch in his teeth and worked the instrument into the lock. A few seconds later, the lock sprang open. Frank lifted the lid of the bin and Sammy shone the torch inside.

Yellow containers marked 'flavour enhancer' lay at the bottom in a jumbled heap. Frank examined them one by one until he found a can with enough residue for a sample. Sammy snapped the lock back on the security bin and they climbed back over the wall.

Frank struggled on the swaying ladder, sweating under his overalls and balaclava. He collapsed in the van while Sammy removed the ladder and sacks from the wall and threw them into the back.

'Where's Lewis?' Sammy asked. 'I don't like it; he should be back by now.'

Vincent checked his watch. 'The guard might have clocked him. It could spell trouble. Go and look but be careful.'

Sammy tiptoed up the alley and peered around the corner towards the bakery entrance. He could see Lewis deep in animated conversation with someone on the other side of the gate.

Sammy slipped back to the van. 'He's still talking to the guard. I could give him a whistle.'

'No,' Vincent growled. 'The guard will get suspicious. What the bloody hell can they be talking about?'

Thirty minutes passed.

Vincent looked at his watch again. 'Fuck him, another five minutes and we're off.' The rear door of the van opened. Vincent swung round, drawing back his fist.

'Whoa,' Lewis held up his hands as he climbed in.

'Where the fuck have you been? We've been stuck here like sitting ducks, you idiot.'

'Oh, sorry boss. Turns out that Kieran the guard used to work at the meatworks. He knows my sister's second cousin's husband George. Funny old world, isn't it?'

Vincent sighed and started the van. He drove slowly down the alley. Once they reached the main streets, he hit the accelerator.

They stopped at a cafe for a late dinner.

Frank recognised the pungent aroma of oil and perspiration in the Golden Gates Cafe. The owner shuffled over with pad and pen in hand. Frank smelt the stale odour of perspiration as he leaned over.

'What'll it be Vincent?'

'Usual all-round Gastro unless you want anything special Franky?'

'I'd like a toasted focaccia with chicken, avocado and goat's cheese please?'

Gastro looked at Vincent. 'Is he trying to be funny?'

'No, he's a City wanker, give him the usual.'

'After we've eaten, you can take your stuff from the back of the van. You're free to go Franky.'

Gastro dumped overflowing plates on the table. On each one sat a sausage, a curled up leathery piece of steak, a mound of chips, two fried eggs, tomato and mushy baked beans. Frank clutched his stomach as a bout of queasiness rose in his throat. He picked at the chips while the others vacuumed their plates into their mouths.

'Not hungry Franky?' Vincent eyed Frank's plate. 'Can't waste it.'

He descended on Frank's dinner, mopping up the last of the grease with a slice of bread.

Frank slipped away. He stood in the dark outside the cafe, Frank had no friends to help him and no idea where he was.

Vincent drove away from the Golden Gates cafe leaving Frank alone.

CHAPTER 59
POSITIVE ANALYSIS

Vincent stood at the council office reception desk waiting for Lucy to finish her call.

'So, I said to Mandy he's a two-timer. I know what I saw. It was that tart from the gym.'

Vincent banged the reception bell and gestured that he was waiting. Lucy sighed and ended her call.

'I want to see Winston Fagg.'

'Have you got an appointment?' Lucy asked.

'He's expecting me.'

Lucy sat back in her chair, quickly picking up the phone as Vincent's angry face loomed closer. 'Winston, there's a Vincent at reception. OK, I'll send him up.'

She pointed to the lifts. 'Second floor, he'll meet you.'

Vincent read a poster on the wall as he waited for the lift:

"People & Community. Working together for a healthier town".

Below the heading was a photo of a smiling Winston.

The lift arrived and Vincent went to the second floor. An agitated Winston met him as he emerged from the lift.

'This way.'

He led Vincent up a long, dimly lit corridor. On one side was a series of large panes of glass, set chest high.

Beyond the panes Vincent saw an open area. It was full of identical workstations containing a chair, desk space and a computer screen. *Poor buggers,* he thought, as he looked across the sea of staff tapping away at their keyboards.

Winston ushered Vincent into a small meeting room and closed the door. 'Have you got the stuff?' he whispered.

'What?' Vincent's boxing career had affected his hearing.

Winston moved closer. 'Have you got the stuff from the bakery?'

'Oh, yeah.' Vincent removed a container wrapped in newspaper from his coat pocket.

Winston took the container and hid it under his jacket. He ushered Vincent quickly back to the lifts.

'I'll let you know the results,' he whispered to Vincent as he re-entered the lift.

Winston's colleague, Max, peered out of his office cubicle. He had seen Winston with Vincent and wondered who he was.

Max had been Winston's second-in-charge for two years. His father was a good friend of the chief executive and Winston was forced to appoint him. Max was ambitious for promotion but Winston continued to downplay Max's achievements in reviews. At thirty-eight, Max was frustrated and looked for any opportunity to undermine his boss.

Max was curious. Winston had been acting strangely lately, disappearing for days without an explanation. Then he reappeared, looking haggard.

Max could see the bulge under Winston's jacket as he said goodbye to Vincent at the lift.

'What's going on Winston?' He ushered Max into his office and closed the door.

'Wrapped up in this newspaper is a container of an unidentified substance. We need to get the contents analysed without delay. It could prove to be the most serious breach of our regulations in history. It could be bigger than the Siamese Cat pie incident of 1992.'

'What cat pie incident?'

Winston explained. 'The cat pie incident is the yardstick we rate other cases by. It was an historic moment in the department's history. My predecessor George Lindberg led the investigation and it featured on national news. They caught the owner of the Pie Surprise shop redhanded in a raid from the department. They discovered him skinning a Siamese cat in his shop kitchen. It transpired that he lured them into his premises with fish paste after dark, then turned them into pie meat for customers. The department first became suspicious after a complaint from a member of the public who found cat fur in their pie. They promoted George to Director of Environmental Wastewater projects.'

'Wow, so what do we do now Winston?'

'The measures we used to get this sample are unorthodox. I have every reason to believe it's an illegal substance. Max, this is important. If you're asked, don't say anything about this sample. I want to check if the allegation is true first.'

'What's the next step?' Max asked, keen to be part of the conspiracy.

'We have to organise an analysis before doing an official raid. Things will go pear-shaped if we charge them based on this sample because we can't prove where it came from. Once I get the lab results, we'll know its legit. Then I'm happy to pretend we're investigating a tip off from a member of the public. We can conduct a full-scale raid.'

'I'll get this to the lab straight away Winston and mark it top priority.' Max hurried out of the office.

CHAPTER 60
A CARDBOARD BOX

Frank rang for a taxi from the Golden Gates cafe to take him to his apartment.

Frank locked his door and slid on the safety chain. He peered out the window but couldn't see any mysterious cars in the street. He felt faint and sat on his couch, head between his knees.

'I am breathing in, I am breathing out, I am breathing in, I am breathing out.'

He hated the smell of the clothes Vincent had given him. Frank ripped them off in a sudden frenzy and threw them in his kitchen bin. He stood naked in front of the bathroom mirror. The bruises on his body were turning from red to dark blue and his ankles were red raw where the ropes had broken the skin.

The hot water from the shower stung his body. He cried out as the water reached his ankles. The soap made the pain unbearable forcing him to cut short his shower.

He dressed in his silk Versace dressing gown. With a coffee cup cradled in his hands, Frank stared at the box on the table. His whole career at Mack 'n' Morti's reduced to a cardboard box. He burned with revenge against Chuck.

He had no one he could trust. Ned had tricked him into thinking Winston Fagg was dead. He felt deceived but he was in no position to debate ethics with the Cleghorn crowd.

Exhausted, Frank collapsed on his bed drifting into a deep, dreamless sleep. He woke with a start, the sun streaming into his bedroom. A car backfired outside his window and for a moment he thought it was a gunshot.

He mulled over his options.

'First thing is to secure my payout from Mack 'n' Morti's before the shit hits the fan.'

His hand trembled as he rang the company's head office.

'Sal, it's Frank Wilson. I need to sort out my pay and return some files and keys. What's the best way to do it?'

'Hello Frank, stay on the line and I'll check.' She put him on hold.

'Bitch.'

A short time later Frank heard a click and Pete Crabshaw was on the other end.

'Frank, how are you keeping mate?'

'How do you think I'm keeping Pete? They sacked me. I didn't even get the chance to discuss it. No warning, nothing. Just sacked.'

'Yeah, Chuck's a tough bastard Frank. But in all honesty, you should have come in and explained the mess you created, even if you were sick. You know Chuck's got a zero-tolerance work ethic policy. Anyway, it's too late now I'm afraid. The boss won't change his mind. You know I stood up for you Frank but once Chuck's decided, that's it.'

Yeah, sure you did, thought Frank.

Pete Crabshaw continued. 'I've got your payout cheque here Frank. How about I drop round in half an hour and we swap it for the files and security keys? Tie up the loose ends so you can move on.'

'Okay Pete, see you soon.'

He tidied the apartment and changed before the intercom buzzed.

Pete sat on the couch, flicking through the files Frank handed him.

'Nothing else Frank?'

'Nothing. Here's my laptop and keys. That's the lot.'

'Gonna miss you Frank, you're a good operator. Got anything lined up yet?'

'There's a few offers on the table but I'm planning a break. I'm thinking the Bahamas.'

Pete Crabshaw left. Frank downed a double whisky. He poured another.

CHAPTER 61
RADIO INTERVIEW

SID SLATER CHILDREN'S RESERVE. EQUIPMENT GENEROUSLY DONATED BY SID SLATER.

The sign stood prominently at the entrance to the two-acre plot of land designated for the Bueno Vista children's reserve. Apart from an area roughly cleared for the playground equipment, it remained a weed-infested field surrounded by houses under construction.

Should have made my name bigger and included a photo, thought Sid as he drove away.

Sid had called the local radio station, 96.5 Hackradio, to tell the producer about his generous donation. Hackradio was looking for feel-good community stories to shore up their Local People, Local Stories funding initiative from the council.

The producer agreed to give Sid a five-minute on-air slot on the breakfast programme hosted by Laura Lee. This was Sid's first time on-air and he was sure once they heard him, he'd get a regular feature slot.

He arrived at the radio station early. Sid was convinced he would be mixing with celebrities in the Green Room with cups of coffee and biscuits. Instead, the receptionist told him to wait in the reception area. They would call him when they were ready.

The producer came to collect him as his time approached.

'You know,' Sid said, as they walked to the studio, 'it would be great for your station to give me a regular spot. I can talk to listeners about property.'

The producer ignored him, focussing on her run sheet. They arrived at the studio and she ushered Sid to a chair opposite Laura Lee. Sid guessed she was about thirty-five. He liked her large round glasses but wasn't sure about the close-cropped green hair. Sid was surprised she was allowed to dress so casually in well-worn jeans and a loose-fitting red top Laura had been hosting the breakfast show for more than two years and attracted a younger demographic of listeners for the station. Her program concentrated on popular music and local news with the occasional soft interview.

Laura Lee pressed the audio button. 'Well listeners, that was the latest hit from Bo Morris's album: "Where have all the fish gone?" In the studio today we have estate agent Sid Slater. He's going to tell us about his plans for the playground at the Bueno Vista estate.'

'Thankyou Laura.' Sid leaned into the microphone. 'When I first got involved with the Bueno Vista project, I wanted to create a safe and carefree environment for young families and children. I like people to think of me as a caring and compassionate man with only the best interests of the community at heart. To that end I have personally donated twenty thousand pounds for state-of-the-art playground equipment. I'm going to install it at the new "Sid Slater Children's Reserve".'

'Thank you, that sounds wonderfully generous Sid. If

any of you would like to ask Sid a question, please call or text in now.'

The lights on Laura's board lit up like a Christmas tree.

'We have Jenny on the line. Go ahead Jenny.'

'You bastard Slater, why did you evict my—'

Laura stabbed the console button, cutting the call.

'We seem to have a technical glitch with Jenny. I'll read some texts for Sid to answer while we get that fixed.'

Laura quickly read down the scrolling list of abusive texts, trying to find something suitable. 'Here's a text from James in Stratford. *As a tenant, how can I force the agent to stop the property owner from sleeping in the shed?*'

'Over to you Sid.' Laura felt one of her anxiety attacks coming on.

'It's the agent's responsibility to act on your behalf and ensure your rights are upheld. I suggest you get on to the agent and remind them of their obligations,' Sid said, winking at Laura.

A new text popped up on the screen from James in Stratford: *You are the agent, wanker.* Flustered, Laura said, 'Well, that's all we have time for today, here's another track from Bo Morris's new album.'

Laura sat with her head in her hands. The producer gestured frantically at Sid to leave the studio.

'I think that went quite well, have you thought about my idea for a regular spot?'

The playground equipment was due in a few days. Sid organised for the press to attend and photograph him with a group of smiling children. The Bueno Vista Residents' Group was suspicious but agreed to attend. Sid wrote an article for *Property News Today*. His article described his personal commitment to developing world-class facilities. He mentioned how proud he was to support the community and fund play equipment. He wrote of his desire for all developers to follow his lead and described his dream to show the public how developers could take a truly proactive role in supporting community projects. Sid went on to describe his concern regarding public perception of developers and estate agents, seeing them as shifty, money-grabbing thieves. They were, wrote Sid, professional and caring human beings.

My article is a real winner, Sid thought. *It will boost my chances of getting elected to the board of the NAEA.*

Mandy typed out Sid's article and showed it to the receptionist. The two women rocked with laughter, they dabbed at tears streaming down their faces.

CHAPTER 62
THE RAID

Max was impatient to get a result for the sample Winston gave him. He called his golfing friend, Cyril Smith, who worked at the lab.

'Cyril mate, I need your help.'

'What's the problem Max?'

'I've got this case I'm working on. I need an urgent analysis on a suspect fluid. It's some kind of toxin.'

'We're overstretched but I'll see what I can do for you Max.'

'Thanks Cyril, I owe you a big one,' Max replied.

The analysis took two days to complete and Cyril emailed the results through to Max. He burst through Winston's door, clutching the paperwork.

He tossed the report on Winston's desk and bounced into the visitor's chair.

'Move over Siamese cat pie, here comes the hot and smoking bakery.'

Winston read the report, then whistled aloud.

'Not a word to anyone about this Max. We don't want someone else taking the credit, now do we?'

'I'm with you Winston,' Max whispered, tapping the side of his nose.

Winston slipped the report into the bottom drawer of his desk and locked it.

'I'll get onto Jim Croker and make sure we line up the right publicity. We need to organise the raid and get the story published straight after. Jim knows the score.'

'You'll make sure I get a mention, won't you Winston?'

'Of course Max, we're a team. Full credit where it's due mate.'

Winston grabbed his phone and rang Jim.

'Jim, it's Winston, great news. Mack 'n' Morti's are drugging toddlers.'

'That's quite the statement.' Jim said, sounding shocked.

'Oh, you know what I mean Jim. The lab came up with an analysis of the samples Vincent stole. It shows a strong concentration of nicotine. There are several other chemicals that act as masking agents. The report showed that a low level of chemical injected into the dough would be undetectable. We need more sophisticated equipment to detect it in the toddler buns. But the nicotine in the sample is strong enough to kill a bloody horse. The report suggests that nicotine addiction would develop if you ate the buns once a week. It's all here Jim, in black and white. I've got enough to lay criminal charges now but we've got to make it stand up in court. We have to raid the bakery, grab the evidence, conduct another quick test and we'll be bloody heroes.'

'I'll get the police for the raid,' Winston added. 'Can you bring a photographer along, so we get photos for your paper?'

'How can you get the police to come along Winston?'

Winston thought through his plan. 'I'll say the raid has the potential to get violent and the department has concerns for staff safety. And I'll claim the guilty party may try to destroy the evidence.'

'Would two o'clock this afternoon be too soon for you?' Jim asked.

'Sounds good to me Jim, the sooner the better. See you there.'

Winston rang Inspector Bob Mathews, his contact at the local police station.

'Bob, it's Winston Fagg here. The department is onto something big. I'm calling to see if a couple of your boys can help us out. There is a serious health threat to children and we must secure the evidence before it's destroyed. We're expecting trouble. Reliable sources have told me to expect fierce resistance from the guards when we raid Mack 'n' Morti's bakery.'

'Sounds big Winston. Do you think the press are on to it yet? Are they likely to turn up?'

'Every chance. Don't know how they do it but my money says journalists will be there.'

'We don't want anyone to destroy evidence,' Bob said. 'Especially if it affects children. Sounds like I'll need to supervise this operation myself. I'll bring my team and meet you outside the bakery this afternoon.'

Bob's career was disappearing fast down the toilet. He'd received a roasting from his chief inspector the day before because he had the lowest arrest rate in the region. Bob was desperate for positive publicity.

At two o'clock everyone connected with the raid assembled outside the bakery gates. Inspector Bob Mathew's team were equipped with batons, flak jackets, helmets and carried shields. He led the way through the gates of the bakery towards the main entrance. Winston and Max followed. Jim Croker's photographer danced around them, firing off shots.

They crammed into the small reception area. Bob found himself jammed against a desk; his officers unable to move.

'Get back officers, give me some room,' he commanded.

They squeezed back against the entrance. Bob looked around to assess the situation. Reception was empty. A solid locked door lay to the right of the reception desk.

'OK team, they've seen us coming. We're going to have to break in before they destroy the evidence. Constable Jennings, break down the door.'

Constable Jennings gave two hefty kicks. He winced in pain as he twisted his knee but the lock on the door gave way. Bob led the entourage down an empty corridor with Jennings hobbling behind. Bob heard music and the sound of excited voices. He held up his hand, put his finger to his lips, gesturing that they keep silent. He remembered the SAS training video on counterterrorism; surprise was the key to success. He motioned everyone to flatten themselves against the wall. A long line of police, health officials and newspaper staff worked their way slowly toward the noise. They reached the door of the targeted room and heard a voice shouting above the music.

'Throw me the matches, Ted.'

'This is it,' Bob whispered. 'They're destroying evidence. They must be on to us.'

Bob motioned Constable Downer to kick the door in. Constable Jennings was still clutching his knee in pain. As Downer lifted her size ten boot ready to slam into the door, the room fell silent.

Bob paused to listen. The crowd behind the door broke into 'Happy birthday to you, happy birthday to you, happy birthday, dear Raymond, happy birthday to you!'

The door swung open into the corridor taking Constable Downer, who was still on one leg, by surprise. She lost her balance and fell backwards into the inspector. The inspector fell, pulling the rest of the group with him. Batons, cameras and helmets flew in the air. Constable Jennings cried out as Winston landed on his injured knee. Winston yelled in pain as Jennings elbowed him in the side of the head.

Judy, the bakery supervisor, stood in the open doorway, open-mouthed, unable to speak. The security guard joined Judy at the door, confused by the tangled pile of bodies lying on the floor.

Bob Mathews struggled to his feet, straightening his uniform.

'I'm Inspector Bob Mathews from the Met. We have reliable information that this establishment is distributing drugs to minors. We have the authority as drug law-enforcement officers to seize illegal substances and will arrest any persons involved. You are to remain in this room with Constable Jennings while Mr Fagg and I examine the equipment.'

'What's all this about?' Judy asked.

'That flavour enhancer you put into the toddler bun dough is nicotine,' Winston explained. 'The same drug used in cigarettes. Your bakery is getting toddlers addicted to the burgers.'

Judy's face crumpled.

'It can't be true; they wouldn't do that, not to little kids.'

'I'm afraid it is Judy; I've had a reliable source confirm it. It's hard to detect in the buns but the concentrate shows a positive reading. It's why you have such secure storage for your chemicals.'

'That can't be right. The security is to protect the harmless secret ingredient, nothing more than that,' Judy pleaded.

The Hackney Gazette photographer took shots of the equipment as Judy unclipped the canister from the dough mixing machinery. Judy handed it to Winston. He asked Judy to open the safe and retrieve the logbooks and unopened canisters. They returned to reception and Bob Mathews made an announcement.

'I've ordered transport to the station for the bakery staff to answer questions and make statements. We are closing the bakery until we complete a thorough investigation of the premises.'

The photographer took shots of people entering the police van, with Bob Mathews pushing them in. He took photographs of Winston holding the canisters and logbooks. Max craned his neck to get in each shot. The police van disappeared through the gates with Judy's sad face peering out the rear window.

Bob Mathews turned to Winston. 'That went well. I'm

CHAPTER 63
PLAYGROUND EQUIPMENT

'Sid Slater here, I need to talk to Chuck Adams urgently.'

Sal replied. 'I'm sorry Mr Slater, Mr Adams is in a meeting.'

Sid grew impatient. 'This is the fourth time I've rung today. I must speak to Chuck, it's extremely important.'

'I'm sorry Mr Slater, Mr Adams is in meetings most of the day. I'll call you as soon as he's free.'

Sid tried again. 'I only need five minutes of his time. Tell him it's Sid Slater, he'll want to talk to me.'

Sal's nerves were on edge. She sat at her desk, looking through the open door to Chuck's empty desk. The police had arrived the previous afternoon. They escorted Chuck from his office to a waiting police car. She'd watched from the window in Chuck's office. He looked bewildered as he looked up at his office window before they pushed him into the back of the car.

Chris Atkins, the company secretary spoke to Sal. 'If anyone calls, say Chuck is in meetings. It's especially important to make things look as normal as possible. We need time to get all the facts and make a public statement.'

'I can't interrupt him Mr Slater but I'll try to help you. What do you wish to talk to Mr Adams about?'

'It's about my playground equipment. Chuck promised delivery in the next couple of days but I've heard nothing. I need to know when to expect it. I've got the official opening of the Sid Slater Children's Reserve next week. I've lined up the press and resident's association.'

'I'm sorry Mr Slater, I don't know anything about your playground equipment. Mr Adams hasn't mentioned ordering it to me and I haven't seen anything in the files about it.'

Sid's mouth started to twitch. 'He promised me this equipment. Go and remind him that it's Sid Slater. I can make it extremely uncomfortable for him and Mack 'n' Morti's if he screws me around.'

Sal reached for a tissue. 'Please don't shout at me. Mr Adams sometimes makes his own arrangements. He doesn't always tell me what's going on. I'm sure your equipment will be there on time.'

Sal hung up the phone and burst into tears.

When news broke of Chuck's arrest, Chris Atkins the company secretary called the company solicitors in for an emergency meeting. Rumours swirled around the office. Office staff knew Chuck's arrest was somehow connected with the bakery raid but didn't know why. Pete Crabshaw left through the rear entrance in a panic when the police arrived.

Chris Atkins called the bakery to talk to the supervisor but she had disappeared. He suspected the police were holding her.

Chris finished the meeting with the company solicitors and phoned Sal.

'Put me through to Vine's head office in the States.'

CHAPTER 64
BREAKING NEWS

The door flew open and Harry rushed into the cafe with a broad grin.

'Couldn't sleep Harry? Jack said. 'Didn't expect to see you until lunchtime.'

Harry held a rolled-up copy of *The Hackney Gazette* in his hand and threw it onto the counter.

'I know you haven't had a chance to read the paper, so I came to show you this.'

Jack and Ben leaned on the counter and read the headline: "Mack 'n' Morti's Burger Chain Drugging Toddlers". Below the headline was a photo of a man in handcuffs. He stared out of a police car's back window with a blank expression. The caption read "Raid on Mack 'n' Morti's Head Office. CEO Chuck Adams arrested by Inspector Bob Mathews". The rest of the front page detailed an account of the raid on the bakery. It described the undercover operation involving the police and health department. "Operation Steaming Buns, masterminded by the police department's Inspector Bob Mathews was a complete success. Several arrests were made."

The story continued on page two with more pictures. One showed Winston Fagg holding a container of the drug with Max's hair and eyes peering over his shoulder.

Another photo showed Inspector Mathews guiding the bakery staff into the police van. The headline on the second page read: "Mack 'n' Morti's plan to turn our toddlers into druggies".

Jack put down the paper with a broad smile. 'Couldn't have happened to a nicer bunch of people.'

'Have to hand it to Ned,' Ben said. 'He nabbed all the right people. I still can't understand why he went to so much trouble for us. It was risky. If any of his victims, I mean, helpful informants went to the police, they could charge him with kidnapping and assault. Why did he help us Harry?'

'For Ned it's family first, then business. The Starlight's been great for me and Cassie and Ned's proud of what we've done here. Closing the Starlight was a red rag to a bull.

'As for someone blowing the whistle, I'm sure Vincent made it clear to everyone involved that it wouldn't be a good move.'

Customers began filling the Starlight.

'I can't remember being this busy Ben.' Jack looked up at the clock. 'It's only eleven and we're packed. Lunchtime might be crazy. I'll ring Stan, see if he can help.'

'Why don't you call Cassie as well? I'm sure she won't mind.'

People queued into the street as arguments broke out about taking other customers' orders. The talk was all about Mack 'n' Morti's selling drugged food to children.

'Wonder how they found out about the nicotine burgers?' questioned a young girl in the queue.

'According to the paper, the police and health department conducted an undercover operation. They were like secret agents,' her friend said. 'The health inspector looked a bit creepy; Winston Hagg or Blag or something. But he must be brave to take on that gang. I read he got hit on the head.'

Stan overheard the conversation.

'Did you hear that Jack? Bloody Fagg is a hero, the slimy toad. No justice in this world.'

'Not much we can do about it Stan. At least he helped close Mack 'n' Morti's down. Look at the crowd we've got now.'

CHAPTER 65
WINSTON'S PROMOTION

Winston Fagg sat in his office, feet on the desk. He clasped his hands round the back of his head, contemplating his new hero status. The Chief Executive rang to see him as soon as he arrived. He looked forward to discussing his promotion and pay rise. The only person who didn't seem pleased was Max. He'd been sulking all morning.

Some of us are born to lead, Winston reflected and *others must learn to follow.*

He made his way to the executive floor, straightening his tie and combing his hair. The carpet was thicker in the chief executive's section, expensive looking paintings hung on the wall. Betty the PA, greeted Winston with her usual indifference and escorted him to the boss's office.

'Fagg, come in and take a seat. I'd like to have a little chat.'

The chief executive despised Winston. He wanted to be rid of him but Health Department policies made it difficult to sack anyone without solid evidence of misdemeanours. Winston being the hero-of-the-hour didn't help.

'Didn't know you were a man of action Fagg. You showed a real sense of duty, going above and beyond.'

'Oh, I like to think of myself as someone prepared to go that extra mile if the public's safety is at risk sir. I'm happy to see the department receiving positive media coverage. My leadership philosophy is lead from the front. No challenge too great.'

The chief executive gave a thin smile and reached for a folder. He removed a document headed with the logo of Barton Laboratories. Winston caught sight of the subject heading: 'Bakery Sample Analysis' before the chief executive closed the folder again. Winston was surprised he hadn't seen it and hadn't expected such a quick turnaround on the final report.

'Max came to see me this morning Winston. He said you've been acting oddly lately. He reminded me that the department had to issue an apology after you accused an innocent cafe of having a cockroach infestation. Then you disappeared for days without letting anyone know where you were. And now this. Organising a raid with journalists and police in riot gear on a reputable fast-food chain like Mack 'n' Morti's. You've made a serious accusation against this company of drugging kids, got their executives locked up in jail and plastered the whole story on the front page of *The Hackney Gazette*.

'But sir, if that's the final report in front of you it must conclude that the bakery injected the toddler buns with nicotine. We tested a sample last week.'

'Max said you received the sample from a thug, a member of a known gang of criminals. That can't be true can it? Please tell me that Max is mistaken.'

'Well sir, we didn't collect the original evidence ourselves but I know for a fact that the sample came from the bakery.'

Winston's hands became clammy.

'The report sir, the report. You've got it there. It must confirm what I'm saying.'

The chief executive turned the folder round and slid it in front of Winston. Winston read the introduction and background to the test. He scanned the methods used and then focused on the conclusion:

The unopened and opened canisters from the bakery contained an identical liquid compound. The company describes this as a flavour enhancer. It consists of natural honey, apple extract, cinnamon and brown sugar. No traces of illegal drugs were present.

Winston felt faint. His mind raced; nothing made sense. *I know Mack 'n' Morti's drugged the burgers. I saw the stuff, I smelt it, I read the fucking secret email.*

The chief executive interrupted Winston's thoughts.

'Good man Max. He spoke to the lab this morning and got me the report straightaway. I need time to think this through before more goes public. Your cowboy antics have embarrassed the department considerably. The minister has summoned me in person.'

'There's something terribly wrong sir,' Winston pleaded. 'I think Max is jealous of my position, trying to undermine my authority. He might even be on the take from Mack 'n' Morti's for all we know. I mean, how can someone on his pay afford a new sports car and own a house on the Bronte Estate? It doesn't add up.'

'Now look here Fagg.' The chief executive glared at

Winston over the top of his half glasses. 'Max comes from a particularly good family. His father and I belong to the same golf club. They are not the type of people who resort to bribery or find themselves in the company of villains.'

Winston couldn't think straight. His career was hurtling down the toilet at frightening speed.

'Please sir. I wouldn't do anything to harm the reputation of the department. Give me a chance to sort this out. I'm sure there's a logical explanation. I'll do anything you want.'

The chief executive leaned across his desk.

'I'm pleased to hear you say that Fagg. Because there is a way you can redeem yourself. I have a request from Central Office, asking us if we could give them a hand with a special job. It should take a few months at most. It needs a man of your quick-thinking ability and heroic actions.'

'Er, I'd love to help out but I want to see this Mack 'n' Morti's thing through. I know there's more to this case.'

'Don't worry about that Fagg. Max can take over Mack 'n' Morti's. I want to tell you about your new project. The United Nations has put out a call for help. They need experienced inspectors to work in a country called Stivaniska. They need assistance with general hygiene and food standards. We want to send our most experienced people of course and as soon as I read this morning's paper I thought of you Fagg. Think of it as a kind of promotion.'

An overseas post didn't sound so bad after all. Winston realised it got him away from the heat when the media ran the story about his supposed stuff-up with Mack 'n' Morti's. He'd heard the United Nations postings were cushy and envisioned a nice house, servants, chauffeur.

'Of course sir. It's my duty as a true humanitarian. Is the house furnished or unfurnished?'

'More like a tent or a Portakabin. These war zones are pretty devastated.'

Winston swallowed. 'Did you say war zone?'

'Of course, you must have read the papers. Stivaniska is in the middle of a bloody civil war, terrible casualties. You'll be helping stem the tide of typhoid that's rampant in the refugee camps.'

'But I'm not the right man for that type of work,' Winston pleaded.

'Don't be so modest. I won't hear another word. You're booked on a flight tomorrow night. I checked with HR and your passport is up to date. I've fast-tracked a visa because your trip is for humanitarian purposes. It'll be great publicity for the department. You'd better start packing. By the way, send Max to see me.'

The chief executive beamed as he watched Winston shuffle out of his office. He had made Central Office happy by supplying a resource to the UN humanitarian effort and this was so much better than just sacking Fagg. If things got too hot with Mack 'n' Morti's, Fagg was the perfect sacrificial lamb. They would blame him for everything while he was away.

Now, time to organise Max's salary increase and promotion.

CHAPTER 66
A GENTLEMEN'S AGREEMENT

Sid Slater continued ringing Chuck Adams at Mack 'n' Morti's but he was permanently in meetings. He came out in a cold sweat when he saw the toddler burger article in *The Hackney Gazette*. The playground equipment was due for delivery and the BBQ invites sent out. The VIPs had replied including the residents' action group, members of the council and the media.

If Chuck didn't respond, Sid planned to drive over to Mack 'n' Morti's head office.

He rang again. Sal answered.

'Look Sal, it's Sid Slater here. I've been trying to get hold of Chuck for days. I'm expecting a delivery of playground equipment for the Sid Slater Children's Reserve. I've got a lot of important people coming to the opening and we have to make sure everything's finished.'

'Please hold the line Mr Slater. I'll put you through to someone who can help.'

The line went on hold. Sid paced impatiently around his office.

The phone clicked and a drawling American voice

spoke. 'Mr Slater, It's Larry Stoker here, how may I help you, sir?'

'Nice to talk to you Larry but I have important business with Chuck Adams.'

'I'm afraid Mr Adams is no longer with the company. I've flown in from the States to sort things out, so please tell me the nature of your enquiry.'

Sid explained that he uncovered Mack 'n' Morti's plot to discredit Starlight Burgers. He told Larry about the deal with Chuck for playground equipment.

'Mr Slater,' Larry drawled. 'We don't seem to have correspondence in our file for this arrangement. Could you kindly email me a copy of the offer that Mr Adams made.' Larry read Chuck's handwritten note again:

> *"Verbal agreement only, no written correspondence to Slater. Delivery arranged with supplier Playtime Children's Equipment to Bueno Vista as agreed."*

'It was a gentleman's agreement. An offer from Chuck in exchange for me protecting your name from the Starlight cockroach scandal. I'm sure you don't need more bad publicity after the bakery raid.'

Larry sat back, half listening to Sid. He scribbled CLOSED over Chuck's note and slid the file into his briefcase. Larry had flown in the day before to manage the damage. Chuck had total responsibility for the toddler burger project and he failed. It was a major setback. As soon as the damage control plan was in place, Larry would conduct a full investigation to see what went wrong.

'Mr Slater, Mr Adams has been under a lot of strain lately. He made many wild and impractical promises to people. To propose that we install playground equipment in an area without a Mack 'n' Morti's franchise is unthinkable.'

Sid became desperate, his palms grew sweaty.

'OK, I'm prepared to renegotiate. As an exception we will allow a Mack 'n' Morti's franchise at Bueno Vista.'

Sid couldn't think how he would explain this to Burger-a-Day. But anything was better than forking out thousands of his own money for the playground.

'Well, this is the thing Mr Slater, unless you have a written contract with Mack 'n' Morti's, there is nothing to renegotiate.'

'I don't think I've made myself clear. I am prepared to allow you to open a franchise in one of the city's leading developments. I would also like to remind you that I know all about the cockroach incident with the burger. Got it straight from your own employee.'

'Ex-employee Mr Slater,' Larry corrected. 'Do not take on our corporation Mr Slater. If we end up in court because you make libellous accusations you will need deep pockets to challenge us. I am reviewing the global strategy of Mack 'n' Morti's. I can tell you now that it does not include provision for any children's playgrounds. I must go now Mr Slater. Goodbye and have a nice day now, ya hear.'

Larry put down the phone and pressed the intercom.

'Sal, ring a company called Playtime Children's Equipment and cancel an order placed by Chuck. It was for a development called Bueno Vista.'

Sid banged down the phone in a rage. He misjudged

a kick at his Italian-designed executive chair, cracking his shin on the pneumatic lift lever. Holding his shin, he hopped around the office, tears of pain blurring his vision. Sid failed to clear the edge of the thick Chinese rug. He tripped and fell headlong into a bag of golf clubs, sending them crashing to the floor. His receptionists, Mandy and Judy heard the commotion, followed by a long silence.

'What was that about?' Judy asked.

Mandy looked up from her desk. 'Expect he dropped his wallet.' They howled with laughter and went back to their filing.

Larry Stoker leaned back in Chuck's chair and yawned. His eyes were bloodshot. After a long flight, he never fared well with jetlag. He looked across the desk at the two men he had summoned.

'Any more surprises I need to know about guys?'

Chris Atkins shrugged. 'Not sure, Chuck acted first and told us later. He's in a mess right now, the shock of getting carted off to jail rocked him. He's even worse since he's seen the newspaper headlines. You sure we can't tell him we're in the clear?'

'Not yet Chris, I want to make sure we've covered all our bases. Check there isn't other evidence that screws us. We've uncovered the mastermind but we need to make sure there aren't others. Now Frank, how about you bring Chris up to speed and we can plan our next moves? 'Frank Wilson leaned forward in a conspiratorial pose. He couldn't believe he was back in the inner sanctum of Mack 'n' Morti's. He opened a folder titled 'Operation Mole Hunt—Code Red'. Frank made up the title from his favourite Mission Impossible movie.

'I suspected something was going on for some time and must have been getting close. Mr "X" compromised our operation with Starlight Burgers and convinced Chuck I was to blame. So, Chuck sacked me. For a while I thought Craig Robinson was the mastermind as he blew the cockroach story to Sid Slater. Now I've discovered he was only a pawn. After intense investigation I've uncovered hard evidence and know who the real Mr "X" is.'

Frank removed two sheets of paper and with a flourish, gave Larry and Chris a copy each. He waited while they read the pages.

'As you can see, Pete Crabshaw sent this email to *The Hackney Gazette*. It reveals our top-secret strategy to inject nicotine into toddler burgers. This compromised our entire Hook 'Em Early campaign. I suspect Crabshaw and Robinson have been on Burger-a-Day's payroll, passing on all Mack 'n' Morti's strategic plans.'

'What about Chuck, do you think he knew what was going on Frank?' Larry asked.

'No, he was naïve and to be honest too arrogant to listen. Took his eye off the ball.'

Larry shifted in his seat and farted. He turned to Chris.

'We would have been history if it hadn't been for Frank telling me about Crabshaw stealing the nicotine additive from the bakery rubbish bins. You did a great job getting the canisters swapped over in the bakery before the raid Chris. Just in the nick of time.

'We've taken a caning in the press but when the council do their analysis, we'll be in the clear. They're gonna have to come grovelling and boys we are gonna have a field day in the press. We will make sure we look like the greatest victims in history. Chris, I want you to scour this place for all files on the Hook 'Em Early campaign. Destroy everything, then go to the bakery and do the same.'

Chris nodded and with a curious glance at Frank left the office. He was in a state of disbelief over Pete Crabshaw. Pete was fiercely loyal to Mack 'n' Morti's. Things didn't add up.

'Well my boy,' Larry said, smiling at Frank. 'We are in your debt. Did you find out who roughed you up?'

'No, they must have known I was on to them so I'm guessing Burger-a-Day.'

'Your loyalty and sacrifice will not go unnoticed back in the States.'

Back in his office, Frank leaned back in his chair, put his feet on the desk and reflected on his ordeal.

Vincent had abandoned him at the Golden Gates cafe. Back in his apartment he kept staring at the contents of his cardboard box, looking for inspiration. His future was bleak: no friends, no job, no money.

If they'd found out he'd hacked into Pete's email account and sent the incriminating email to the *Hackney Gazette,* Mack 'n' Morti's would murder him.

He recalled his anger at the injustice of being sacked after his beating and torture. The desire for revenge had consumed him.

His lucky penguin had been with him from childhood. Crabshaw jammed it between the *Little book of Calm* and jellybeans in the cardboard box. After straightening the penguin's wings, Frank placed him on the coffee table and stared into his small beady eyes.

What if he could frame Crabshaw for the email and somehow save Mack 'n' Morti's from the scandal? He would become a hero and get revenge on Chuck. Frank remembered his satisfaction as he hatched out the plan.

He would call Larry in the US, saying the nicotine program had been compromised and he couldn't trust any of the existing management team. Say he had been trying to find the 'mole' in the organisation but was unfairly sacked.

He expected Larry to fly over once the nicotine story broke. He would show Larry a printed copy of the email sent to *The Hackney Gazette* from Pete Crabshaw's email address compromising the nicotine programme.

Then he'd tell Larry how he was abducted and beaten. And when he overheard the plan to expose the nicotine programme he managed to escape.

He would warn Larry the bakery was about to be raided and it was his idea to swap all the nicotine in the safe. A shadow would be cast over the whole management team, including Chuck.

'You OK, Frank?' Larry stood in Frank's doorway. Frank whipped his feet off the table.

'Sorry Larry. I haven't slept for days.'

'We need to protect you Frank. A lot of crap's happened and I wouldn't want anyone coming after you. We are going to move you to the States for a while. You can spend some time in head office until things blow over.'

Shit, thought Frank. *Nothing wrong with hanging out with the American bigwigs to help him climb the ladder.*

America seemed like an excellent plan. 'Thanks Larry. I'd feel much safer over there.'

CHAPTER 67
CELEBRATION

Jack invited friends for a victory celebration at the Starlight. The first to arrive was Magpie. They heard the familiar death rattle of Magpie's van pulling up outside. He entered the cafe in a purple shirt, blue shorts and brown boots. He'd parted his hair in the middle and his ears sported traces of dried shaving cream.

Jack shook Magpie's hand. 'You look smart tonight Magpie.'

'I like to dress up if I'm invited to a function. This shirt is genuine Hawaiian; a mate of mine gave it to me in return for a welding job. It's one hundred per cent acrylic, says so on the label.'

Ben looked Magpie up and down. 'Looks great Magpie, it's your colour.'

Julie arrived wearing a navy-blue figure-hugging business suit under her raincoat.

'Sorry Jack got held up at work. I didn't have time to change.'

Jack kissed her and took the raincoat.

'I'll fetch you a drink, what do you think about the decorations?'

Multi-coloured balloons and rainbow streamers hung from the ceiling. The walls were covered in vintage-style bunting saying Starlight Rocks in bright-blue Starlight colours.

'Looks fantastic Jack, who did it?' Julie yelled, raising her voice above Pharrell Williams singing *Happy* and the noise of the crowd.

'Who do you think?'

'Of course, it must be Cassie.'

'Yes, she insisted. Worked with Ben on it all afternoon, she'll be here soon.'

A crowd gathered at the door signalling the arrival of Ned and the Cleghorn clan.

Harry went over to meet Ned. 'Great to see you Ned, come over and I'll get everyone a drink.' Ned followed Harry to the counter.

He moved a collection of empty sparkling white wine bottles and discarded corks from the counter to crates on the floor.

'Glass of sparkly Ned?'

Ned grimaced. 'A beer Harry, dark one if you've got it.'

Two party poppers went off in rapid succession. Vincent turned quickly.

'Relax Vincent, have a drink,' Ned patted Vincent's shoulder.

Ben balanced a tray of mini burgers with one hand and carried a pile of napkins in the other.

'Something to eat?'

Vincent's huge fingers delicately picked a mini burger from the tray.

The throb of a high-powered sports car drew up outside. The cafe door opened. Julie caught a glimpse of

Cassie's bright-orange hair bobbing up and down. Through a gap in the crowd Cassie sighted Julie.

'Hey Julie, I want you to meet my favourite cousin Des. Well, equal favourite to Harry of course. Des, this is Julie, my adopted big sister I was telling you about.'

Julie smiled.

'Heard you had trouble with Mack 'n' Morti's?'

'Yes but Jack and your Uncle Ned sorted them out. Shame it only got picked up by the local media.'

Cassie laughed.

'Don't be so sure, we've still got a few surprises for those creeps.'

Julie looked puzzled.

'Wait and see,' Cassie winked at Julie.

'There's Harry,' Des waved and wandered over to meet him.

Julie and Cassie stood at the counter drinking sparkling white wine.

'Have you had any more art commissions Cassie?'

'I finished the work on the buildings at the shunting yards. The manager loved it and sent some photos to his mate at a railway depot in Staines, so fingers crossed.

'Best news is, I got a call from the Beans A Go-Go coffee head office. They've given me a contract to create a whole new look for their franchise operators. They saw the photo of the Starlight in *The Hackney Gazette* when the cockroach apology came out.'

'That's wonderful, things are really taking off for you.'

'I'm excited about it. Even Uncle Ned approves.'

Ben appeared from the crowd. 'There you are Cassie; can I steal you for a few minutes?'

Ben took Cassie's hand and led her through to the storeroom.

He locked the door.

'What's all the secrecy about Ben?'

Ben fished out a folded piece of paper from his wallet and gave it to Cassie with a smile. She unfolded the paper and read it slowly.

> *"An Agreement between:*
>
> THE VENDOR: *Agnew Properties and*
> THE PURCHASER: *Mr Ben Harrington.*
>
> PROPERTY: *'The Daisy Queen, 102 Blomfield Road,*
> *London W9 2QY."*

'You're moving out of that dingy old flat. Congratulations Ben. That's a funny sort of address, though?'

Ben pulled her closer.

'Cassie, I love you. I want more than anything in this whole wide world for us to be together. Please say yes and share our new home.'

Cassie's face lit up and she flung her arms around Ben, kissing him.

'Yes, yes, yes.' Tears of happiness rolled down her cheeks.

They heard banging on the door. 'Won't be a minute,' Ben cried.

Cassie wiped the tears from her face. 'Why is the flat called *The Daisy Queen*?'

Ben grinned. 'Because it floats on the Regent's Canal.'

'No!' Cassie exclaimed. 'A narrow boat on the canal! Ben, you're a genius.'

'It needs a lot of work but we can live in my flat until I've fixed her up.'

'Stan!' Ned shouted. 'Come have a drink with us.'

Ned greeted Stan like an old friend. They sat together talking and laughing like schoolboys.

'Funny looking at those two,' Julie whispered to Jack. 'If you spent most of your life making sandwiches, what do you have in common with someone like Ned?'

'They're not that different. Stan was a wild boy when he was younger, according to my mum. I reckon Ned and Stan enjoyed every moment sorting out Mack 'n' Morti's.'

Stan was in deep conversation with Ned. 'I'm trying to work out a way of getting rid of the neighbour's cat. They'll suspect me, so I've got to be careful.'

'I'm sure we can come up with something Stan. You'll be in the clear; leave it with me.'

Stan felt a small hand tap him on the shoulder. He turned around. 'Hello Grandad.'

Stan stared at April in disbelief. 'April, what...' He looked up to see Ginny and Rebecca walking toward him.

'How are you Dad?' Ginny bent down to kiss him.

'This is wonderful, I can't believe you're both here! And April's grown so much.' Stan hugged his grandchild.

Rebecca put her arm around Stan.

'Jack rang last week to tell us you sold the business. He invited us to be here tonight. We couldn't believe you'd ever retire. It must be a real wrench. Now you have more time, how about you stay with us sometimes?'

'Nothing would give me more happiness.' Stan wiped tears from his eyes.

'Can I have some chips Grandad?' April said.

'You can have as many chips as you like.'

'The old place looks amazing,' Ginny said. 'I never thought you'd give it up Dad.'

'It's all Jack's doing. I nearly had a heart attack when I first saw it. The old place has a new lease of life now and I love it.'

Magpie cornered Jack about his latest scheme.

'What do you think of this idea? Might be the big one? I've finished a new prototype—'

'These burgers get better and better,' Harry interrupted Magpie. 'What about franchising the Starlight Burger name Jack? You'd make a fortune.'

'I don't want to end up like a Mack 'n' Morti's. I need to maintain great burgers. It's hard to keep that quality if you start franchising.'

'It's depends on the agreement Jack. You sign off on standards and the consequences if an operator breaches them. Even with a fleet of vans you can't grow much with the size of this cafe. Running a franchise gives you more opportunities. You'd need an office to manage the operators and marketing. You wouldn't have to cook or serve another burger for the rest of your life.'

'I'm not sure it's for me, imagine negotiating with people like Sid Slater? It would give me the shits. I'm starting to understand how Stan feels about the place now. When he suggested working at Starlight, I did it because I was desperate. I didn't understand the value of our customers as friends, real people. The Starlight is a community. It's where people relax, catch up with others. I prefer to stay as I am.'

The last of the partygoers left after midnight.

Julie finished filling crates with empty bottles.

'Let me get those.' Harry carried the crates to the laneway. 'Great party Julie.'

Harry took the last crate from Julie and stacked it on the pile. 'Yes, it was nice to meet everyone tonight. Your Uncle Ned's a character Harry.'

'He's been like a father to me but I worry he'll end up in jail one day.'

Cassie dried her hands. 'Tables and chairs are clean Jack, what's next?'

'Bens finished the griller. Can you give him a hand with the decorations and I'll mop the floor?'

'Sure.'

Jack carried the remaining case of sparkling white wine into the storeroom. Ben came in carrying the discarded decorations.

'Funny how things turn out, isn't it Jack?'

'How do you mean, Ben?'

'Well, first you took on Harry who tried to rob us, then the cockroach business and now we've beaten Mack 'n' Morti's. I wonder what's next for the Starlight Jack?'

'Let's see how things go. We can do a lot more here before we expand. Julie thinks the tobacconist is thinking about retiring in a few months. I'll ask him for first refusal on the shop. Wouldn't be hard to knock through a doorway.'

They lapsed into silence.

'How are things going with Cassie?'

'I still can't believe my luck that she wants to be with someone like me.'

'I can't believe it either Ben.'

'Why do you say that?'

'It's obvious, why would a bright, intelligent girl look at an ugly bugger like you, smelling of burgers and chips.'

Jack burst out laughing.

'Do I really smell of burgers and chips Jack?' Ben sniffed his armpits and shirt front.

'Why don't we have a nightcap at the Speckled Duck on the way home?'

'Great idea Jack. How about I lock up with Cassie and meet you and Julie there?'

'Ben looked really happy this evening', Julie said. 'Chatting away to people, seemed more confident. Anything happened?' Jack drove into the Speckled Duck car park. 'Not that I know of Julie.'

The Speckled Duck car park was crowded. They fought their way through the packed wine bar to the lounge off the main restaurant. The pub was one of the few that stayed open until 2 a.m.

As Ben and Cassie arrived, Jack ordered drinks from the bar and they crowded around a small table.

Cassie snuggled up to Ben and they started softly singing 'Cruising down the river on a Sunday afternoon...'

'What's going on?' Julie asked.

'You tell them Cassie.'

'Ben and I are going to live together on the canal in a narrow boat.'

Julie hugged them both. 'Congratulations you two.'

Jack bought a bottle of champagne.

'Here's to the future. The Starlight not only created great burgers and friendships but a great romance.'

If they hadn't been so distracted, they would have heard the steady throb of propellers from the Hercules Transporter. It passed overhead at 20,000 feet on its way to Stivaniska. Winston, the health inspector, sat strapped into a small, hard seat clutching a paper air sickness bag. He was about to vomit for the second time that evening.

CHAPTER 68
MEDIA POWER

'I'm gonna have someone's balls for this,' Larry Stoker ranted from his office at Mack 'n' Morti's. 'Some fucking limey protestor group calling themselves MAKOK dressed as cigarette butts are yelling at customers in our restaurants. They're telling parents their kids are getting cancer. Chris, who are these people? Can't we get the cops and shoot a couple?'

'Calm down Larry. They call themselves the Mack 'n' Morti Are Killing Our Kids collective. And the British police don't usually have guns. And they're not allowed to shoot protesters. We're not in the States now.'

'That's the problem with this fucking country? No backbone.'

Groups of parents were gathering across the country at Mack 'n' Morti's restaurants chanting 'Stop drugging our toddlers! Go home, Mack 'n' Morti!' The protests went viral on Twitter and Facebook and trended on Instagram and Snapchat. A pack of press photographers started to gather at the entrance of the company's head office. Sal told him a similar group had gathered at the bakery.

Larry picked up his briefcase and left to visit Chuck Adams. He stopped at Sal's desk on his way out.

'Any news from the cops?'

'Not much. They think the Facebook group was set up by a student. It's not illegal and they won't arrest protesters while it's peaceful. I've just had calls from Luton and Woking. They're getting worried. The restaurants are empty.'

Larry looked grim.

'I'm going to see Chuck. I want you to set up a meeting with Chris and Frank Wilson to discuss our approach with franchise owners. Keep in touch with the cops and give me a ring if it gets uglier.'

Larry mulled over his telephone discussion with the US strategy team. He had to convince Chuck to take the blame. In return he would falsely promise to send him back to a job in the States.

A blaring car horn broke his train of thought. 'What the—' The headlights of a Ford Mondeo flashed as it came towards him head-on. Larry wrenched the steering wheel, swerving into the left lane.

'I hate this place; they can't even drive on the right side of the road. Christ, that was close.'

Chuck was pacing around his lounge room when Larry arrived.

'Thanks for getting me out on bail Larry.'

'A lot has happened since your arrest Chuck. Luckily, we swapped the nicotine before the raid. So, unless there's evidence we're unaware of, Mack 'n' Morti's will be in the clear. We've discovered that Crabshaw and Robinson were in Burger-a-Day's back pocket. Crabshaw leaked an email to the newspaper with our Hook 'Em Early campaign report.

'We're gonna deny everything. Bluff our way through. I've spoken to the strategy team and come up with your best option. Your name connects you to the Hook 'Em Early campaign on the leaked email, so you will have to take full responsibility. We'll say that you made it up as a practical joke, not realising the trouble it would cause. You will announce a full apology to the public and Mack 'n' Morti's staff. You can say your private life was a mess and you weren't thinking clearly. It was an internal staff joke that got out of hand and, in retrospect you realise it was in poor taste. We will arrange a psychological report from the States that says you are suffering from acute stress disorder. The tasteless joke was a result of your confused mind.'

'Larry, how can you expect me to take the whole rap? I followed the plan that you guys set up. Why should I trash my reputation and career for you?'

'Let me finish Chuck,' Larry hissed. 'The legal team will fix everything and we will find you a good position back in the States at Head Office.

'We knew the nicotine concentrate was risky and we're disappointed that you didn't conduct thorough scenario testing. You left us exposed which is why Mack 'n' Morti's is in this mess now. You should have checked your team more carefully. It's a good job you had Frank Wilson, or we'd be in even deeper shit. Chuck, for the sake of the greater good you've got to take the rap.'

Chuck struggled to see a way out. He knew he would be blamed no matter what happened.

'OK Larry, I'll wear it. But get me out of this lousy country.'

CHAPTER 69
THE COMPROMISE

The council's Standards Committee met in their CEO's office the night before meeting Larry Stoker. The chief executive called the meeting to order.

'Fagg has left us in a compromised position. While I think he was on to something, we have no hard evidence. I believe we have no alternative but to issue a statement clearing Mack 'n' Morti's in tomorrow's paper.'

There were no objections and the following day *The Hackney Gazette* ran a story on page 2 saying:

"Mack 'n' Morti's Cleared of Toddler Drugging Charges".

The council issued a statement explaining that it acted on fabricated information from disaffected employees of Mack 'n' Morti's. The health inspector in charge of the case was currently on a humanitarian assignment overseas...unable to comment further.

Larry waited impatiently for the council's chief executive to take his call.

'Mr Stoker,' the chief executive said in a formal tone. 'I am pleased to inform you that the analysis is clear and you are free to reopen. An apology appeared in the media yesterday.'

'Is that it? You useless bunch of bureaucratic halfwits

make wild allegations about my company, our franchise operators are going out of business and all you can say is sorry? I want compensation and full-page apologies in all the major dailies, or we'll sue the arse off you.'

'Before you go any further Mr Stoker you need to understand our position. I do have a report on another sample taken from one of your containers. This sample shows strong nicotine content. Also, locked in my safe are emails from Chuck Adams explaining how your company planned to use it and a number of logbooks from the bakery.'

'Hold it right there,' Larry interrupted, 'that's complete crap. A disaffected employee planted that sample and sent the email. They were working for our competition. This is a clear case of industrial espionage, nothing more.'

'Mr Stoker, that's exactly what I thought. Trouble is, we've got other evidence that I can't seem to reconcile.'

Larry began to smell trouble and shifted in his seat, letting out a short pungent fart.

'Go on,' he waved his hand to dissipate the smell.

'We interviewed the security bin service for the bakery. We inspected the bins the morning after the raid. The department managed to take a spilt sample from the floor of one bin. Well, what we found was an awful shock to us Larry, not at all what we expected. The new sample matched the earlier sample our inspector brought to our attention.

'Larry, are you still there?'

Larry's cheeks turned fiery red.

'So what's next?' Larry snapped.

'I'm a reasonable man Larry. I don't see why we can't

work something out. You want Mack 'n' Morti's name cleared and I want to end this matter quickly. We've dealt with the inspector involved. He's out of the way because I didn't want him to become a bloody hero. So why don't we forget all this nonsense about full-page apologies and compensation? Let's allow things to take their course with the apology statement we released yesterday.'

'I see your point. Prolonged litigation won't look good for either of us. I need your assurance that the security bin sample will disappear.'

The chief exec coughed. 'What sample Larry? I have no idea what you are referring to. I take it that we have a deal?'

'Yes, we have a deal. Tell me one thing, I'm curious. Who leaked our strategy to the Press and Burger-a-Day? Who told you about the security bin?'

'Burger-a-Day, what are you talking about?'

'I'm talking about our ex-employees, Pete Crabshaw and Craig Robinson. They were in cahoots with Burger-a-Day. I want to know which one organised the raid on the bakery.'

'Our information was from someone called Frank Wilson. He emailed *The Hackney Gazette* with the Hook 'Em Early strategy paper. He also organised a team to break into the bakery to get the sample. Sorry, I wasn't aware that there was a Burger-a-Day element to this fiasco?'

Larry's stomach tightened in a knot. His bowels gave way to a stream of toxic wind.

'Gotta go.' He slammed the phone down on the desk. 'Sal, get Chris in here now.' Larry plunged the metal letter opener deep into the top of the desk.

The chief executive summoned Max into his office.

'Well Max. That was a stroke of genius, creating the story of a second sample. It's a pity we didn't find any before they scrubbed the bins clean. But all's well that ends well as they say. This deserves a celebration; how about joining me at the club for lunch?'

CHAPTER 70
ALL ABOARD

'There's Ben's Golf.' Jack pointed to the car parked in Warwick Avenue.

'It's hard to find somewhere to park around here.'

'Quick, over there Julie, in the centre. Next to the silver Merc.'

'Don't forget the wine Jack.' He reached into the back of the car, grabbing the bottle of red.

'Have Ben and Cassie done all the work on the boat themselves?' Julie asked.

'Yes, it's taken nearly six months with the settlement and repairs but they moved in last week. It was the cheapest boat they could afford so it was in a bit of a state.'

'The canal is this way.' They walked along Warwick Avenue past white stucco three-storey Regency-style buildings.

'Ben said to turn left at Blomfield Road and look for a small gate to the canal.'

Waiting for the traffic lights, Jack spotted the gate.

'This must be it Julie. Look, it leads to the canal.'

They walked along the canal, checking the name of each boat they passed.

'Here it is Jack, the *Daisy Queen*.'

Double wooden doors opened at the end of the boat. Ben appeared, wearing a sailor's hat.

'Come aboard.'

They heard Bob Marley singing *I shot the Sheriff* as they stepped onto a small deck at the rear of the narrowboat.

'This is great.' Julie examined the boat. 'I love the combination of dark blue sides and red roof.'

Jack peered down the side of *The Daisy Queen*. 'Looks long, what's the length, Ben?'

'Forty-six foot, it's got plenty of space inside. Come and have a look.'

Stepping over Colin, fast asleep at the entrance, they descended the steps into the cabin.

'Wow.' Julie looked around at the warm and cosy interior furnished with soft furnishing in vibrant colours. 'This is fabulous Ben.'

Cassie was in the kitchen at the far end of the boat. She turned to see them come in.

'Hi, Julie. Hi, Jack, welcome to our home.'

THE END

www.ingramcontent.com/pod-product-compliance
Lightning Source LLC
Chambersburg PA
CBHW020012120726
47903CB00004B/1249

* 9 7 8 0 6 4 5 1 3 3 7 0 7 *